THE GLOAMING

Also by Kirsty Logan

The Rental Heart and Other Fairytales
The Gracekeepers
A Portable Shelter

The Gloaming

KIRSTY LOGAN

Harvill *Secker*
LONDON

1 3 5 7 9 10 8 6 4 2

Harvill Secker, an imprint of Vintage,
20 Vauxhall Bridge Road,
London SW1V 2SA

Harvill Secker is part of the Penguin Random House group of companies
whose addresses can be found at global.penguinrandomhouse.com.

Penguin
Random House
UK

First published by Harvill Secker in 2018

penguin.co.uk/vintage

A CIP catalogue record for this book is available from the British Library

ISBN 9781911215936 (hardback)
ISBN 9781911215943 (trade paperback)

Typeset in India by Integra Software Services Pvt. Ltd, Pondicherry

Printed and bound in Great Britain by Clays Ltd, St Ives PLC

Penguin Random House is committed to a sustainable future for
our business, our readers and our planet. This book is made
from Forest Stewardship Council® certified paper.

For Ross. I'll deny it, but I love you.

It is a joy to be hidden, but a disaster not to be found.

– D. W. WINNICOTT

PART 1

PART 1

Let the Sea Take It

That last summer, the sea gave us jellyfish. Every morning when the water slid back and revealed the stony beach, there they'd be: dozens of squishy, silvered things with their purple threaded innards. The girls shrieked to see them, especially when Bee prodded them with sticks to make them shudder. Dead or dying, they didn't know. And it didn't matter – no one was giving them back to the sea, so they'd die in the end, and when evening came the tide would creep back in and steal the corpses. The sea takes everything.

But it was a dark, drawn-out summer, and there is much to tell, so let's look at one night in particular. First there's Islay with her long curls red as blood, long limbs bare in her floaty nightdress, seventeen years old and as perfect as a painting. Then Mara in her swimsuit, fifteen and a half, boxy and fierce and sharp but still thinking one day she'd be beautiful, somehow, without having to give up anything for it.

Islay had the light: an old brass lantern, glass sides spidered with cracks, but still bright enough. It was never really night in the summer, not this far north, and the best the moon could do was a greyish glow from behind the clouds. There was only one way to get to the beach, and that was through the trees, so through the trees the girls went. Mara barrelled on ahead, bold in the darkness, leaving strands of her hair snagged on branches. Islay picked a delicate way, not wanting to jag her skin on twigs, the light held out to the side so she wasn't blinded by it.

Then there was Bee, of jellyfish-prodding fame. Forgive him: he'd only known this world for five years, and there was so much still to learn. He was squat, pretty, golden-haired, strange in the best way. The girls hadn't invited him to the beach, but as they passed his window Islay's light pulled him from sleep and he pattered from his bed, pushing up the sash to lean his soft little body on the sill. Even in daylight, even standing at the end of the garden, you couldn't quite see through the trees, but if Bee closed his eyes and stretched his ears hard he could hear the girls and know what they were doing. The snap of twigs changed to the clatter of tiny stones, and the girls were at the beach.

Mara ran straight into the sea. Wide leaps through the long shallows. An involuntary yelp at the chill. Arms arrowed and a dive into the depths past the sandbank. On the brightest days it was possible to stand on the sandbank, lean forward, dip your face below the surface, and – if your eyes could stand the salt water – look down into a drop-off so deep its end was invisible.

'Come on, move your arse!' Mara, treading water, flexed her toes so they wouldn't go numb. 'It's not even cold!'

Islay emerged from the trees, walked twenty steps across the stony beach, and stopped just before the lap of the tide. She loved the sea, just as all islanders love the sea – because why else would they want to live surrounded by it? But loving something did not mean you wanted to leap into it and let it drown you.

Islay didn't yelp at the cold and she didn't dive off the sandbank. Instead she took small and steady steps, letting the water creep up her calves until she began to feel unsteady, the yawn of the sandbank dropping away just in front of her. She stopped there in the shallows, the water licking her legs. The moonlight turned her floral nightgown monochrome. She held the light high, but the sea's black surface was unbroken. Mara, breath held, waited underwater.

'Are you ready?' called Islay.

A stream of bubbles broke the surface.

'I see you, Mara! Hurry up, I'm not standing here all night.'

Mara's head followed the bubbles, her sleeked hair dark as the sky.

'And you can start with that. Sin number one: making my sister wait while I fanny about instead of getting on with naming my sins.'

'Let the sea take it!' announced Mara. She emphasised her point by turning away from the island and pushing the seawater away from her, then turned it into a backwards somersault, fish-slippery, making hardly any splash until she misjudged her feet and they ow-wowped in the water. She wouldn't have admitted it to her sister, but she felt that if she kept moving, then all those ghostly dead jellyfish wouldn't float over and brush against her legs.

'Will we do another one of yours?' called Islay. The lamp was heavy and her shoulder was beginning to ache.

'I don't have any more,' Mara called back.

'Liiiiiar,' sang Islay. 'You've got loads. I saw you eating after Mum said no snacks before dinner. Be honest. The sea can't take it if you don't tell.'

'Fine,' said Mara. 'The bread and sugar I stole from the larder – let the sea take it.'

'Let the sea take it!' repeated Islay.

'The tea I spilled on my dress and then blamed my brother – let the sea take it!'

'The time I told my sister to piss off – let the sea take it!'

'The shed window I broke and then just went away like nothing happened – let the sea take it!'

Between each of their confessions, Mara did somersaults and dives and flips, her awkward body effortless underwater.

'The earrings I took from Islay's jewellery box and then broke – let the sea take it!'

'What? Mara! Which earrings?' said Islay, but Mara had dived underwater and didn't hear.

The things I took that weren't mine, the things I said that weren't true – let the sea take it! Let the sea take everything!

When the confessions were done, Islay held her light high to guide her sister back. Mara had to kick hard to get ashore – she'd drifted north-east, into deep water. It was easy to do.

The girls traipsed back through the trees, Mara leaving a trail of seawater and Islay letting her extinguished lantern catch against low branches. If they'd glanced up, they'd have seen Bee, asleep with his head resting on the windowsill. His eyes closed, his ears open, listening to it all.

Dwam

The world was so full of magic then that Mara didn't always know when she was awake and when she was asleep and dreaming. At night she'd lean out of the window to see the sleeping island lit by stars. She'd watch the silvery flicker of midges catching the moon on their wings. She'd smell the coppery, sweet-rot scent of the enchantments she knew lurked under the earth. She'd hear the steady breathing of the sea, slow and deep as a giant's. She knew that if she could stretch up over the treetops, she'd see dozens of jellyfish glistening on the stones. She knew that behind her and beneath her was home, this rambling storybook mansion of fifty rooms, some shut up for years, a sanctuary for tiny creeping things – four stone walls enclosing a land of mysteries, each of them belonging to her. She'd feel the cold breeze and jag herself on splinters from the buckled windowsill, and it would all feel as real as a dream.

Once she crept into Bee's room and whispered him awake, asking him to please hit her as hard as he could, because the splinters didn't hurt enough to be sure. He wouldn't, and got upset, and cried soft little huffling tears until she tucked him in and said it wasn't real, what she had said wasn't real, he was only dreaming.

She never asked Islay to hit her, because she knew that she would, and then Mara might wake to find it all gone.

Fankle

‘on’t forget about tonight, Mum,’ said Mara to Signe’s
back. They were forever talking to Signe’s back as she
was always at the cooker or bending over to clean
under something or at the sink staring down at her motionless
hands in the water. ‘It’s the special dinner. You said lamb stew.’

‘Now then,’ said Peter with a frown, ‘I’m not so sure about that.’

‘What? But you!’ Mara’s voice went up so high she couldn’t say
more of the sentence.

Peter made his black eyebrows go up and down. ‘I’m not sure,’
he said, ‘that these ladies will manage to eat much of their lamb
stew with such a distractingly handsome boy in our midst.’

‘Man,’ murmured Signe into his ear as she bustled past,
spooning porridge into his bowl.

‘Man,’ amended Peter, adding sugar and cream, though when
did a scrawny sixteen-year-old boy with a shaving rash on his
throat earn the right to be called a man? ‘Such a handsome
man.’

Mara looked smugly into her porridge. Islay made a sicky face.
Bee didn’t notice because he was wiping the sugary dust from his
cereal into his fists and hiding them under the table. Islay watched

him while piling her toast crusts up to make a barrier around the edge of her plate.

'Now listen, because I have to tell you about today,' said Peter. 'Today you all have to go away and stay quiet and not bother me with questions every five minutes, and definitely not come to me telling tales about your sister, because I'll be working.'

'Windows?' asked Islay.

'Floors?' asked Mara.

'Roof,' said Peter. 'The clattery tile that keeps you awake when it's windy, Islay – that will be gone. The drip-drip-drip in the corner of your room, Bee – that will be gone.'

'Finished?' signed Bee with his sugary fists, confused because he wasn't listening.

'Yes, finished. I'm going to patch it up. I'm going to fix all the tiles on that whole roof. Our roof will be perfect, like something from a magazine.'

'A magazine of roofs? Sounds thrilling,' murmured Islay, but under her breath so Peter didn't hear. Mara heard, though, and snorted, then regretted it when she remembered that ladies with gentlemen coming to dinner didn't snort.

'This house will be fixed up in no time. I'll be done with the tiles in time for dinner. Tomorrow I'm going to do something else, and that will be done in time for dinner too. The floors. Or the replastering upstairs. By the end of the month – the end of the week! – we'll all be living in paradise.'

Signe didn't think that was likely. It wasn't likely that the roof would be fixed at all, never mind in a single day. And who on earth could replaster twenty rooms in a week? They'd been in this house for six years now, and it seemed that every time Peter managed to fix something, another three things broke. But she said nothing.

'Finished,' signed Bee as he pushed back his chair, the legs shrieking on the stone floor. He held his clenched fists out to his sisters.

'I'm finished too. Thanks, Mum, love you, Mum.' Islay slid sideways off her chair so it didn't shriek and wrapped her hand around Bee's wrist. They had to squash together to fit through the doorway, but Islay didn't let go. Mara spooned up her porridge in three bites, but she was too late. She followed as close as she could.

Peter lifted his porridge bowl and licked the last of the cream from the rim. He patted his wife's bottom as he passed, aiming a kiss towards her forehead.

'Thanks, my dove. You won't believe how beautiful I will make these tiles for you. They'll be the loveliest things you ever had above your head.'

'Lovelier than the sky?' Signe asked, in what she hoped would sound like a teasing way, but Peter had already wandered out - to be wildly optimistic on the roof, presumably - and her words fell down to her bustling hands. She ate the leftover porridge from the pot, standing at the kitchen sink. She tried to think: not about what she had to clean or move or organise in the house today, but about something bigger than that. Something noble and dramatic. But she couldn't grasp hold of a single thought. Her mind was loud and white and chaotic, like a dozen swans taking flight.

Toty

Bee stamped down the hallway, one arm raised, dragging his sister behind him. This made him look angry, except that he stamped whatever mood he was in, and his fists were only clenched so he didn't lose any of his cereal. He headed for the front door, which was usually to be avoided because an enormous shark jaw was hung, open, in the doorway, and you had to walk through it to get outside. The jaw was there when they bought the house, and at least once a month Signe asked Peter to take it down – it would scare the tourists, she said, and he agreed, but said that's exactly why he wouldn't take it down, because tourists liked to be scared sometimes; why come to a rocky little island and stare out to the endless, ravenous sea if you don't want to feel small and temporary? They knew the jaw couldn't be real. No shark was ever so big. But that didn't make its teeth any less sharp.

Through the doorway, past the empty paint tins and splintering ladders piled up against the front wall of the house. Skirting the mass of lavender, scent clouding, stems twitching under questing bees. Ducking under the frayed washing line. Clambering over the drystone wall. Pushing aside the branches of the pear trees to creep in under them.

Bee came to an abrupt stop and Islay tripped over him, her arm thwacking against a root.

'Shitting shitty shit!' She sat up and rubbed the sore bit. Bee didn't notice. Under the branches' canopy, he spread his arms like wings. Sugar-dust scattered.

'Hide,' he signed, and shuffled back behind a tree. The girls followed – Islay a little grumpily – and sat beside him, bottoms on the hard earth, arms around knees.

Bee had always been the golden boy, but that summer he gleamed. Buttercup sun lolled through the branches, catching the fuzz on his bare shoulders and back. Their tiny haloed lion. Islay pulled him closer so his heavy head rested on her lap and began twisting a thin braid in his hair.

The orchard had a dozen trees, and the pears hung pale and heavy from the branches. Mara reached up and pulled one from its stalk, letting the branch rebound with a swish. She made sure Bee was looking at her, then rolled the pear to him. It trundled an arc across the ground. He sat up, shaking off Islay's hands, and rolled the pear back. Mara grinned and returned it. The pear trundled back, and halfway through its arc, Islay snatched it up and took a big bite.

'Thanks, Mara,' she said, grinning as she chewed, pretending that the pear wasn't sour and underripe and grainy with dirt. 'So kind of you.'

Mara resisted the urge to kick Islay in the face. She was barefoot, so it wouldn't even hurt. She pulled down another pear for herself. Bee wouldn't eat one; he wouldn't eat anything that looked like it had grown rather than been made in a factory. They crunched their spiteful fruit among the silent trees.

They waited. Before long an assortment of insects emerged, tempted by the sugar. Blood-bright ladybirds, oily beetles, spiked and fidgety caterpillars: all convened in the dirt. Bee leapt forward with a shriek and grabbed a fistful of ladybirds. Islay followed, plucking up a caterpillar. Mara trusted to luck: she laid her hand palm up on the soil and waited to see what would climb it. A black beetle, pincers twitching. She closed her hand tight. The inside of her fist tickled and she clenched it harder, so the beetle was all nice and cosy and couldn't move.

'What now?' she said.

Bee mimed a dance, then raced out of the orchard and across the grass. With his ladybird-filled fist he did heads, shoulders, knees and toes (knees and toes). He tried somersaults. He shook his hands like maracas.

Islay joined in, turning flips and cartwheels, her red curls twisting in the breeze, her dress flipping up to show her silky black under-wear – and where had she got that? It wasn't fair! Mara's underwear was all white cotton, little bows, stitched pink flowers. She wanted black. She wanted silk. She watched from the shade of the trees.

Bee ran to Mara and opened his hands, spilling ladybirds at her feet. 'Look,' he signed at the ladybirds. They lay tumbled, legs twisted at the sky.

One by one, Bee flipped them red side up. 'Look,' he signed again. Still they lay.

Mara didn't want to open her hand. She knew without looking that her beetle was dead. It died the moment she clenched her fist.

Bee pushed away the dead ladybirds, which, being dead, still weren't looking at him. His face twisted goblinish. His chest expanded as he pulled in a scream, ready.

'No no no, Bee! Hush hush hush.' Islay ran over and put her arm around his shoulders. Mara copied her, enveloping Bee's chubby body.

His chest softened as he pushed down the scream. He extricated himself from the arms and prised open his sisters' hands to extract the insects, which he arranged in a neat line at the edge of the orchard. He dropped cross-legged to the ground.

'Where?' signed Bee.

'Maybe they'll go to the cliff,' said Mara. 'Maybe everything goes there eventually.'

The day was already too hot; sweat pricked behind Mara's knees. From the orchard, a muffled thump as a ripe pear fell. Islay picked a daisy and pierced its stem with her thumbnail, ready to chain. Before you could count to ten, Bee got bored.

'Sea,' he signed.

'Good idea, Bee,' said Islay. 'Let's go and give the bugs to the sea. Maybe it will give us something back.'

Together they scooped up the dead bugs and ran back through the jaws of the house, leaving Mara alone on the grass.

Hame

The island is not neat. Not a single straight line on it. Not edged with tall white cliffs like meringue, or skirted with little beaches patted flat as the edges of a pie. You couldn't compare it to any foodstuffs at all, and definitely not sweet ones.

It's cliffs and clusters of defiant trees and rain-blown sheep bunched around wire fences. It's a low row of stone cottages painted chalky pastels. It's a harbour, a shop, a cafe, a pub. It's green and grey and the orange bob of buoys between the pale sky and the silver sea.

It's not so far from the mainland, but travel is tricky: no flat hilltops for planes or helicopters, no calm bays for ferries. It's all rocks round about, nasty spiked ones just under the water's surface.

But it doesn't matter how hard it is to get there, or how dark and rocky the sea. We'll all still try. What other choice do we have? Every childhood is an island.

Chapping

He arrived through the front door apologetically, the hem of his trousers catching on a tooth. His suit had been his father's suit, and perhaps his grandfather's before that; although it fitted him fine, the fabric was faded to shining at the elbows and knees. His name was John, or Joe – James? He was so forgettable. It's an achievement just to be able to mention his existence. Most people forgot him moments after meeting him. Even Mara forgot about him sometimes. Not his existence, of course, not his name – but the heft of him, the details. What colour were his eyes? Did he smell of soap or sweat or aftershave? What kind of shoes did he wear? Nobody knew. Just think of the blandest teenage boy you know, remove any identifying features, and imagine him standing gawkily in the ramshackle hall of a dilapidated guest house, smiling at his girlfriend's mother. That's John. Or James.

Mara had been waiting for him at her bedroom window, so she could get the timing just right. She'd watched him approach the house, his polished shoes dulling as he scuffed up the path, bouncing on the balls of his feet. She'd smiled to herself, in the indulgent and affectionate way she sometimes saw Signe smile at Peter.

She counted to ten to give him time to settle himself in the hallway; to catch his breath before she took it again. Then she arranged herself at the top of the stairs, ready to make her grand entrance. Of course she was still clumsy and sharp; still boxy as a woodlouse in her party dress – but why ruin the illusion? She hadn't even looked in the mirror, to better preserve the vision that she was Cleopatra, Cinderella, Scheherazade. It was probably for the best that Islay chose that moment to clatter out of her bedroom and down the stairs, obscuring Mara just at the moment that her boyfriend glanced up.

'Hello, Islay,' he said, trying not to look at the way that her too-tight, too-short floral frock showed a rather large quantity of skin. Trying to look, in fact, as if not only was he not looking, but he hadn't realised there was anything there to be not-looked at.

'Hello,' said Islay, breathing deep so her cleavage rose like bread. Just to wind him up, of course. Islay got so bored, so starved of consequence, and it was satisfying to make men look. This one was a boy, not a man, just a silly bit of nothing; but it was fine to toy. Islay thought his name was Joseph, Signe and Peter thought it was Jonathan, though it didn't matter as none of them ever used it. He was My Boyfriend to Mara, Him to Islay, The Boy to Peter and Signe.

Mara took a moment to collect herself, then continued her grand entrance. She paused after each step and trailed her finger-tips along the banister. She was an illustration in a storybook. Her nails weren't bitten and her hair didn't frizz and her chin wasn't spackled with spots and everything she saw in the mirror was a lie because this – this was her true self.

'Mara,' said J (which we'll call him, since we can all agree that whatever his name was, it began with a J). 'You look beautiful.' And Mara smiled, because if he said it then it must be true. She reached for his hand, which was large and damp. She held it anyway. She swung their linked hands slightly to catch Islay's attention.

Signe hadn't noticed her younger daughter descend, as she was too busy frowning at Islay. 'Your dress,' she said.

'You told me to put it on.'

'Well, let's get you a few new dresses, shall we?'

'Now?' asked Islay in confusion.

'Later. We'll order them, get them posted. The same, but … with more coverage.'

Islay plucked at the front of her dress as if trying to stretch out the fabric.

'Peter,' called Signe, her tone sweet and high, 'Mara's boyfriend is here!'

A squeal from the kitchen as a chair was pushed back. Three thudding footsteps.

'Welcome!' boomed Peter, smiling so his eyes crinkled, trying to hide that he had forgotten anyone was coming. In his defence, the promise of J was no more memorable than his physical presence.

Peter shook J's hand and clapped him on the shoulder. 'Welcome, welcome. We're so glad to have you here. Please do come on through so my wife can feed you up. It's her favourite pastime.' Peter grinned and patted his belly, which was large, but no larger than the rest of him and solid as packed earth. He scooped up his family and deposited them around the kitchen table. The room was thick with steam and the smell of lamb stew.

Signe had already set the table, and although she knew its pine surface was scudded and stained, the embroidered tablecloth was thick enough to hide it. She'd brought out the second-best cutlery, the ones with the bone handles. The coasters were silver, engraved with thistles.

'We won't always eat here,' Signe murmured as she scooped the stew into bowls. The cupboard doors were still mauve. In one corner, she'd started to steam off the floral wallpaper, only to reveal two other wallpapers underneath, each with a different floral pattern. 'There's a dining room,' she said.

'And what a room it will be!' Peter reached for his spoon. 'What do you think, my dove? Would you like some reclaimed cornicing? Stained-glass panels in the window?' He was still reaching for his spoon, having not quite managed to grasp it the first time. 'Stained glass would be nice.'

Peter had got a start on the roof, but he was only one man, no matter how huge his plans. He'd gone outside straight after breakfast and climbed the ladder and made his unsteady way above the choked gutters and started work. After a few hours he decided to go down for a tea break. But before that break, he'd need a break. He got a shake in his hands sometimes – nothing serious, nothing to worry the wife about. A shake in his hands, and sometimes his legs and body and brain. He would give himself a moment, just so he didn't wobble on the ladder.

And then something had happened. He wouldn't have been able to tell you what, exactly. He knew that he sat on the tiles and raised his eyes to look out across the house and garden. He knew that he saw the driveway, sweeping and structured but clogged with dandelions – he must get some weedkiller on that. And the shed, one window broken – a new pane, easy enough. The trees around the sides and back of the house – too close, they'd need pruning back. He'd do all of it, fix every broken thing. He'd make the perfect home for his family. But why was he on the roof? Was he meant to be clearing the gutters?

And then, somehow, his wife was calling him in so he could get washed for dinner. Where had today gone? Where had all of the days gone?

Telt

When Mara was little, she thought that babies hatched from eggs. When mums were making the eggs, their bellies got bigger and bigger, and when their bellies were tight and round and the egg was ready, they went into hospital where the egg was removed somehow (through the belly button? some sort of hatch? the details were unclear). The mums had to stay in hospital for a few days while the egg sat under a heat lamp to make it hatch, which was why when new babies were brought home, they were red and wrinkled like they'd just come out of a hot bath.

In Mara's defence, this was what Islay had told her. Long before Signe began to fatten with Bee, Mara put down her dolls one winter morning and asked where babies came from. Islay told of the eggs (though she left out the detail of how the egg was removed, as she wasn't sure herself), and of the heat lamps (if Islay had stopped to think about what she was saying, she'd realise she'd invented this, though as it did make sense she took it as fact). She added a further fingerprint to the tale: the mums kept mementos, and in every mum's bedroom there was a container with little bits of shell inside. And that was the proof.

Mara kept watch at the door while Islay crept into Signe and Peter's bedroom. She crawled under the bed, but found only lost socks. She laddered her way up the wardrobe shelves, but found only a dead fly. She stretched to tiptoe and ran her hands along the mantelpiece and her hand caught on something cold: a little china box in the shape of a heart. She kept her back to Mara so she wouldn't notice – just for a moment, she wanted these shards of their beginnings to belong to her alone. Islay opened the box. It fell to the carpet, spilling its contents as she ran out of the room.

'What? What?' whisper-shrieked Mara as she passed. Too afraid to go in and check what had frightened her sister, Mara ran to her bedroom and slammed the door. Later, Islay crept back into the room to return the teeth, counting them into the china heart. The teeth smelled sweet and bad. She slipped one into her mouth to feel its sharp edges on her tongue.

Mara never told Islay this, but she went back into Signe and Peter's bedroom to open the box and see the thing that had given her sister such a fright. She was disgusted and disappointed by the teeth. She'd wanted something other-worldly, something horrifying, something that would teach them a truth. But it was just old pieces of herself.

Although neither of them found the pieces of shell, for years after that both Ross girls still believed that babies hatched from eggs.

In Islay's defence, this was what Signe had told her. And as the hallway of their house featured a photo of a young Signe on stage, crowned with feathers, her limbs as thin and pale as bird bones, this seemed perfectly believable. If their mother were part bird, then of course they'd come from eggs.

In Signe's defence, the subject of pregnancy was a difficult one, and it seemed easier to make up a story. Soon after she met Peter she fell pregnant with triplets, and all the beauty and possibility of life was laid out in front of her. She should have known that nothing is that simple. During Signe's sixth month of pregnancy, one of the babies died. She would have done anything in the world to keep the other two, or even just one of them. Any living child; it did not matter which. She would have promised anything, climbed anything, killed anything, eaten anything, avoided anything. But we cannot make deals with nature. Just when Signe thought she'd suffered the worst possible grief, another triplet slipped away, and a further depth was revealed. But one child held on and Islay emerged, wrinkled and wailing, into a world that would never contain her sisters.

Two years later, another girl-baby followed without fuss. Signe had never told anyone that she planned to name two of the triplets Islay and Iona, a pair of islands; and the other Mara, to be the calm one, the sea between. Surely there was no harm in using one of the names for this child – and so she named her Mara.

Signe felt lucky enough with two living children, and was content to stop – but Peter wanted a boy, and she wanted what Peter wanted. They tried again, and lost two more. She agreed to one more try. One, and then her heart could not take it. And then came Barra, her little Bee, as solid and beautiful as the island for which he was named. He was her seventh child, the one blessed or cursed, depending on which stories you believed.

But Signe didn't need stories to love this child. He was her final creation, her last grasp at perfection. The marble-carved mounds of his cheek, his thigh, his shoulder, showed her where she'd fallen short before. She thought she knew love and grief already – but the thought of losing this child was past bearing. She would do everything she could to keep him in this world with her.

Signe never did tell her daughters that children were not hatched from eggs. They must have found out the truth somewhere else. When she thought about it, she felt sad that she'd missed that moment: the flash of realisation, the firmer grasp on the world, the click as things fell into place. The letting go of old fairy stories. But then, she soothed herself: we cannot be held responsible for every pretty lie we tell to our children.

Dram

'Shall we?' said Peter, standing from the table and leading them away from their empty plates.

In the front room, Islay plopped down on the smaller couch, which was scratchy with horsehair but meant no one would sit beside her. Peter took the leather armchair, rubbing his thumb over the white ring stained onto the arm.

'A drink?' said Peter.

'No thank you, sir,' said J, though he must have wondered whether it was actually more polite to say yes.

'A wee one,' said Peter. 'Puts hairs on your chest.' He nodded at Signe, who took two glasses from the sideboard and tipped whisky into them. One finger for the boy, four fingers for the man.

When Mara was little, Peter always took warm cream in his whisky. If she was good, he'd let her collect the silver jug from the kitchen, where Signe stood at the cooker heating pans of milk and cream for their bedtime cocoa. Mara would carry it through with perfect posture, head up, back straight, like she had books on her head. Peter's face would light up to see her step so ladylike into the room, the jug held before her like a prize. 'My best girl,' he'd say, and scoop her into his lap, where she'd pour the perfect dollop of cream into his glass, watching it swirl. Peat, warm cream, her father's soapy cheek. It was still her favourite smell.

Signe considered going into the kitchen, taking down a pan, fetching the cream from the fridge, heating it, finding the silver jug ... she lost the pattern of her thoughts to the white whoosh in her head. This endless house and its endless demands. She handed the glasses to Peter and the boy.

'*Slàinte*,' said Peter, tapping his glass against the boy's.

'Story,' signed Bee, because Signe had sat down in the story chair.

'Not now, Bee,' she replied. 'We have a guest, and I'm sure he doesn't want to hear me wittering on.'

'No, I would,' said J. 'If that's all right with you. Not that you witter. I mean, a story might be nice.'

'Go on, Mum,' said Mara, who had realised that if Signe told one of her stories, then she wouldn't be able to tell an embarrassing anecdote about Mara, of which she had a wide stock, and which Mara would like to hide from her boyfriend for as long as possible. Most of them involved her as a small child, puking or shitting at an inappropriate place or time. Mara didn't know whether Signe thought the stories were cute, or knew that they were embarrassing and relished it.

'Well,' said Signe, surprised, 'if that's what you all want.'

Peter knocked back his whisky in a single gulp and put his glass on the arm of his chair, perfectly aligned with the white ring. Islay got as comfortable as she could on the horsehair couch. J sipped his whisky and did a terrible job of hiding his grimace. Mara arranged herself beside her boyfriend and pulled Bee onto her lap. Signe began her story. She'd read it aloud so many times over the years that she knew it by heart, and did not need a book.

'There was once a handsome young fisherman,' she said, 'who could not find himself a wife. The island girls were pretty enough, but he felt something missing. Every day he took out his boat and set his lobster pots, and every night he sat alone in his cottage and watched the peat fire rise and fall.

'One evening he heard soft laughter over the dunes. His footsteps silent on the sand, he crept closer. In the moonlight he saw a trio of women, all silvery hair and long limbs, dancing on the damp sand. One woman in particular captivated him. Her eyes were black as the night sea and her hair was starlight. He felt quite bewitched.

'As he watched, the women stepped over to the rocks, where sat a pile of greyish skins. They slid the skins up over their own pale limbs – and when the fisherman blinked, the women were gone, and three seals slipped into the water.'

In Mara's arms, Bee began to fidget. 'Finished,' he signed. Mara held him around the waist, making shushing sounds into his ear with the rhythm of her breathing, and he settled.

'The next night,' continued Signe, 'the fisherman was waiting. When the women began their laughing dance, he crept to the rocks and snatched up one of the skins. He ran and hid it in a wooden box under his bed. When he returned, two of the women had disappeared, but the black-eyed selkie woman was still searching for her skin. She begged the fisherman to let her go home. But desire made him selfish. He promised that if she became his wife, he would love her and care for her and make her happy each day of her life. You may love me, she replied, and I may even love you back – but I can never be happy here.'

Bee arched his back and tried to prise Mara's hands away from his middle. 'Finished,' he signed again. Mara stroked his hair and tried to soothe him.

'They married,' went on Signe, 'and had seven fine children, all happy and strong and full of life. The fisherman loved his selkie-wife, and in time she loved him in return. But every night she slid from her marriage bed to stand on the shore, gazing out at the water and mourning the other world now lost to her. The fisherman lay sleepless in the empty bed, the stolen skin beneath him.

'One day their youngest son was exploring the house, and found the sealskin under the bed. The seventh child, you see, is always closest to the other world. He brought it to his mother and asked her, what was this strange thing, so soft and smelling of the sea? The boy knew nothing of his mother's history; he was simply curious. The selkie –'

Bee began a wordless wail. Mara tried to hold him, but he made his body rigid, his head thrusting back to hit against her chest. She let him go with a gasp of pain. He thudded to the carpet and wailed even louder.

'Bedtime for bees,' announced Signe.

Bee wailed louder.

'Now,' said Signe.

Bee stayed on the ground, his body still rigid. His hands, his arms, his legs did not move. His chest did not move. His face grew pink.

'Bee, stop it!' said Mara.

Bee was silent. His face went from pink to red.

'Bee, little love, don't do that,' said Islay. 'If you go upstairs now, you'll get a story.'

'Och, leave the lad!' said Peter. 'He's fine. Just stubborn.'

Bee was still silent. His eyes began to bulge.

'Oh, Bee,' sighed Signe. She scooped him up, his body stiff as a doll, and carried him out of the room. Everyone held their breath. Finally, from upstairs, the wails resumed at a quieter volume. And they breathed again. Since Bee was born, none of them had heard the end of a story.

'I remember this story,' said J. He sipped his whisky and, this time, managed not to grimace. 'My mum used to tell it. The selkie takes her skin and puts it on, and she goes back into the sea. Her husband and children never see her again. Sometimes the husband wanders the shore feeling sad and missing his wife. I remember I didn't like the story when I was a kid, because it was too sad and I –'

'No,' said Islay, indignant. 'That's not how the story goes. Who told you that?'

'It is,' persisted J. 'It's the only way it can go. The selkie can't be happy on land. That's not her true nature, and even if she loves her kids it's not enough.'

'That doesn't make sense,' said Mara. 'It's a love story. How can it be a love story if they're not together at the end?'

'I'll tell you the end,' said Islay. 'The selkie decides she doesn't want the skin after all, because she loves her husband and her wee ones too much. She gives up her other life and stays with them. Happily ever after.' This was the version that Signe had told Islay and Mara before Bee was born, back when stories still ended. Islay smiled pityingly at J. 'Sorry your mum told you a weird version. When you get home you can tell her the right one.'

'I can't tell her anything,' said J. 'She went up to the cliff last year.'

'Oh,' said Islay. 'I forgot. Sorry, I - whatever. She's still wrong, though, the way she told you it.'

'Well!' said Peter, getting up to refill the boy's glass, the slosh and clink filling the silence. 'Let's agree to disagree. It doesn't matter anyway, now does it? It's only a story.'

Entrelacé

O nce, and only once, Signe told her daughters how she had met her husband. What she didn't tell them is that there are two versions of the story, and both of them are true.

The version she told her daughters is about a swan maiden whose feathered cape is snatched by a man who she then marries. They have children, and love them, and the swan maiden never misses her old life or her old freedom or the feeling of spreading her wings and flying high over the trees without being bound to anyone or anything. She chooses her family and forgets everything else. Happily ever after.

The other version, the one she didn't tell, is about a dancer and a boxer who meet in a bar one night after a performance. Both of them are in jeans and shirts - no pointe shoes, no wrapped hands - so they meet as total strangers, and don't know until much later that they are a dancer and a boxer.

At least, as far as the boxer is concerned. Because the real story inside the real story is that the dancer had seen the boxer before. On television, which was a thing she often watched and always enjoyed, sleepless and secretive in hotel rooms. The only channel with clear reception showed a boxing match: a replay from that night's fight. Its staccato thuds were almost lost under the excitable stream from the commentators. Fists connected. Blood spattered. Signe jolted up in bed and stared at the screen. Then she stared at the man: not the one who bled, but the one who caused the bleeding. His face split into a grin, triumphant – but for a moment it faltered, and she was sure she caught regret. She leaned so close to the TV that the image dissolved into pixels. She wanted to crawl in beside him. She wanted to lick the blood from his fists. That night, in her dreams, the boxing match replayed at quarter-speed. It was a brutal dance, but a beautiful one.

She woke in her own personal pool of blood: her period, missing for years, finally returned. Leaving the hotel sheets to soak in the bath, she dressed and went to find out where the boxer would be that night. A theatre round the corner from her theatre. His name was displayed in lights. She made note of the nearest bar.

That evening, after her show, she went there with her fellow dancers. She made sure to sit in the middle of the room, under the brightest light. When he arrived, he wouldn't fail to miss her. She knew that out of costume, the dancers still commanded an audience: their sharp cheekbones, their wide deer eyes, their endless limbs. But he didn't come that night, or the next night. Still she went. Still she waited. And then, finally, he walked through the door. Happily ever etc. etc.

The thing is, there is another real story inside that real story inside the real story, which is that the boxer had seen the dancer before.

He wasn't a fan of dance, but was trying to show the girl he was seeing that he wasn't just a meathead with scarred knuckles. So, the ballet. From the moment the lead dancer appeared on stage, he was bewitched. She played two roles that night, the good swan and the bad swan. He had to resist the urge to chase her backstage and fling her over his shoulder like a caveman. After the show he ditched his date and lurked near the stage door. Even out of her swan costume, she was easy to recognise: the bones of her face were strong and sculpted, each movement as graceful as a bird opening its wings. He watched which bar the dancers disappeared into. He went to follow, then stopped. Although he'd won last night's fight, he'd ended up with a lumpen, purpled eye. He couldn't meet her like this, the beast to her beauty. So he waited until he looked mostly human again, and then he went to the bar, and found her there under the brightest light.

They never meant to lie to one another. The truth of how they met was just a thing that they didn't say, and didn't say, and still didn't say. The longer it went unsaid, the more it became a lie.

Dunt

t first, Mara and J climbed the cliff holding hands, but it was hard going over the tussocks and rocks, and they soon had to let go. It was halfway between dinnertime and bedtime, and the sky was streaked with pink. It wouldn't get completely dark, but it would get darker than this. Mara had told her parents that she was going to walk her boyfriend home. She'd said it just like that: *I am going to walk my boyfriend home.* Signe had hidden a smile and nodded her solemn approval. She'd learned from her older daughter how vital it was to take teenage girls seriously. While the cliff was technically on the way to J's house, in that nothing on this small island was out of the way, it was a bit of a detour. It was J's idea; Mara would have been happy with a quick kiss at the end of her driveway, but he wanted something more private. That was fine with her too. Everything J said or did was fine. Never wonderful, never terrible, just fine. As he climbed, J hummed a tune under his breath.

Mara was distracted, thinking about the selkie story. About how desirable it was to be desired. To be so beautiful and so sad. To never be hasty or clumsy; for all your movements to be slow and elegant with grief. To have a man want you so much he'd steal from you and lie to you every day, just to keep you. If only life could be a pretty story like that.

This part of the cliff was steep, and Mara's breath came harder. She tried to wipe her palms on her thighs without J noticing. Finally, they emerged at the top of the cliff. The wind shrieked around them, lifting Mara's hair, chilling the sweat on the back of her neck.

The first statue had only been here a few months. Elinor, from the other side of the island. She'd looked like stone even when she was still made of flesh: grey hair, grey skin, wrinkles carved deep into her cheeks. Her every movement was slow, considered, as if she carried pebbles in her pockets. But then, maybe hers was a gradual change, and she'd started to turn before Mara even arrived on the island. Maybe she hadn't always been the way Mara saw her. Maybe she'd been young and black-haired once, flirting with boys and knocking back whisky and dancing until her feet bled.

The next statue stood alone, away from the group. This was one of Mara's favourites, and she took the time to break away from J and touch the stone hand. Caleb, with his forward-slanting forehead and his underbite, as if every part of him was leaning forward, impatient. Caleb was different because although his body faced out to sea like all the other statues, at the last minute he had turned his head to look over his shoulder, back at the island. Before he came up to the cliff, Caleb had a sheep farm on the south edge of the island. The sheep were stupid and stank of shit, but Mara liked to find the fluffs of wool they left in the knots of the barbed wire. They looked like tiny clouds, but felt rough and oily. Now that Caleb was here, Mara's boyfriend's dad had the sheep farm. One day Mara's boyfriend's dad would come up to the cliff too, and

Mara's boyfriend would have the sheep farm, and Mara would help birth lambs and get used to the smell of sheep shit and have all the oily clouds she could ever want, happily ever after.

And there was J's mum, Eilidh, short and curvy and curly-haired, smiling wide to show the gap between her front teeth. She stood like most of the others, but if you looked you could see how her hands were cupped open, ready to hold the hands of her husband and son when their time came. Mara remembered when Eilidh came up to the cliff last year.

Eilidh had been changing for a few months by then: her movements stiffening, her eyes darkening to grey, her skin flaking grit when she rubbed her hands together. Finally, when she could only just walk, she called the islanders together. People didn't always come together when someone went up to the cliff, but Eilidh was popular. The islanders, holding candles, lined the path. J and his dad stood at the end of the line, right at the top where the land dropped away to the sea. Eilidh made her slow, jerky way up the path. Her hair had already turned to stone, and instead of blowing in the wind it stayed in neat, solid curls, framing her face. She was so stiff that Mara could hear the creak and crack of her knees as she walked. Mara reached to hold her sister's hand – but Islay shoved her fists into her coat pockets. She never liked when people went up on the cliff; she said because it was boring and creepy, but really because she didn't want to think of a time when she would have to stand at the top of the path as one of her family made their final walk towards her. Bee, too big to be held so long in Signe's arms but accepting nothing else, fidgeted and mewled into her neck.

As Eilidh made her slow climb, each person leaned in to her and whispered in her ear: a memory they shared, a wish for her happiness, a reassurance that they'd look in on her husband

and son. No one tried to convince her to change her mind; it was far too late for that. Finally, Eilidh made it up to the top of the cliff, just as her movements slowed to stillness and the black centres of her eyes faded to grey. And there she stayed.

It was getting dark now, and most of the daisies had closed. J and Mara spent a while searching for flowers that still showed their faces. Mara tied one long-stemmed daisy around the rest to make a bouquet, then placed them in Eilidh's open hand. Around them, dozens upon dozens of stone figures, all ages and heights, all facing out to sea. They stood in proud formation, heads high, like soldiers marching into battle.

J reached for Mara, pulling her down onto the grass. Close to the ground, out of the wind, they could hear one another speak.

'You always touch Caleb's hand when we go by,' said J. 'Do you think you'll look back like him?'

'When?'

'When we're here.'

'But we are here.'

J laughed. 'I know, but I mean when we're here like they are.' He motioned to the statues. 'When we're here forever.'

Mara felt her innards swoop to her throat, then back down. Her blood throbbed in her temples. But this was what she wanted. This was all she wanted. Everything was good good good and she pushed out a smile.

'We don't need to decide now, do we? That won't be for ages. We've got our whole lives to live before then. Travelling, and adventures, and a whole world to see.'

'Travelling?'

'Yeah. Interrailing around Europe. Or backpacking in Australia, or South America, maybe. Like people do.'

Most young people did leave the island when they were old enough, and rarely seemed to come back. Of the few hundred islanders, Mara and Islay and J were the only teenagers.

'Sure.' J draped his arm around Mara's shoulders. 'If you want to.'

'Don't you want to?'

'I said, if you want to. I don't really care. I don't see the point in going anywhere, when we'll just come back here anyway. Everything we need is here.'

'Okay, fine,' said Mara, but she didn't think it was fine.

J laughed, lifting Mara's hand to kiss her palm. 'You're so cute, with your plans and things.'

Mara bit down on her irritation. J was only a year older than her, but to hear him speak you'd think he was an adult and she was a child. He'd been like that ever since he'd seen his mum up onto the cliff. As if not crying was what made a man.

'If you say so.'

'Come on, Mara. I'm only saying. You love living on the island, don't you?'

'Yes, but I don't - it's not -' Mara let the wind steal her words. There were a lot of things that J understood that she didn't - mostly to do with sheep - but she knew better than him what it was to love and hate at the same time.

Six years ago, when the Ross family had bought their house, there was no handover of keys, because there was nothing to unlock. There was no front door and no back door. There were no windows in the downstairs rooms. Dead leaves blew along every corridor. If you stayed quiet, you could hear things skitter. For a month they lived in one room while Peter and a hired crew made the house habitable. Doors, windows. Portable gas heaters in the bedrooms until the electric could be connected. Then Peter got rid of the hired crew and said he'd do the rest of the work himself. Mara didn't care; she loved the house the way it was. They had a place to eat, and a place to sleep, and they had each other. The longer they all lived in it, the more they moulded the house to their shape. How could anyone else live in it now?

And so she would live there, and then she would get married and live on a different bit of the island, and she would spit out a brood of babies and be the queen of everything she saw, and before long she would come up to the cliff too, and she'd be majestic and candlelit and loved, and then seabirds would shit on her forever.

'Mara! Where are you going?'

Mara stopped walking, looking at her feet as if she wasn't in control of them. Ahead of her was only this: dozens of bodies turned to stone, and then the edge of the cliff. The glimmer of rocks. The lure and chew of the waves.

'Nowhere,' she said. The sea, the island, the sky. 'I'm not going anywhere.'

Clype

Mara sloped back to the house alone. Her chin was tender from J's stubble; as she walked she pressed the back of her hand to her face to cool it. The taste of his saliva was still in her mouth, an unfamiliar staleness like old chewing gum.

A single light was on upstairs, her parents the only ones still awake. They didn't need to wait up for her – it wasn't that late, and anyway what could happen on this island, where every story ended the same way? Still, she knew Signe would keep that light on until she heard the click of the front door closing. She scrunched across the gravel.

A light blinked from the warped door of the shed. What the hell was Islay doing? Mara was torn between curiosity, and not wanting her sister to know that she was capable of arousing her curiosity. Pride won; she turned away from the shed.

Then she stopped. What a shame to pass up the chance to spy. It was always useful to have material for blackmail. She crept closer, straining her ears, trying to hear over the sound of her throbbing blood. She kept her steps as light as breath. She was delicate and elegant: a ballerina, a bird about to take flight. A high-pitched giggle burst from the shed.

'I can heeeear yoooou!' sang Islay.

Mara sulked into the shed.

'Nice job, elephant feet,' said Islay, exhaling a long stream of smoke. 'I heard you coming from a mile off.'

Mara stuck her tongue out at Islay and slumped down in a torn armchair. Dust bloomed. Tea lights were lined up along the base of the walls, and in their flickering halo Islay perched on the window-sill, long legs dangling. Looping curls of cigarette smoke emerged from her hand. The tip glowed as she inhaled. Mara was disgusted and envious.

'They smell horrible,' she said. 'Where did you even get them?' She whipped the cigarette packet off the arm of her chair.

'Watch it!' snapped Islay. 'You'll dent the corners. I have to sneak it back into the first-aid box later. Mum won't notice a couple missing.'

'How do you know?'

Islay shrugged. 'She never does. And you,' she added, 'can't have one.'

'I don't want one! They're disgusting.'

'Convenient for you.' Islay pouted, exhaling a perfect stream of smoke. 'Seeing as how I won't let you have one.'

Mara lifted her feet, hugging her knees to her chest. The shed was always cold, lurking in the shadows between the house and the trees, away from the sunlight. It was a dumping ground for haunted things. Old objects from people who'd passed through the house, evidence of all the attempts that had been made to turn it into something. A three-legged milking stool and gauze that still smelled faintly of rancid butter; cardboard files, chewed by mice and rotted with damp; jars of pickled somethings, their contents blackened and sticky.

The shed wasn't meant to be a playroom. When they'd first moved in, it was just a place to keep garden tools and furniture that Signe was going to do up for the house – but then Bee was born, and shrieked through every night. Signe and Peter took it in turns to jounce him on their hips and wander the corridors, his cries eventually filling the whole house, and the shed became a secret haunt for unsleeping girls. Islay and Mara would sneak out, make a fire from candles in the middle of a circle of bricks, pull all the damp cushions onto the floor, toast marshmallows over the flames, and tell fairy tales where all the characters were called Islay and Mara, and they were all the prettiest and cleverest, and they all got to marry the youngest and bravest prince, and be the queen of something or another. If Mara dug through the flowerpots up on the shelf, she knew she'd find old packs of cards and tins of sweets, wrapped in months of grime. Someday soon Islay would leave the island, and no one would eat the sweets or play the cards or light the candles ever again. The thought made tears itch the top of her nose.

'Mara,' said Islay.

Mara's head jerked, twinging her neck. She'd slipped half-asleep to the whisper of the waves.

'Remember that time we went down to the sea?' asked Islay, her voice slow and sweet.

'There have been literally hundreds of times.' Mara blinked fast so Islay wouldn't see her tears. 'I'm not bloody psychic.'

'That first night on the island. We crept out of bed. We were still trying to figure out how things worked here, and we were so frightened, and so excited. We went down to the sea and stood there on the stones and let the freezing water eat our feet bite by bite.'

Mara felt the world reduce to the glow of Islay's cigarette and the low hum of her voice. She wondered if she was asleep after all.

'We talked about what we thought happened to people after they died, and you said ... ' Islay's voice slid lower. 'You said maybe this was dying. You said the sea would keep going, keep licking and licking at us until we were all gone. Until there was nothing of us but sunken bones, and then we would have to stay here forever.'

Mara breathed in her sister's smoke. Her eyes burned.

'So what?' said Mara. 'You had weird ideas too. You said ... '

Islay had said that people might turn into stars and shoot up into the sky, or turn into ants and slip down into the soil, or shatter to glitter and get inhaled by a passing cow. She'd said that death might be just like this world but all over again, or flooded or burned or suspended from chains in the sky. She'd said that we might forget who we were and live the same life over again. She'd said we might be stuck in that final moment forever. She'd said ... she'd said ...

'You said lots of things, Islay. And I never made you feel silly about them.'

'That's not what I mean. I mean – what if you were right?'

'No.' Mara loved to say no to her sister, even if it meant admitting she was wrong about something. 'It's magic here. It's the best life. You know it is.'

'But what if?' Islay looked at her sister. 'What if it's not?'

Mara watched as the glow from Islay's cigarette burned out to nothing.

'Mara, I think you were right. I think this is dying.'

'No,' said Mara, and she got up and walked out of the shed without looking back.

Stramash

One summer, many years ago, the Ross family visited the funfair. There were carousels and twisters and haunted houses with chipped, flicker-eyed movie monsters. There were people screaming and laughing and doing a mixture of the two. The lights were so bright they outshone the stars.

The air was heavy with the smells of sugar and frying dough; it made Islay feel hungry and sick all at once. Signe got candyfloss for the girls. Islay unwound it with her fingers and made it into a crown, which she regretted as after ten minutes of prancing around giddily declaring she was the fairy queen, she went to take off the crown and eat it, only to find it was half melted and studded with loose hairs and dead midges. She put her lips to the clean edge of the cloud and it dissolved to sand on her tongue. She didn't feel like she was eating it, as there was no chewing or swallowing involved.

Mara was too small and Signe too nervous to go on any of the strap-in tumble-round rides, so they all had to stick to the sideshow games. Islay sulked that she wanted to have a shot on a roller coaster, but when did it ever matter what Islay wanted?

They failed to throw hoops over wooden blocks, failed to shoot ducks with pellet guns, and failed to make a spinning wheel land on the smiley face. After yet another failure, Mara, ever the brat, stormed off and caught her toe on a stone. She opened her mouth to wail – but before she could, Peter scooped her up and onto his shoulders, kissing her toe where she'd stubbed it. From the ground, Islay scowled up at her sister. Mara's head was practically in the stars. She was the tallest and happiest girl in the world. From up there, she would win every game.

The last in the line was a boxing game. In the front of the stall, three skull-size balls hung down, striped yellow and black like bees. In the back sat rows of cheap toys, leading up to the very top prize: a doll's house.

'Look!' shouted Mara. 'Look at that! Can I win that?'

'Fear not, my princess! I shall win it for you.' Peter spread his stance and flexed his arm muscles, making Signe giggle and Mara squeal and grab his hair.

'Will I? For old times?' he said to Signe.

Signe looked at him with soft eyes. 'For old times,' she said.

Peter won the boxing game, which wasn't a surprise as it was rare for him to meet a man or a machine he couldn't knock out. The stallholder congratulated him and did an announcement where he put his mouth too close to the tannoy so the speaker popped and squeaked and shouted in drawn-out vowels 'WE HAVE A WINNER!' and made everyone clap. Then when everyone had stopped looking the stallholder tried to give Mara one of the big cuddly penguins.

'No thank you,' said Peter. 'My daughter wants the doll's house.'

The stallholder gave Mara and Islay a cuddly penguin each, and a tiger too. Islay would have been fine with them. She knew that even Mara, despite her sulks, would have been happy with any prize. But it was too late for that.

'No,' said Peter. 'The doll's house.'

The stallholder waited until the crowd had drifted away. 'Mate,' he said, his tone reasonable, 'I can't. The boss will kill me if I give that away.'

'Mate,' said Peter, equally reasonable, 'I'll kill you if you don't.'

Signe leaned up and whispered in Peter's ear. Sulkily, he gathered his daughters and let them hang off his arms like monkeys. Signe waited until her husband was out of earshot, then she spoke to the stallholder. They did not speak for long, but it was enough.

Peter carried the doll's house home. Mara skipped along beside him, high on sugar and attention. Islay barely noticed, too busy trying to find a stone big enough to stub her toe so she could have her turn on Peter's shoulders.

Bairn

ara woke early, so she was the first to notice that Bee was not in his bed. She noticed it gleefully, sneakily, like she'd discovered a secret. She'd find him and bring him home before anyone else noticed, and then everyone would be grateful, and Bee would sit on her lap for ages and not fidget.

But finding him was not easy. He wasn't in the garden, or in any rooms of the house. Not hiding in a cupboard, not playing in the shed, not marching up and down the drive looking for bugs. He wasn't even in the trees behind the house. Mara had to twist to avoid stabbing her legs with twigs, and to duck to avoid branches pulling out her hair. Finally she emerged at the beach to the pink summer dawning. Around her, long trails of seaweed draped the rocks, sopping green, parted in the centre like hair. The crowns of heads buried deep, sleeping warriors about to rise.

Bee definitely wouldn't be at the beach. He never went there alone; he was too frightened of the skittering crabs and too unsteady on the pebbled surface. He never would – unless, maybe, he'd given a beetle to the sea, and wanted to know what it had given him in return.

Mara's body shivered hot and cold. In the distant flip and forge of the waves she saw something. The glimpse of a round head. A reaching arm. A splash.

'Bee!' she tried to shout, panic shrinking her voice, even as she told herself it was a seal, just a seal and not a boy. 'Bee, swim this way!'

She yanked off her boots, fingernails scraping her skin, and stumbled into the shallows. Because this was stupid, so stupid, and she was no good at saving people, but there was nothing else to do so she kept going even as the chill of the water hit her harder than a punch. Off the edge of the sandbank and her feet kicked out into nothing and her fingers were already numb and she couldn't see anything at all, not the curve of Bee's head nor the splash of his arms. She let herself sink, let the black water close silent over her – then thrust herself up. Her shoulders cork-popped up out of the water and she could see him, his dark gold hair. She looked back at the shore. She was much further out than she should be, and the waves were pushing her further still, and at the same time they were bringing Bee closer to her. One more kick through the burning in her legs, one more pull through the ache in her arms – and there, just a glimpse of his grasping hand, and she was so close, and she could see that his face was tilted to the sky and his eyes rolled towards her just as a lolling tongue of water swallowed him up.

She dived down and came up empty-handed. The waves clawed at her clothes, dragging their fingers through her hair and grinding salt into her eyes. It was fine for her to reach Bee but she couldn't have him, she couldn't bring him back; the sea wanted them both. Something bumped her leg: she reached out for Bee but couldn't get a grip on the drenched fabric or slippery skin. Another dive, and a wave whipped at her closed eyes with something hard and solid, and the water was so cold that she didn't know if it cut her but there was a warm stinging and all the air pushed out of her lungs and she flailed in the water and her hand found the silkiness of Bee's hair. She held on, kicking until she met air, and then there was heat on her cheek and her left eye wouldn't open and she realised that something was wrong, and that was stupid because everything was wrong.

Hauling Bee under her arm, making sure that his face was out of the water, she turned for shore. But she couldn't swim like that, with only one arm and trying not to jolt Bee, and she saw then that she didn't know how to be in the sea, not really. She could laze through the warm shallows with her legs kicking angles like a water beetle's, but now her muscles juddered and her eyes swelled and she couldn't fight the waves and the cold and the sodden weight of a child. She held one hand under his body so his face wouldn't go underwater and she pulled at the water with the other arm and she kicked harder and harder through the ache and the sharp and the panic.

The water was up around her ears, and her spine ached from keeping her head tilted back, and the sky spun above her, and she felt like her body was more sea than skin, and she wanted to just give up. Sink down. Know quiet. But the weight of Bee, the sea pulling at him, and she wouldn't let it have him. She made a last desperate kick and felt sand graze her toes. The sandbank.

She staggered upright with the sea pulling at her knees and lifted Bee out of the water and stumbled onto the beach. She lay him down on the stones. She was shivering so hard that she retched. She couldn't open her left eye. Icy water dripped from her hair onto Bee's body. Breath gasping, she pressed her hand to his bird-fragile breastbone. There. Again, again. A fast pulse, heavy in her fingertips.

He was fine.

Everything was fine.

She rocked back on her heels, tiny stones embedding into her shins, and sobbed out a laugh. She reached for Bee, ready to scoop him into her arms and carry him home for hot chocolate and a bath and a proper scolding about never ever going anywhere near the sea by himself. She'd never let him go anywhere by himself again. She'd be with him, always.

It took far too long for her to realise that his chest was not rising. The pulse had not come from Bee, but from Mara's own heartbeat, hard in her fingertips. She snatched her hand away.

The eyes rolled back, all white.

The blood clotted black in the mouth.

The skin already clammy.

The body was dead, and she was afraid.

Mara skeltered into the house, her hands held over her left eye, her cheek and throat sheened in blood, shrieking fit to wake the dead. Signe and Peter rushed for wet cloths and telephones, but she grabbed at their hands, trying to pull them back out of the door. Her terror made the whole house tilt. Signe forced Mara – still stuttering about Bee and the beach, Bee is at the beach, the beach, Bee, Bee – into a kitchen chair. She was shaking so hard that her feet drummed on the tiles.

'We'll go and get him,' soothed Signe, 'we'll go now, it's fine, it's all fine, hush now.'

It took all of Islay's nerve to keep Mara upright in the chair and hold the sides of her face together. Mara's cheek was a mass of red.

Islay's hand slipped in the blood and the wound gaped, revealing the teeth underneath. She couldn't hold in a sob. Peter had phoned for an air ambulance and then dropped the phone onto the table in his haste to go for Bee, and Islay could still hear the operator's voice, a soothing muffle through the plastic. She wiped the blood from one hand onto the thigh of her pyjamas and reached for the phone.

'It's okay,' said the operator, 'stay calm, it's all okay,' and it didn't seem like she was even listening to herself, but she must have known that it didn't matter what the words were as long as someone was there to say them.

Signe and Peter rushed into the garden. Somewhere in Signe's mind she wondered if she should be running harder. But to run would be to accept that there was a reason to run. Mara's panic was so extreme, so theatrical, that Signe couldn't join it. She was so calm she felt drugged, as if she was floating above them all, observing.

Together, Signe and Peter fought through the dark trees. They emerged from the shadows into the bright day. Before them the beach stretched, a vast nail clip. Every inch of the stones was covered with a mass of jellyfish. Peter strode towards the water, his boots slip-sliding, squealing on the juddering bodies. Signe followed, trying to step in the wet dents he'd left, her ankles already nipping from the stings. Together they waded into the water. A red drone was getting louder in their heads. There was nothing and nothing and nothing. Becoming more frantic, their shouts for their son beginning to waver and break, they searched the shore and the sea, wading out past the shallows, reaching off the end of the sand-bank. But Bee was not there.

The sea had taken him.

The sea takes everything.

PART 1½

Birling

At first there were helicopters. Hospitals. Police and needles and stitches and search dogs. A persistent high panic whining through the house. Rooms usually populated only by mice and the upturned bodies of dead beetles were opened and searched. Every cupboard was checked. It was unlikely – impossible – that a small boy would have prised the nails from the door frames, forced open the heavy wardrobes, crept past three locks into the attic. But maybe, maybe – and so they checked, and checked again.

Nobody found Bee. Not in the house, and not outside it. After a week the search became slightly less frantic – by then, it was not a rescue effort to save a living boy, but to find a body. Crime was almost unknown on the island, and Bee hadn't left, because the fishing boat was the only way on or off and he hadn't been on it. But accidents can happen anywhere. Every islander knew of someone lost to the sea.

After two more weeks the search cooled. After two months it stopped – not officially, but in practice. For a while no one on the island let their children out of their sight. All the island men were interviewed. Signe and Peter were interviewed. Islay and Mara were interviewed. Posters were put up, the gappy grin of Barra Ross on the wall of the shop and the cafe and the pub. Everything came to nothing. The sea had taken Bee, and it would not give him back.

There was no funeral. No memorial service, nothing to mark the cut-out space left behind. Signe wouldn't allow even the mention of it. The missing did not need funerals, they needed to be enticed home. He'd crept away from her and was surely hiding somewhere. Deep down she knew that he –

She knew that he –

He must be somewhere, run off in a huff, his tiny temper burning bright – but all of him fine, all of him safe. This must be true, because any other thought was too terrible. All she had to do was get the house right – get it perfect, the perfect home, everything perfect from the top of the chimney to the end of the garden. She would be the perfect mother in the perfect home, and then her perfect boy would come back.

She worked on the house from the moment she woke. Every time she blinked, she felt a coarse scraping in her eyes. Every crease of her body itched with dirt and paint flecks. Every muscle felt stiff and hot, as if they had rusted. She arranged old sheets along the bottom edges of the walls, tipped paint into trays, pushed fluffy rollers through greys and blues and pale pinks, put the kettle on, left the mug in the sink, hefted in more paint tins, left the brushes in turps. She put bricks in a wheelbarrow, wheeled a grubby trail through the kitchen, tipped the wheelbarrow out into the back garden. She sanded floorboards and mixed plaster and screwed in new switch plates. She painted ceilings and wiped drips of paint off the floor where the dust sheets had slipped.

The days fell away, and Bee did not come home.

Everything that Signe made, Peter unmade. He had decided on his own deal: he would give back what he had taken from the island. He would make the house exactly as it had been when he had found it. Then perhaps he would get back what had been taken from him.

His was a sneaky destruction. There was no tearing up of floorboards, no smashing of walls. It was important for Peter to pay attention to exactly what Signe did, and undo it all again. In the same order, if he could.

It was all going well, until it wasn't. He'd thought his work would soon overtake Signe's - after all, isn't it always easier to destroy than to create? But every day, Peter got slower. His bones ached. His joints shrieked and cracked. Powdered stone snowed from him each time he moved. He pushed his body harder, but it was no good; the ghost of his son hung around his neck, and pulled.

Islay moved among all this making and unmaking. If she saw an open door, she closed it. If she saw a lid left off a paint tin or a jam jar, she replaced it. A sticking plaster is no good on a broken back, but what more could she do? What bothered her most was how mundane it all was. This terrible thing had happened - this huge, life-changing thing that meant the world would never be the same. But outside their house, whose life had changed? Even inside the house, what, really, had changed beyond repair? They still had to get up every morning. They still had to eat breakfast. They had to pay bills and buy toilet paper and smile at the postman. They didn't wander through moonlit rooms tearing at their hair. They didn't curse an unfeeling god. The whole world should have shifted on its axis, should have shaken the petals from every flower, uprooted every mountain. And here they were, going through the motions, as if they'd lost a pet cat or a set of keys.

Islay said none of this to her sister. Before long, they weren't saying anything much to one another; just *pass the pepper* and *I borrowed your top* and *it's fine, I'll wash up*. It wasn't that they were relying on telepathy, some secret sisterly code. Inside their heads was silence.

Summer bled into autumn, the trees fell bare, and in the lengthening red nights Islay lay outside on a bed of crunching leaves, watching the glint and dart of insects over her head. She let them flit across her face; let them tangle in her hair. After a while, a single thought settled on her: if I don't leave here now, I will never be anything but the sister of a lost boy. She was eighteen. She could do what she wanted. She packed in the silent moonlight, then left before dawn to catch the morning boat.

Signe came down to the kitchen a few hours later and found Islay's note on the table. She read it once, then folded it up and put it in her pocket. She'd need to take the butter out of the fridge now, to let it soften enough for pancakes. She'd do eggs too, and crispy bacon, and perhaps there was some bramble jelly at the back of the pantry. A breakfast wouldn't bring back a daughter or a sister, but it was all she had to give Peter and Mara. The Ross family - what was left of it - carried on.

Stravaig

To Mara, the months before they lost Bee felt like the last real summer. For the rest of the season, she wandered the darkened house. She needed to heal, and her stitches itched worse in the sunlight. Loss felt cold and quiet, and the world through the windows looked too hot, too bright. It would hurt her eyes to see things lit so clearly. The house closed in around her, silent, velvet.

Before, Islay would have slipped into bed beside her every morning and together they'd do their schoolwork. Now, they worked in silence in separate rooms, heads down, eyes aching. Before, they had an enthusiastic but unstructured education from Signe: the stories of ballets, the use of flowers as medicine, Renaissance painters, the wildlife of the taiga, the history of space exploration, Achilles tendon stretches, how to gut a chicken for roasting. But there were other lessons to be learned now. Maths, English, languages: when the guest house was finished, someone would have to do the books and speak to the tourists.

Somewhere among it all, J left the island. Maybe he didn't want a sheep farm after all. Mara forgot to say goodbye.

Mara and Islay did their exam papers together and sent them off to the mainland. They passed. Signe stuck the certificate to the fridge. Islay left. Mara stayed in bed.

Some days she watched the first pale line of daylight expand to paint the whole room gold. Some days she watched the leaves on the trees outside redden and fall. She smelled cut grass and fresh paint. She left her bed twice a day to go into the kitchen, open a tin of soup, and eat it lukewarm from the pan.

When the world outside the window turned white, Mara put on her coat. Her boots scrunched on the snow. Every breath burned ice in her lungs. She cupped her hands around her eyes and tilted her head to the sky, letting snowflakes fall into her open eyes. When her eyelashes were jewelled, when the snow fell so heavy that she couldn't see further than her own feet – then she started walking.

That was the beginning of her island exploration. Everything looked unfamiliar, the houses and hills shrouded. The packed snow on the paths supported her, and she stepped as light as a bird. There were white mounds off to the side where only gullies had been before, and she knew that if she stepped on them, she'd end up hip-deep and numb. Sheep stared as she passed. Birds rose like smoke from treetops. Her leg muscles ached, and her breath came harder, and it felt good. Walking the island's perimeter took four hours, though on the days of the thickest snow it was more like six. Every day Mara changed her route, spiralling in to the island's centre, traipsing through gardens and across roads. The snow erased all the boundaries.

Right at the centre of the island was a loch. Under the grey clouds the water reflected silver. The surface was salted with snow, lying for a moment before melting. Mara stepped closer to the water. What a shame it would be to spiral all the way round the island and then have to stop just before reaching the centre. Chains of white stones gleamed in the shallows like a string of pearls. The middle of the loch was black, reflecting nothing. Mara didn't know how deep it was – the water was too peaty to see far, even if you were to dip your face under the freezing surface, but it was certainly too deep to ice over completely. The edges were uneven, the slow beat of the waves sounding in a slushy whisper. The ice here, although broken up, seemed like it might go deep. If she spread her weight ... if she stepped fast ... Mara inched forward. The ice split under her foot, revealing black water under the white, soaking through the stitch-holes of her boot. She stepped back onto solid ground. Her foot was already numb. She limped away, back to her house, stamping to get the blood going.

But she couldn't stay away from the frozen loch. She was pulled to it with as much force as she was pushed away from the sea. Day after day she returned, never going further than the slushy bank, never again dipping her toe into the icy water. She stood on the edge until her hands turned blue inside her mittens, until her feet felt like blocks of wood, until her ears numbed and thawed in painful needlepricks. The loch was dark and deep and if she cupped her hands around her eyes and looked right into the middle of the water, she could almost pretend it was the sea. The sea, but safer.

After two weeks of padding around the shore of the loch, Mara found something she'd never seen before. Rounding a hill, she stepped onto what looked like hard-packed snow, but wasn't. She thudded knee-deep into the loose drift. By the time she'd managed to extricate herself, winded and exhausted, all she could do was lie back in the snow and catch her breath. She saw now that the hill was hollow, and there was something inside. Something big and boxy, taller than her head. Toy-bright colours were just visible under the patchy drifts. She approached with gentle steps, not wanting to sink again. With a mittened hand, she scrunched snow off the metal surface, letting it stutter in clumps to the ground. RARY, in bright painted letters. She swooped the arc of her hand wider. LIBRARY.

Mara couldn't help laughing. A library bus, suddenly, now, where before she had seen nothing. Where before, she was sure, there had *been* nothing. So the island still held secrets after all. And here was the door, and here were three steps leading up to it. Inside, the bus smelled of cold and metal and the sweetness of old paper. Every shelf, floor to ceiling, was crammed full of books. Mara tapped on the roof; it felt firm, though the metal panels on the sides let in starpricks of light. She took a step inside. The floor creaked, but held – and she took another step, and another. Tiny beams of light slid across her body as she walked. In here, she couldn't hear the loch, or the birds, or the crunch of snow under her boots. She couldn't see the sky. In here, hidden, contained, it was just her and the books.

Mara slid the first book off the first shelf and read the first page. Everything disappeared. The island, the loch, her placid father, her frantic mother, her absent sister, her scars, her sadness. Gone. She sank into the familiar invisibility of stories.

Over that winter she read a hundred deaths – and when the book ended, she could turn to the first page again, and the death was undone. Every Sunday she went back to the library bus and exchanged seven old deaths for seven new ones. She finished the first shelf and started on the next.

When she wasn't reading, she was working on the house. When she was stripping paint, when she was sweeping up bent nails, when she was screwing on new cabinet handles, she wasn't seeing any of it. Behind her eyes, stories flickered – death after death, forwards and backwards, nothing done that couldn't be undone.

The year slipped away and winter came again. Every week Mara walked across the island, back to the library bus for more new deaths. She hadn't counted, but she guessed there were a few thousand books. Someone's lifetime of reading, waiting to be found. When she emerged with her new armful, she could ignore the loch. She knew it lay there, black-centred, just on the other side of the white hill. A tiny trapped sea, calling to her. But she wouldn't respond. She couldn't help noticing, though, how the whispering slosh of the ice chunks matched itself to the rhythm of her footsteps, the water calling to her.

PART 2

Fae

There was a time, a few generations ago now, that there were four fine houses on the island: one at the northern-most shore, one at the southernmost, one at east, one at west. The house on the southern shore sat snub at the top of a hill, all sandstone and curved picture windows. It was owned by a grand lady, heir to a fortune accumulated from a popular brand of tinned soup. Even in the early days, most of the houses on the island clustered in a semicircle on the south-east shore, looking out to the mainland – which was just another island, looking south-east to another mainland. As the island's population grew, the new-built houses crept up the hill, closer to the big house, like saplings sucking all the water from an old tree's roots. Who could say why that house fell down? The sea brought up a storm, the foundations were shaky, the stones were poorly made. All anyone knew was that it fell.

The easterly house was knocked down to make room for a new mansion. A multimillion pile designed to look old, but in a new way. Perfect for a family who wanted to escape the rat race, move to a quaint and pretty little island where life would be simpler, better. The owner, who was not an island man, went bust halfway through after one of his uninsured cargo ships sank in the middle of the Pacific. He abandoned his half-finished home. It still sits there, roofless, empty-bellied, left to the seabirds and the sky.

The westerly house looked out across the sea over days and days and days of nothing. It was a stark and stern thing, flat white walls and tiny-eyed windows. It was built as a home for a man who soon realised that it was not, and never could be, a home. He finished construction, setting the costs as a loss through some accountant alchemy. But he couldn't stand to stay for more than a night in its cold, dark rooms, and caught the first boat back to the mainland. The house still stood, and for a while there was talk of turning it into a prison – the location ensured no prisoners would be able to escape to the mainland, though it would have to be minimum security, for the safety of the islanders. It hadn't happened, and the house stayed empty.

And then there was the northern house. Built as a folly, a rich man's gift to a wife who was not as silly or as girlish as he thought. As soon as she saw its pink granite walls, its smiling doorways, its little white-hatted turrets at each corner, she refused to ever live there. The rich man, unfazed, finished the house and promptly sold it. After that it passed from hand to hand, employed as storage or underused civil service buildings. It crumbled, but not as much as you might expect. Perhaps it was waiting for the right person to take possession. But you've already visited that house, because now it belongs to the Ross family: the fighter, the bird, the beauty, the changeling, and the golden boy.

Islands are about balance, and they each have their own rules. It's tricky to get it right: the sea always wants things to change, the land wants them to stay the same. Everyone finds their own balance, and sometimes they get it right. But sometimes – far more often – they get it wrong.

Drouthy

Mara hated daytime shifts. The pub slouched. Everything was grey and brown. Everything was aimless noise: the bleep of the quiz machine, the thud of a glass on a beer mat, the lethargic conversations. A single line of sun struggled through the skylight, brightening a square on the bar. Mara could spend hours watching the dust glint in that beam. Even when she was roused to pull a pint, refill the orange juice, slap a packet of crisps on the bar, count out change, answer questions about how her mother was faring – still she was dazzled. After she'd performed her role, she resumed her position in front of the optics, watching the sunbeam.

'Pint please, love.' The man winked at Mara as he put his money on the bar. Mara winked back, then regretted it as she felt the tug of scar tissue in her cheek. She still didn't know what had caused the injury, and no one could tell her. She remembered two moments of sudden, burning agony: one when she was in the sea – splinter-edged debris from a boat, maybe, or a handful of mussel shells kicked up by the waves – and one when she was running through the trees, the snapping and slapping of branches in the wind. She could blame the sea, or she could blame the island. But it didn't matter. Knowing the cause of the injury didn't take away the scar.

She pulled the pint. The man looked at her for a bit, then made a point of not looking at her for a bit, as if her face was just like any other face. Mara tried so hard to stand straight and hold her head high that her spine twinged. She smiled achingly and passed the pint. The man thanked her and sloped back to his seat.

To strangers, Mara displayed her face with hostile bravado. She held their gaze a few seconds longer than necessary. Let them stare. Let them keep staring. She'd never see them again – these tourists who came in all seasons to watch birds or eat scallops or hope for Northern Lights. A dozen new faces a week braved the wind and the waves, suffering through a rollicking trip on a fishing boat just to get to this little paradise full of quaint and kind islanders living the good old-fashioned life. Fuck them. Let them stare at the angry scarred girl. She smiled so wide that her face twisted into a mask.

But most of the people in the pub were not strangers. They'd known Mara since she was nine years old. They knew Peter and Signe. They'd known Bee. Mara's face was familiar to them, but now it could never really be familiar. Her scar ran in a bracket from the outer corner of her left eye to the corner of her mouth, splitting her cheek. When she thought of nothing and her face was still, the scar lay pale and flat, barely visible. But with any emotion, any thought, any movement in her eyes or mouth or cheeks, her face distorted. Her eye pulled almost shut, her mouth twisted to one side, her scar deepened. The line running through its centre tugged snow-white, reddening the skin around it. Mostly people were torn between staring, and proving how much they didn't care about it by directly mentioning it in a helpful sort of way. Mara had heard every home remedy for reducing scarring, and had tried exactly none of them.

The pub had always been called Bennett's, just as the shop had always been called McConnell's, though it wasn't always the same Bennett at the pub, and as far as Mara knew it had never been a McConnell at the shop. The current Bennett was Ida, 24-year-old daughter of the older Bennetts, trusted to run the pub while her parents enjoyed a sort of retirement, spending their days experimenting with Indian cooking, collecting old vinyl, and watching for seals in the harbour. Everyone on the island had at least three jobs, but now the Bennetts had none at all.

'Help me restock?' asked Ida. Mara nodded and followed her into the storeroom.

As well as running the pub, Ida also did palm reading and crystal healing, and could do any vintage hairstyle you cared to request. She was dark-eyed with a dimple in her chin. She smiled a lot. When she was nervous, she fidgeted with the way her fringe lay across her forehead.

They restocked the shelves in silence. Mara wasn't sure whether the silence was companionable or awkward, but it didn't matter as she couldn't think of anything to say to break it.

'Hear from your sister much? What's she up to these days?' said Ida, hands chinking-full of tiny bottles of tonic.

Mara shrugged. 'She calls. She's busy.'

It was true, sort of. Islay had called a few times, though their conversations were laboured and clock-watching. Underneath every word that Mara said to her sister was what she did not say: *come home*. She wouldn't say it. She wouldn't even think it. She could handle this, all of it, alone.

'And your mum? Your dad? Haven't seen him in here for a while.'

'They're fine.'

Mara knew how the islanders gossiped about her family. She didn't blame them; she'd do it too, if it was someone else's fascinating tragedy. Although everyone has lost someone, there was extra depth to the gouge left in the Ross family. Such a small boy, gone so strangely. The younger girl was there, did you hear? She pulled him out of the sea. She says he was already dead, but who can know? And how did he disappear, if she pulled him out? She always was an odd one.

'Right,' said Ida, shoving the last box into the corner. 'Great chat. That's my shift over. See you later.'

Mara resumed her place behind the bar. She and Ida could be friends. Probably they should be friends. But they weren't. Soon her shift would be finished, and Ida would come to take over, and Mara would go back to the house. She'd walk home in the dark, and if she looked up, the stars would be as tiny and distant as the passing boats far out to sea. She'd help Signe to paint something or scrape something or paper over the cracks in something. Her exam results were still stuck to the fridge: a promise, a hope for the future, a daily reassurance to them all that she would help to run the guest house when it was finished. Someday, someday.

Mara wished for a storm, for the clap and slash of the splitting sky. She wished for something to break, to change, to be undone – so that it could all be over; so that she could go up onto the cliff and be still forever. But until then – she reached for her latest book, ready to read and unread another death.

Tumshie

When Mara was Bee's age, Islay told her that sugar was made of ground-up teeth, and if you ate too much of it then the tooth fairy would come and pull out your teeth and grind them up to replace all the sugar you'd taken. Islay felt a spiky, slippery sort of pleasure in seeing that Mara still had to blow all the powdered sugar off the tops of pastries before she could eat them.

Islay told her that if you put a part of an animal in your mouth, you could speak its language. Mara spent a week collecting hedgehog spines and cat whiskers, holding them in the pockets of her cheeks, sliding her tongue along their lengths, trying to twist their sharp edges inwards. Neither of them ever told Signe why Mara ate her dinner so hesitantly, her mouth aching and swollen with cuts.

Islay told her if she bit her nails then a goblin with knives for fingers would come in the night and cut off her hands, and that if she took extra portions at dinner then her stomach would explode, and that if she told tales to Mum and Dad then her tongue would turn into a slug. Mara believed all of it – well, why wouldn't she? Islay was big, and she knew everything.

And then they grew a little bigger, and moved to the island, and life felt endless. Magic was real and the girls roamed wild as cats. The sea encircled the entire known world. The grimy remnants in the shed. The chalky float of steam in the bathtime air. Pieces and jam for supper. Stacks of books on the hall floor, used as stepping stones over shark-infested seas. A dead bee put to rest in an acorn cup. Bright orange lobster creels piled clattery in the harbour. Crabbing on the quayside with bacon and string. Marshmallows held over candle flames, toasted hot enough to blister.

The days stretched slow as toads. Stitching squares for a quilt, the jab of the needle into a thumb, blood beading bright. A stray cat at the harbour, licking fish guts from the stone. Crows biting out newborn lambs' tongues so they can't suckle and die the day they're born. At low tide the land changed, the waves sucking back to reveal caves and shores gaping wide like open mouths, the sharp jag of rocks that weren't visible before – but they were always there, ready to rip at your sea-kicking feet, waiting to tear the bottom out of your boat.

And among it all: two girls, ten and twelve, not ready yet to be women, but ready to think about starting to try, if not now then very soon. Then came Bee. They both told him stories, but not the stories that Islay had told Mara. They told him tales of friendly sea-creatures, tales of lovely objects washed up on the shore, treasures meant only for him. Only pretty things. Sweet things. For Bee, they would remake the world, newer and better. A world worthy of the bright gold of him.

Bonny

The first day of a new year, much the same as all the other years, except that it was Mara's eighteenth birthday. As a gift to herself, she had traipsed through the snow to the library bus. The spines rainbowed out before her. Still more deaths to be read and unread. She breathed in the cold air and sighed out a white cloud of happiness. She reached for the next week of books.

She paused. Just for a moment, she thought she heard faint music. But when she strained her ears, the sound was gone. Snow did funny things to sound: muffled it, or amplified it, so that things said miles away could be overheard, and a whisper close to your ear was lost. Then, a noise she definitely didn't imagine, but one she couldn't understand: the squeal of the bus door opening.

Mara turned, her arms full of books. 'Oh,' she said.

'Oh,' said the woman standing in the doorway of the library bus.

Mara stared at her as she stared back at Mara. The woman was tall, dressed all in black. Her hair was cut in a smooth bob, sleek to her head, emphasising the rounded curves of her cheeks and the long line of her throat. A few scattered snowflakes crowned the top of her head.

'Oh,' said the woman again, but this time with a smile. 'You'd better come into the house. I was just making tea.'

Mara swithered by the shelves, all her muscles twitching. Her face burned. Should she put the books back? On the shelves, or on the floor? Or should she bring them with her? But the woman had disappeared from the doorway, so Mara crammed the books back onto the shelf and followed her outside.

The world was white, snow-blanketed, and of course there wasn't a house, there had never been a house, it was just the hill and the bus and the slushy-beating loch, but the woman in her sleek black clothes and her sleek black bob was swaying through the snow and into the lee of the hill – and she was walking towards the hill, and she was opening a shadow, and then the shadow congealed into familiar shapes and there was a door set into the side of the hill. And there was the music, released from inside. The woman lingered in the doorway, waiting for Mara. Against the snow, her skin was the colour of pennies. Mara felt dizzy. She followed the woman through a tiny wood-panelled hallway and into a kitchen. A fire flickered in a wood-burning stove, its window silver with ash. The music swooned from a record player balanced on a kitchen chair. Everything in the room felt old, as if had been there for a long time – and yet temporary, as if no one really lived there. There were no windows – Mara realised that the house must have been built right into the hill. A hidden home, with a ceiling of turf; a true part of the island. Candles in glass lanterns lit the room buttery-soft.

'Take a seat,' said the woman. 'I'll get the tea.'

Mara slid into a kitchen chair and tried to stare at the woman without making it obvious that she was staring. She looked a few years older than Mara. Her black clothes clung to her curves, and her neck and wrists were layered in fine silver chains hung with tiny charms. The dark line of her fringe framed her eyes. But – those eyes. Mara couldn't help staring then. One eye was blue, one brown. Earth and sea.

Mara wanted to read the woman. She wanted to stop blinking so that she could look at her more and more and more. Then she realised that if she was close enough to scrutinise the woman so intimately, if she was close enough to see the colour of her eyes, then the woman could see her in detail too. Pores, scars, flaws. She hunched her shoulders and let her hair fall forward to hide her face.

'I'm Pearl,' said the woman. Mara watched as she lifted a copper kettle off the stove. Her skin was dark, but at the join between each finger it was silver with scar tissue.

'Pearl. I'm Mara.'

Pearl paused, the kettle still steaming in her hand. She was gazing at Mara. 'Say that again,' she said, her voice low and soft.

'Mara,' said Mara. She tried to pronounce it clearly in case Pearl couldn't understand her island accent.

'No, not your name. Mine.'

Mara frowned. 'Pearl?'

Pearl closed her eyes and smiled. 'The way you say it,' she said. 'That rolled R. The rounded middle.'

Mara felt huge and clumsy. She resisted the urge to raise her hand and cover her scar. 'Am I saying it wrong?'

'No! No.' Pearl seemed to wake. She poured the tea and set the kettle back on the hob. 'It's just,' she said, 'it's just that I like hearing my name said like that.' She took a chair next to Mara, so close their arms almost touched.

They sat in silence, sipping their tea. Mara felt her muscles relax, her jaw unclench. She straightened her spine and let her hair fall away from her face. She couldn't remember the last time she was comfortable with a silence. The pub was forced noise; the house was forced silence. Here it was warm, sleepy-making, and without thinking whether it was rude, Mara pulled off her coat and hung it on the back of the chair.

'So,' said the woman. Pearl. Her name was Pearl, and Mara rolled the name around in her mouth as Pearl spoke. 'You've been nicking all my books.'

'No! It's not like that. I didn't mean it to be like that. I'm not a thief.' Mara realised that technically she had been taking things that didn't belong to her, which was the definition of theft. 'I mean, I did take them. But I only wanted to read them. I kept them as good as I found them – I didn't turn down the page corners or crack the spines. And I brought them all back.'

'I'm teasing. Help yourself – not as if anyone's using them. I like a book with a cracked spine. Better they're getting read than just sitting there rotting. So what books did you read?'

'All of them. Or, almost all. I still have a couple of shelves to go. But I prefer the ones with –' Mara stopped herself, not wanting to look like a freak in front of Pearl.

Pearl grinned. Dimples deepened in her cheeks. 'Ones with what? Dirty bits?'

Mara could smell the scent from Pearl's throat: salt and spice and something she couldn't name. She sipped her tea and put her cup back on the table, but that didn't help – now she could feel the heat from Pearl's skin. Her head spun.

'No. With – with deaths.'

'Crime novels? Mysteries? I don't have that many out in the bus, I don't think, but I could find –'

'Not crimes. I mean, it doesn't have to be crime. It doesn't have to be murder. There just has to be a death.'

Pearl stopped grinning. 'You only want to read books about death?'

'It's not that. You can't tell from what it says on the back, but most books have a death in them somewhere, so you have to read all the way to the end. And in the book they die, but then you can go back to the start and they're not dead.'

'Ah. I see.'

Mara wished she could sew her mouth shut. She drained her teacup. 'I'd better go,' she said. 'It's my birthday. I'm eighteen.'

'Many happy returns,' said Pearl. She was still looking at Mara, but now her head was tilted, thoughtful. Her grin hadn't returned, but she didn't look annoyed or disgusted, and Mara could be content with that.

'I'm sorry,' said Mara, and she was getting up from her chair, and she was pulling on her coat, and she was blundering through the wood-panelled hall, and the music was fading, and the air outside burned frozen in her lungs, and –

'Wait!' Pearl called.

Mara turned back, heart beating too fast.

'I have something for you.'

Pearl disappeared down the hall. Unsure, light-headed, Mara followed. Through the blood-warm kitchen with its woozy soundtrack and flickering candlelight. Through a cold hall to an open door that led to shadows. Mara lurked in the doorway. Pearl's bedroom could only be called that because it had a bed, of sorts: a sofa almost hidden under the pile of faded floral duvets and bedspreads avalanching off it. A trio of silky pillows was propped on one arm. The walls were bare, the floor unwaxed boards. The room smelled of Pearl, that salty, spicy, mysterious thing.

But what mattered was Pearl, her skin warm in the dim light, bending over a book-stuffed crate beside the sofa, picking up a slim paperback. 'Here,' she said, holding out the book to Mara. Its title, in silvery capitals on a black cover, was *Mine*. 'It's a birthday gift,' said Pearl, smiling a dimpled smile. 'No one dies.'

Laldie

T he Ross girls were raised on fairy tales. The kind of books that would curdle your blood. Ravening beasts and hand-less maidens and hacked-off toes. Stepmothers dancing to death in red-hot shoes. Mermaids turning into sea-foam, ugly sisters having their eyes pecked out by birds, little red-hooded girls being eaten by wolves. All sorts of lovely things.

Signe read them the stories – but the stories she told weren't the same as the ones in the books. Every single tale she told was given a happy ending. Terrible things happened, of course they did – a story couldn't be a complete lie, especially not a story told to small girls, who are very good at recognising the grate and catch of a lie. But the terrible things weren't the endings. No matter how dark things looked, there was always a happily ever after.

Islay and Mara spent a lot of time acting out the fairy tales they'd heard. They were most interested in the part just before the end, where the princess dies. They weren't quite so interested in the part where she comes back to life and gets married and lives happily ever blah blah blah. They mostly argued over who got to play the dead girl. It was clear that the dead girl was the most-desired one.

Islay was the best Snow White; her cry of pain and sudden swoon after she bit into the apple was so perfect that Mara got nervous that she really had died. She was also great as the Little Mermaid; she could stay underwater for so long, and under the waves her red hair looked like an illustration from a book, like a pool of spreading blood. She was perfect as Beauty (the one with the beast) and also Beauty (the sleeping one).

One of Mara's happiest memories is of the time she was allowed to play Rapunzel. In the story that Signe told, Rapunzel didn't technically die, but Islay had read somewhere that a corpse's hair keeps growing after death, and it was clear to them that a single lifetime couldn't be enough years for a girl to grow hair long enough to reach out of a tower and all the way to the ground. She must have been dead for an awful while for her hair to grow so much. Mara lay on her bed of leaves for hours, her hair spread out, making her breath slower and slower so her chest barely moved. She stayed there for so long that Islay got bored and wandered off to play something more fun. But still Mara lay there, playing dead, playing beautiful.

Skelf

nother afternoon shift at the pub. Outside the winter wind tantrummed at the windows. Inside the dust glittered and settled. When it was this quiet Mara could sneakily read a book under the bar, and she was now on the third read-through of *Mine*, the book that Pearl had given her. Usually she'd only read a book once before returning it to the library bus, but this one was different.

It was a short book, and a strange one: a sort of fable set in a huge city-size tower. At the top of the tower, a small group of women were concubines to an emperor and wore masses of dazzling, sharp-edged diamonds. One woman, desperate to leave, escaped by shaving her head and then worked her way through many hardships to the bottom of the tower, where she spent her days sooty and claustrophobic but free, mining the diamonds she used to wear. But she couldn't be happy with her new life, as she was in love with one of the other concubines still in the tower. So she left the mine, and had to work her way back up the tower to rescue her. Meanwhile, the other woman realised she was in love with the woman who'd left, and escaped the tower to find her – so while one was going down, the other was coming up, each trying to save the other. Finally they met, so scarred and changed by their quest that each believed the other couldn't love her any more. The book ended with these lines: 'They didn't live happily ever after, like a couple in a story. But they were happy for a while, and perhaps that's all we can ask.' Pearl was right: no one died. But Mara found she didn't mind that.

The hours slipped away as Mara pulled pints, lined up packets of crisps on the bar, took orders for the kitchen, and read her book when no one was looking. Which is exactly what she was doing when she saw a pair of hands on the bar. She looked up – into one blue eye, one brown.

'Hello, Pearl,' said Mara, trying hard not to smile, to keep her face still and beautiful-ish.

'Hello, Mara,' said Pearl. 'Isn't it a thoroughly shitty day?'

Mara, surprised, laughed. 'It is, actually. How did you know?'

'I just know. Is it okay to get a drink? Red wine – and one for you?'

'I can't,' said Mara, her hands and feet already moving without conscious direction from her brain, measuring out a glass of wine, sliding it across the bar, counting out Pearl's change. 'Not when I'm working.' Typically, the scatter of dozing men in the pub had chosen that moment to all come up to the bar at once.

'Then I'll have to come back,' said Pearl, 'when you're not working. But for now ... ' She pulled a chunky paperback out of her coat pocket and held it up. 'For now, I'll get to work on this. Thanks for the drink.' She picked up her glass and turned away.

'That book you gave me,' said Mara.

Pearl turned back. 'Did you like it?'

'It was different,' said Mara. 'I didn't know stories could end like that.' In the corner of her eye she saw a queue beginning to form at the other end of the bar. It seemed like every regular from the whole island, as well as a clump of strangers, had chosen this moment to come in for a pint.

'I know,' said Pearl. 'I thought it might be time for a change. A new story. A love story, maybe.'

She wanted to smile at Pearl, but if she smiled then her scar would pull down the corner of her eye, and her face would twist into its mask again. She kept her voice neutral so she wouldn't be tempted to smile, not even a little. 'You think it was a love story?'

'You don't?'

'It can't be a love story. At the end, you don't know if they end up together. Love stories have a happy ever after.'

'But in a book,' said Pearl, 'love is like death. No matter how it ends, you can go back to the start. It never has to end. They can fall in love again, as many times as you like. I mean, as they like.' Pearl flicked her gaze down to her hands, and back to Mara. As their eyes met, Mara's body beat in twin throbs, in her throat and between her legs: one-two, one-two. She wanted to turn away from Pearl, to cover her face, to hide her scar. She swallowed.

'I should –' She motioned to the restless drinkers.

'Sure, sure. I'll just ... ' Pearl lifted her drink and cheersed the air. 'I'll see you around.'

'I did –' Mara's voice caught, and it was too quiet, and Pearl was already walking away. She swallowed again, tried to steady her hands, and Pearl was further away now, and she'd have to say it louder, and maybe the whole pub would hear and they would think … they would think … She raised her voice loud enough for Pearl to notice her and turn. 'I did,' she said. 'I did like it.'

Mara was kept busy with customers for the rest of her shift, and when Ida arrived to take over, hair tangled and cheeks pink from the wild night, there had been no chance to do more than get Pearl another glass of wine. She counted out her tips and pulled on her coat.

'Are you leaving?' Pearl was grinning her dimpled grin.

'Yep. Shift's over.'

'Maybe I could buy you that drink now?'

Mara smiled. 'Maybe you could.'

She automatically went for the darkest corner, where she'd be hidden away, but Pearl carried the wine bottle and glasses to the brightest and warmest spot in the pub: a table in the middle, just vacated by a giggling couple.

It didn't take them long to rattle through the basics. Mara: lives with her parents; one sister and one brother, neither of them on the island; spending her days on the exciting pursuits of pulling pints and home renovations; waiting for the house to be done so they could let the rooms to tourists; waiting in general. Pearl: performs in a show travelling all around the world; born on the island but only comes back every few years; no family, on the island or anywhere else. Perhaps it wasn't all true, but it was true enough for now.

After they'd emptied the bottle together, Pearl slid out of her chair. 'What do you want?' she asked.

'I don't know, I … ' Mara's head was spinning from the wine, skin glowing warm, thinking: *I don't know if I want you, or want to be you, or want to peel back your skin so I can see inside.*

Pearl leaned over the table towards Mara, her hair soft on Mara's cheek, her words only breath. 'I think that you do know. I think you want the same thing I do.'

Mara, breathless, just stared.

'Wake up, daydreamer!' Pearl, laughing, waved a hand in front of Mara's face. 'I'm asking what you want from the bar. The same?'

When the pub closed at midnight, Mara and Pearl found themselves stumbling up onto the cliff with a bottle of red wine. Their breath came out in clouds, their fingers already numb from the cold. Stars and satellites careered above them. Mara led Pearl through the mass of stone figures, right to the edge of the cliff. Unsteady, Mara leaned on a stone figure, reaching for its hand as if to hold it. The stone was as smooth as skin, but cold. She reached for Pearl instead, and together they tumbled to the grass. Mara propped the wine bottle between them. A rain too fine to hear settled around them, sudden and bright. It fell on their faces, into their eyelashes, blurring their vision, and in the damp moonlight it seemed to Mara that Pearl shimmered.

'What do you think happens after?' said Mara.

'After what?'

'After you're gone.'

'Come up here to the cliff, I suppose. Other places have graveyards, and when you walk across the grass you're stepping over dead flesh, all rotting and being eaten by worms, and that's bad enough – but these statues. I know the flesh and blood has all turned to stone, and there's nothing rotting, so it should be better. But it's not.'

'Is it what you'll do?' Mara drank deep from the bottle and handed it to Pearl.

Pearl scrunched up her face. 'Never thought about it,' she said, 'and I'd like to keep it that way. I don't usually stay long here.'

'But what if you're not here? What if you're not anywhere?'

'Everyone is somewhere,' said Pearl, still cradling the bottle, not drinking.

'Not when you're missing.'

'I think … ' said Pearl, sighing. 'Okay, it's daft, but I'll tell you what I think. And no laughing. I think that when we're dead, we do the things we could never do in life. I think that if we always wanted to breathe underwater, or go to the moon, or have a dozen children, or explore the North Pole, or do a perfect somer-sault, or ride a horse across a desert – after we die, that's what we get to do. I think that if we always wanted to be right in the middle of a big noisy family, then we are. If we always wanted to be alone and quiet, that's what we get. We get to know all the things we never knew, and understand all the things that were mysteries to us. We can get right inside other people's heads, and they don't know we're there, but we're with them, and we can finally understand them.'

'Is that what you want, after? To be with your family?'

Pearl shrugged. She drank deep from the bottle and pushed it at Mara. Rain sheened Pearl's cheeks and forehead, made spider-webs on her hair.

'I wish,' said Mara. 'I wish I believed that too. I wish he could see, now, how much we – But I don't believe it. I wish I – Why do you keep coming back to the island?' Mara struggled to force the words out; her tongue felt swollen, her lips hot. 'Why, if you don't want to come up to the cliff?'

Pearl shivered and took the bottle back from Mara. 'You know, I read somewhere that in the American Civil War, soldiers died of homesickness. Nothing wrong with them, no physical illness. They were away from home for too long, and it killed them.'

'Do you think of the island as your home?'

'Somewhere has to be. And it's good to come up here and see everyone on the cliff, to remind myself of the person I could have been. Stuck forever on this dying little island, telling myself that that's all there is. Telling myself that I don't need to see the world because I can just read about it.'

Pearl lifted the bottle to hand it back to Mara, then saw the look on her face and put it down again.

'Oh God, not you! I didn't mean you.'

Pearl was too close, and the moonlight would shine bright on her scar, and Pearl would see the ugliness of her, and even though she knew she couldn't be beautiful she still wanted to be beautiful for Pearl. She pulled her hand away and tugged the bottle out of Pearl's hand, ducking her head so her hair curtained her face. She drank deep, letting the wine sour on her tongue. She tilted her head back, blinking until the stars steadied. The darkness made her bold. The bottle was empty now and Mara threw it over the cliff, not waiting to hear it shatter on the rocks below.

Pearl put her hand on Mara's. 'I really didn't mean you.'

'Why did you come to the pub tonight?'

'I wanted to see if you ...' Pearl leaned closer on the grass. Their fingers twined. 'I just wanted to see you.'

The world was spinning and the stars fizzed and the grass was as soft as a bed and Mara wanted – she wanted –

'Does it hurt?' asked Pearl.

Yes, thought Mara, yes yes yes, all the time. 'Does what hurt?'

Pearl tucked Mara's hair behind her ear and pressed her hand to Mara's cheek. She stroked her thumb along her scar. Her hands were cool, rough, solid.

'You don't have to hide. I want to see you.'

'It doesn't,' said Mara. 'It doesn't hurt.' Pearl leaned in closer, and they met in the middle. Pearl tasted of wine and salt. Mara closed her eyes. And it didn't hurt.

Sickling

igne knew she didn't have to fuss so much over Mara's scar. At first there had been so much to do, so much busywork. She had to check Mara's stitches and monitor her painkillers. But now the wound was long healed. The pain a memory.

Signe caught Mara first thing in the morning as she stumbled down to the kitchen for breakfast, her eyes crusty, her breath sour. Signe, of course, had been up for hours, cleaning things that she knew didn't really need to be cleaned. Mara, surprised and not awake enough to say no, followed Signe into the front room.

They sat politely on the horsehair couch, which was lumpy and scratchy but was right beside the tray with the coffee pot and cups. Signe had arranged it beautifully: a cafetière of dark roast espresso, a jug of warm milk, and two bone china cups so fine you could see through them when you held them up to the light. She knew that Mara hated those cups, sure they would shatter, but she only remembered that now when it was too late. Mara's cup - a thick ceramic mug, the sort that comes in packs of four at discount shops and only shattered if you threw them hard on a tiled floor - was still in the cupboard. Signe poured the coffee. Mara lifted the cup like it was a bee about to sting her, but she still sipped from it.

'I ordered you some samples of make-up. No, Mara, don't look at me like that. It's proper stuff, medical grade, for burns and deep scarring. Lots of patients have had success with it. The coverage is very good.'

'No thanks, Mum,' said Mara.

'How about you try it before thanking me?' Signe splayed out a selection of beige tubes. 'Give me your hand, and I'll test them and see which is the right colour for you.'

'Do I need it? Medically speaking.'

'Oh, Mara.' Signe tried not to sigh. She held her coffee cup delicately, as if balancing it on the surface of water. 'You want to look pretty for when your boyfriend comes home, don't you?'

'I don't care,' said Mara, draining her cup and pouring another.

'Your boyfriend will care. Don't you want to be pretty for him?'

'I don't want to be pretty for anyone.'

The thing was, since losing Bee, Mara was pretty. Well, not pretty, but striking in an old-fashioned way. She'd never be fine-boned and exotic-eyed and full-breasted and long-limbed. She'd never have small hands or small feet. She'd never walk as if she could slip into a slow dance at any moment. She'd never be so beautiful that a man would lie to her just to keep her close. She'd never, in short, be her mother.

Islay had come closest: she had grown up equal parts scornful and sensual, ready to set fire to anyone who got too close. But losing Bee had made her softer, kinder. There was a void left for a distant beauty, and although Mara didn't quite fit into it, there was no one else there.

'I don't think that's true,' said Signe, who had always been beautiful and always would be, and so never had to wonder about the value of it. She sipped her coffee – black, strong – and closed her eyes as the caffeine thrilled through her blood.

'It is true. And he's not my boyfriend anyway,' said Mara. 'I hope I never see him again.'

They finished their coffee, and Mara obediently put out her hand so that Signe could test the contents of the beige tubes on her skin, and later when Signe went to throw the coffee grounds away she saw all the tubes in the kitchen bin.

Skite

Mara ran the hot tap until the water turned cold. The claw-foot bath juddered with the effort of the pipes, shivering ripples across the water. She turned off the taps and slipped her nightgown off her shoulders, letting it pool around her feet. She looked down at her body. She was not in the habit of looking at herself; she couldn't remember the last time she'd seen her face in the mirror. She'd developed a method of looking in the mirror without really seeing – could brush her teeth and hair with her gaze on the glass, looking at her features separately, as parts, individual things to be rearranged or cleaned.

Now the mirror was steamed over, opaque, safe. She could look at her body the same way: just parts. The dark nipples, almost purple against the pale skin. The cold toes, pale blue, marble-carved. The road map of veins on the belly and thighs, indigo and violet and mauve. A stranger's body to go with her stranger's face.

She stepped into the water and stood calf-deep for three breaths, testing to see if she could stand it. The water was so hot it made her shiver. Her ankles were already numbing to the heat. She bent her knees and knelt in the water, watching her thighs redden, then sat. She let the water settle. Steam lazed up towards the ceiling. The bathroom was tiled in rose pink and teal to halfway up the wall; after that it changed to bare plaster, lumpy and mottled. Signe was going to retile it all in white ceramic, or put in dove-grey panelling, or salvage hammered tin tiles, or rip out the whole thing and have en suites instead.

Mara's skin juddered against the bath's cast-iron sides as she settled. She slid down until her ears were underwater, her face cupped by the water. Her scalp tingled with heat. She traced the blue-green veins at her wrists, the underground rivulets of her body, her own salt blood. The milky water made islands of her breasts and knees. She could hear the muffled thud of her heart, the ebb and flow of it. She tried to put the parts of herself together, to see herself as an island floating on an island. But it was hard to think of her own body, the functions and parts of it, without comparing it to Pearl's. How ridiculous that Mara could want Pearl to look at her body and desire it. Her purple threaded veins like jellyfish innards, her spindly limbs. What was she, compared to Pearl?

Mara had never done any of the things she read in books. She'd never fallen asleep in a lover's arms. She'd never broken a heart, or had her own heart broken. She'd never got drunk on sweet aniseed liquor and woken up in a sweaty hostel bed in a tangle of her friend's limbs. Never got on the first train leaving the station without checking where it was going. Never gone walking through a strange city without a map. She didn't even have a passport.

But Pearl – she was a world made flesh. She was a universe in the shape of a woman. If Pearl had left the island to make sure she didn't turn out like Mara, that meant it had been a possibility. And if Pearl could have been like Mara, did that mean that Mara could be like Pearl?

She took a breath and held it. She closed her eyes and slid down further, so her knees angled up out of the water and her head was submerged. She listened to the boom, boom, boom of her blood.

She flattened the small of her back against the bath. The water pressed heavy against her closed eyes. She bubbled air out of her mouth, then breathed in through her nose, slowly so the water droplets wouldn't go into her nostrils. She kept breathing like that until she felt steady.

She slid her hands between her legs. She felt Pearl lay her down at the edge of the sea, snowflaking kisses down her neck. She put her hands alongside Pearl's, touching where she touched. The water stroked Mara's cheeks. Pearl's hands were gentle and strong at the same time, slip-squeezing, lick-teasing, nipping at the edges of her. She moved firmer, stronger. The sea shushed a lullaby. Above them, the sky was sunset - no, sunrise - no, a warm black night with stars and satellites twinkling white. Pearl was touching her, loving her, owning her. Their bodies merged, became one. Mara was Pearl and Pearl was Mara and they were both - they were both -

Mara's heartbeat pulsed louder in her ears. She breathed hard through her nose. The feeling was building, getting closer - almost there, almost peaking, knees pressed hard to the sides of the bath, knuckles tensing, releasing, the water heavy, hot, hands slick, and just as she tipped over the edge she lost her grip and slipped down: seawater in her nose, her mouth, her throat, seawater freezing and salty, her eyes blinking blind, and she panicked, splashed, she couldn't breathe, she was drowning, she was dying.

She sat up gasping, her body pulling in two directions at once, pleasure and panic shuddering through her from throat to knees before settling again, low and throbbing.

Her whole body shook. Steam clouded the room and she blinked against it, letting objects take their shape.

She breathed in and out, letting her heart slow. She lay back in the water, letting it lap around her shoulders. She felt good and bad and good. The water grew cold, her fingers became as wrinkled as puppies, and then finally, finally, she trusted her legs to lift her out of the water.

Messages

The island shop had everything you needed and nothing you wanted. At one end, a fridge of hard waxy cheese and vacuum-packed venison sausages. At the other end, a congregation of wine and whisky bottles, every label decorated with images of stags and misty hills. In between, shelves stacked with solid white loaves wrapped in paper. Little cardboard boxes of nails and screws and tampons and light bulbs and tea bags and washing-up gloves. Waxed jackets and wellington boots and fishing rods. The hum and flicker of strip lights. Empty rat-traps lurking in the corners.

Mara stood just outside the doorway and stamped snow off her boots. A bell jangled as she pushed open the door.

'Morning,' mumbled Mr Pettersen, then bent his long body back over the newspaper spread out on the counter. His neck was long and pale and freckled. His hair was buzzed short, the rusty red of fox fur. Mr Pettersen had owned the shop for years, as far as Mara knew, so the shop being called McConnell's was a mystery. Mr Pettersen also had a fishing boat and bred sheepdogs, none of whom seemed to be dozing behind the counter today.

'Morning,' Mara mumbled back. She hooked a basket into the bend of her elbow and browsed the shelves, even though there was nothing of interest to browse. She already knew what she had to buy, but it was so boring that she couldn't bring herself to do it.

Once a week, Signe phoned her order through to the shop, and then a boy on a moped chug-chugged round the next day to deliver it in a wicker basket, which he unpacked onto the kitchen table, his feet leaving a flecked double-trail of mud and snow through the hall. Milk, eggs, tea bags, butter, bread. Red meat and vegetables. A whole chicken. Sometimes sugar and flour, so Signe could bake a cake. The boy sometimes changed, but the bike never did. This week, Signe had forgotten to add toilet paper to the phone order, and Mara volunteered to walk to the shop and get it. At first she'd thought it would be a good excuse to swing by the library bus. Now that Pearl was there she felt awkward about it. It felt too much like trespassing. But maybe if she dawdled past, and dragged her feet or coughed, Pearl would hear her and come out. They could have tea. They could talk. She could lean in close and smell the scent from Pearl's throat. But halfway there, she'd lost her nerve.

Behind the counter, Mr Pettersen turned a page of his newspaper. It felt grand to call it a newspaper, really; it was more of a pamphlet, published fortnightly and covering the island's vital news. The results of shinty matches, which days the post was coming, adverts for seal-watching tours, a wedding announcement, a crossword. Unmissable. And yet Mara quite happily missed it every single fortnight. When Islay had first left, Mara sent her the newspaper as a joke, to show her the thrills she was missing. She'd soon stopped; it didn't feel so funny after all.

She put toilet paper into her basket. It seemed stupid to walk so far just for that, so she added a box of sticking plasters, because they seemed like a useful thing to have that no one ever thought to buy before they needed them. Then she added a block of cheese and a loaf of bread. They could all have roasted cheese for dinner, and Signe wouldn't have to cook anything, and she might smile at Mara. She put her items on the counter, on top of Mr Pettersen's newspaper.

'Thanks,' she said.

'You for?' asked Mr Pettersen, nodding at the counter.

Mara stood, her face neutral, her mind frantically turning over the sentence, trying to figure out what it was asking. *Are you four years old? Do you want these four items? Do you know about U4, a submarine, a secret code? Have you met Yufor, a new resident on the island?*

'Yes,' she said, trying not to make it sound like a question.

'Huh,' said Mr Pettersen. 'Fair enough.' He picked up the items and typed their prices into the till, one by one. Mara kept her head down, still turning over the sentence, puzzling over its sounds, trying to see it from a familiar angle. As Mr Pettersen lifted the last item off the newspaper, the headline was revealed. RESIDENTS DIVIDED OVER FINAL PLANS FOR MAINLAND BRIDGE. The meaning of his sentence clicked into place.

'Oh!' said Mara. 'Am I for the bridge!' She didn't know the details, but had heard the regulars in the pub rumbling about it.

Mr Pettersen regarded her steadily. Mara smiled wide, feeling her scar tug. She took a newspaper off the rack and put it on the counter.

'I mean,' she said, 'are *you* for the bridge?'

Mr Pettersen added the newspaper to her bag. 'Doesn't matter much what I think. It'll happen or not happen.'

'That's true enough.' Mara handed over the money, letting go of her smile with relief as she took her bag of shopping outside. She paused in the doorway, trying to decide whether to take the long way home.

It would just be to stretch her legs. It would just be to get some air. It would just be to exist for a moment in the same airspace that Pearl had inhabited. Or – or it could be to run into Pearl's house and grab hold of her and throw her down on the kitchen table and kiss her and kiss her and kiss her. Mara couldn't help smiling, and with that image flashing bright in her mind, she turned – and bumped into Pearl. Every muscle in her body panicked.

'I wasn't –' she said before she could force her mouth to stop.

'Wasn't what?' Pearl was dressed all in black again, gloved and scarfed against the cold, a woolly hat pulled low to frame her face. Those eyes, that skin. Mara wanted to look at her so much she could barely stand to.

'Wasn't ...' She mentally searched through her bag, trying to decide on the least awful thing. Plasters? No. Toilet paper? God, no. 'I wasn't,' she said, 'planning to get a newspaper. But then I saw it and I wanted to read about the bridge. Everyone seems to have an opinion about it, and I want one too.'

'Well,' said Pearl, and her smile was like the sun coming out. She reached out a hand, and for a heart-thud moment it seemed that she was going to press her fingers to Mara's lips, and then she would ... and then they would ... But instead she motioned to the shop. 'I'm glad you got a newspaper. That's what I came to the shop for. Maybe I could share yours?'

'Sure. Of course you can. But then haven't you had a wasted trip?'

Pearl smiled. 'No, I haven't. Not at all. And I can buy two from Stefan next time to make up for his lost business.'

'From who?'

'Stefan. From the shop. Tall? Redhead?'

Realisation dawned on Mara. Mr Pettersen's first name, after all, was not 'Mister'. But ever since she was a child, Mr Pettersen had been Mr Pettersen – nothing more, nothing less, *give your sweeties to Mr Pettersen so we can pay for them, Mara; say thank you to Mr Pettersen, Mara*; the name so familiar it fitted neatly into her mouth, the consonants tucked behind her front teeth.

'Right,' said Mara, 'right, Stefan.' Perhaps it was time to spit old words out to make room for new ones.

'Walk with me?' said Pearl.

Mara looked around at the grey-walled shop, the almost-empty harbour, the row of chalky-painted cottages, the path furling out under the low sky. 'Where?'

Pearl nodded to the harbour wall. 'Sometimes there are seals.'

Mara followed Pearl across the scrubby grass by the harbour. The fishing boats were mostly out at sea, pulling in their nets and creels. The scattered boats in the harbour were the leftovers: the between-owners, the weak-hulled, the rotted, the old. Traditionally they were named for the most favoured girls on the island. Mara had never seen a *Mara*.

Pearl stumbled over a notch in the grass, and without thinking Mara reached out for her arm.

'Sorry,' said Pearl, righting herself. 'I've got sea legs; never was as steady on land.'

They kept walking, and Mara kept her hand just behind Pearl's back - not quite touching, but close enough to steady her if she stumbled again. Her fingers still tingled where they'd touched Pearl's skin.

There were no benches on the harbour wall, because you weren't supposed to sit there. The point of the wall was to stop storms from sweeping right in and taking the village out to sea. But someone from the cottages had put out two folding chairs, because people did sit there, because it was beautiful and because no islander would be daft enough to sit there during a storm anyway.

The few hours of winter daylight were almost over, and the light was silvered and pale. The harbour wall was just wide enough for Mara and Pearl to walk side by side. To their right, the dozing island. To their left, the restless sea. Mara lowered herself into a folding chair, shivering as she settled, the metal cold on her thighs even through her clothes. Pearl was right: there were seals. Unless - no. It was just the kicked-up waves, sheened black, peeping.

'I can't stay long,' said Pearl.

'That's okay,' said Mara. 'I should get this stuff home anyway.'

'No, I mean -' Pearl turned and looked at Mara for slightly longer than was comfortable. Mara felt her scar burn. 'I mean I can't stay long on the island. I have work.'

Mara remembered the feel of Pearl's hand on her cheek, the taste of her mouth. She leaned in. Then she thought of Mr Pettersen in his shop, newspaper abandoned, watching them through the glass. The row of cottages stared, the low sun making the windows blink. She leaned away again.

'Where do you work?' she asked.

'Far away,' replied Pearl. 'I work in lots of places, but they're all far from here.'

'What's your work?'

'I told you. It's a travelling show.'

'I know, but that's not very specific. What kind of show?'

'Oh, it doesn't matter. It's not interesting.'

Mara opened her mouth to tease, to start guessing what sort of show it could be, but then a thought seeped cold into her head. 'Is it –' She couldn't meet Pearl's eye. 'Is it an adult show?'

And it didn't matter if that's what Pearl did for a living – it didn't change what Mara saw when she looked at her. But she didn't want it to be true. She wanted people to look at Pearl the way she did: with wonder.

Pearl tilted back her head and laughed. 'No! No. It's not that. Though I do sometimes wear a bra made of shells.'

'So you perform in a bra,' said Mara. 'But you're not ...'

Pearl sighed. 'Okay, I'll tell you. But don't laugh. I'm a mermaid.'

'A mermaid? Really?' Mara didn't feel like laughing. She felt like she'd been asleep, and had woken to a harbour full of seals, a sky full of stars, a fleet of pretty boats all called *Mara*.

'Not a real mermaid,' went on Pearl. 'Because, you know, mythical and all that. I'm a mermaid performer. It's like underwater acrobatics, but wearing a mermaid tail. There are five regular girls. We each have a solo show, and there are some group shows too. It varies depending on the venue. Sometimes it's a daytime show, kid-friendly, Disney tunes and big smiles. We do residencies at aquariums and water parks, stay there for a month, two shows a day. Even cruise ships – we perform in a big container of water on the deck of a big container floating on water, if that makes any kind of sense. And there's money in the corporate stuff, too. For a while I was at a hotel in Vegas. They had a huge tank in the middle of the restaurant, and me and another performer would do our mermaid thing while everyone ate their fancy dinners. Seafood, of course.'

Mara was so busy gaping awestruck that she didn't realise Pearl had made a joke. It was too late to laugh, so she asked: 'Do you miss it?'

Pearl sighed and shifted on the folding chair. 'I miss the weight of it. The water above you is heavy, and it makes you feel grounded. When I'm out here' - Pearl gestured to the clouds, the sea, the air - 'I feel like I could just float away, like all around me is nothing. And at the same time I'm stuck.'

'But at least you can breathe here,' said Mara.

'I can breathe in the water too.'

'What? You never said you could - you said mermaids weren't - what?'

Pearl gave a tiny smile. 'Sorry, I didn't mean to be an arse. There's a breathing tube. Clear plastic, in the middle of the tank. Timing is important, because going to the tube for breaths has to look like part of the routine.'

'I wish I could try it,' said Mara. 'Someday.'

'You can,' said Pearl, and with a scrape and a screech of metal on stone, she shifted her chair closer to Mara's, as close as it would go, and she laid her head on Mara's shoulder. 'You can do anything you want.'

But Mara didn't see how she could ever go beneath the water again. Her memories of Bee felt like a mass of pebbles that she always carried with her. Every time she moved, she felt a pebble spike in her shoe, making her stumble. Every time she spoke, she felt a pebble sitting sour under her tongue, making her stutter. How could she ever be safe in the water with all that weighing her down?

After a moment, Mara tilted her head to rest it on Pearl's. The coolness of the rain crowning Pearl's hair soothed the ache of her scar. She looked out at the sea, at the bobbing peaks that might be seals or might just be waves.

Loupin

Islay had never loved the island. But the further away she got,
the more she felt its pull. An island is always a destination; you
never pass through it incidentally on your way to somewhere
else. Arriving feels like crossing over an invisible boundary; the
sudden jolt of land after the lull of the sea. The island's secret was
its stone statues, but the more she travelled the more stories she
heard, and it seemed that every place has its own small magic.

In one place, where she fell in love with someone unfortunate,
she heard that people could rent clockwork hearts and return them
when their relationship ended so they were not heartbroken. She
considered trying to track down one of the heart rental shops, but
decided that her own heart was strong enough already. It was
certainly strong enough to recover from being dumped by a
pathetic man-boy who, as she said in an eerily calm voice during
their final fight before clicking the door shut and walking away
down the corridor with one tear rolling cinematically down her
cheek, really needed to grow the fuck up.

In another place, where she worked nights in a 1950s-themed
bar and had to wear a circle skirt and squeaky shoes and cat's-eye
glasses with prescription lenses that made everything looming and

blurry, everyone grew miniature horns: goat, rhino, giraffe, deer or unicorn, depending on their personality. Most people filed them down flat, though increasingly there was a movement to display them with pride. Islay hadn't actually seen anyone with horns, but the stories were common. Perhaps everyone just styled their hair over them.

One entire island was apparently the body of an enormous giant – the rolling hills his ribs, the seaweed his hair, the coast his circled arms. Every hundred years the giant would get hungry, and his rumbling belly would cause earthquakes until a suitable sacrifice could be made. Islay's time there, where she tried becoming a professional shoplifter but realised that was no good since everyone remembered her red hair, and instead tried working as a lookout for a small-time drug dealer which worked well as her hair was a great distraction for his activities, didn't coincide with the giant's waking. She'd have liked to go back in the future to feel the earth move, but when she had to leave suddenly after the dealer disappeared, she thought it best to cross that whole island off her mental map.

Islay fell in love and out of love. She worked many jobs she hated and one that she liked. She got bored, and she moved on. Every place had its own stories. Smoke from chimneys formed ghosts that came tapping at the windows at night. Or a woman could lie with a wolf and a man together and give birth to something halfway between the two. Once, after three days without sleep trying to work multiple jobs and party with her new friends the rest of the time, Islay swallowed some mystery pills and saw small pink flowers growing from cuts in people's skin, mushrooms that grew so huge that people carved them into houses, corpses that rotted down to form mice and moths and miniature rabbits. She'd heard plenty of stories about these things so she knew they were real, even though after catching up on sleep she could never find them again.

She phoned Mara, ready to tell her about how it looked to see a fist-sized white rabbit emerge from a dead man's mouth. But when her sister answered, Islay realised that the image – which had seemed positive and reverential to her, a way to live and love the earth beyond your own life – would seem horrific. Instead, she mumbled something about being busy, and rang off.

Everyone who lived in these places found these small magics ordinary. It's easy to keep a secret when you don't know it's a secret.

Stooshie

The bridge was coming, and it didn't matter what Mr Pettersen thought, or what anyone else on the island thought. The work had already begun, most of which consisted of men in offices drinking bad coffee and arguing over large sheets of printed paper. Plans were drafted and redrafted, contractors were selected, costs were lowered and negotiated and lowered again. The planning had been slow and expensive, as it usually is, but now things were moving. Soon diggers would grumble to life. Cranes would stretch their necks to the clouds.

Peter and Signe discussed the bridge over breakfast. Mara was still in bed; she'd been so distracted lately, and Signe expected she'd wander down sometime after ten, scuffling along in slippers while humming off-key, and funnel some toast crusts into her mouth before scuffling out again. If they were lucky, she might find the time to say good morning, though Signe wasn't holding her breath.

Signe had made a pot of strong coffee, a tower of toast, and bacon the way Peter liked it: so crispy it snapped. 'The bridge is happening then,' she said as she slid the food onto Peter's plate.

'Hmm,' replied Peter, his eyes still on the newspaper, which was unnecessary as he'd already read it. 'Too late to lodge a protest now,' he said.

'Why would anyone protest it?' Signe poured herself a large cup of black coffee, the same breakfast she'd had for the past thirty years. 'It will be wonderful for the island. And the guest house! Just imagine. We thought we'd be scraping by with ramblers and foodie types and people tired of the city, the only people who cared enough to get onto a fishing boat to come here. Soon we'll be open to the whole of the mainland. Thousands of people – tens of thousands.' She sipped her coffee, shivering at its pleasant bitterness. 'Think of it, Peter! We'll be full every night. I'll need another washing machine to keep up with the sheets.'

'But the building of it,' said Peter, finally looking up from his paper. His neck creaked and he was sure he felt stone snow onto his shoulders. 'What will it cost us?'

'Well, there might be a few downsides, when I think about it.' Signe paused to show that she was thinking about it. 'It could affect the fishing, with all the machinery cluttering up the place and making vibrations. It will be noisy for a while. And messy, I suppose. But aren't we used to that? And won't it be worth it in the end?'

'That's not what I mean,' said Peter. 'There always needs to be a bargain. We can't know what this bridge will cost us.'

'Don't be ridiculous. The bridge is a good thing – a vital thing. It will save us all.'

Signe stared at Peter. Why didn't he want them to make a living from the guest house?

Peter stared at Signe. Why wasn't she adding up the only things they had left to give?

Bareknuckle

Peter could not remember ever having a dinner that wasn't stewed meat and over-boiled vegetables. Sometimes, just to shake things up, his mother would serve up turnip instead of potato, or pork instead of beef. Peter didn't care; food was just a way to not be hungry.

But one night, to celebrate something – Peter didn't know what, a bet or a fight or an argument won – his father brought home lobsters for dinner. Live lobsters, their whiskers twitching, their slowly waving claws held shut with blue elastic bands. Peter's father set them to racing across the kitchen floor, and Peter's brothers yelled and cheered and placed bets, and Peter joined in because he knew he was supposed to. Looking around at their faces, gleeful at the lobsters' slow creeping, his stomach lurched. But he made his face match his brothers', and it was only later that he wondered whether they were all doing the same, the row of falsely happy boys increasing in height like a set of Russian nesting dolls.

The prize for the winning lobster was to be cooked last. Peter's mother had filled their biggest pot – big enough for Peter's smallest brother to fit inside, had they wanted to put him there – and brought the water to the boil. Peter didn't know why, but his father chose him to take up the tongs and lift the lobsters and drop them in one by one. As the middle brother, Peter rarely got to do anything special; his older brothers just hit him when he tried to follow them, and his younger brothers were too small for Peter to hit in revenge.

Peter lifted the last-place lobster. It waved its claws helplessly. Its eyes were like peppercorns. Its insect legs twitched. Slowly, Peter lowered it into the boiling water. He knew it didn't scream, but he imagined it did. One by one, he lowered the rest of the lobsters into the pot. Each one twitched. Each one screamed.

Peter held the lid on the pot, hearing the water bubble and thud. His hands looked so small next to his father's, his hands that had never held anything except gently. The things he knew his hands could do now. The pain they could cause while causing him none at all.

Peter hated boiling the lobsters. Making a game of their deaths. Watching them die slowly. Cracking their bodies open and sucking them clean.

He hated it because he hadn't hated it. He'd liked it.

Cabriole

B ee was new to the island, new to the world; nine months inside her body and only two outside it. Signe settled him in his Moses basket and thought about leaving.

She was already running late for her dance class at the town hall. Over the past year she'd built up the numbers, though she'd had to pause in the later stages of her pregnancy. Now she had five pupils: tiny girls, hip-high, hair curled in ringlets, dressed head to toe in pink. Sherbet fairies, a Victorian stage dream. She would lead the girls through the alphabet of ballet: always the same *pliés, grands battements, battements tendus, développés*. The key to ballet is getting the outside right, and then the inside will follow. The dancer can't start by trying to decide which muscles to use to achieve a movement. She must learn to do the movement correctly by observing and mimicking. When her movement looks correct, the correct muscles are in use. Tomorrow there were more classes: all-ages aerobics, barre stretches, beginners' yoga.

If she was honest, she didn't need to do the classes. But she'd always used her body to earn her living, and she didn't want to stop now. Peter had saved almost all his income over his fighting years. He'd always had lean tastes, and his prize money had only needed to cover his one-bedroom rent and more eggs and organic protein than Signe had thought a single person could ever consume. He'd tucked it all away for a rainy day – another of his ways of trying to control the world's vagaries, like knocking on wood and wishing on eyelashes.

During Signe's pregnancy, he had told her not to let moonlight touch her bare skin. It was sweet at first – a silly excuse to keep her warm inside the house while he went out to get more wood for the fire. But soon his superstitions irritated her. When Bee was newborn, Peter had pressed a silver coin in his tiny hot fist for luck. Signe, exhausted after ten hours of labour, didn't find it at all cute that he'd give a newborn a choking hazard. It was even less cute when they got back to the island to find that Peter had left all the drawers and cupboards in the house wide open, to make sure they were unlocked – locks, she assumed, being bad luck.

But Peter said he'd done these things for their girls, whether Signe remembered or not. Together they'd ushered their girls from babyhood to childhood, and so it was their duty to do them all over again for their boy. The strange old things his mother had taught him as a child – and he'd done them all. Suckling the girls from his pinkie dipped in crystallised salt to purify their blood. Not saying their names aloud for the first month. Leaving open scissors near the cot to keep away fairies – though Signe drew the line at suspending the scissors directly over their pillow. The bargains he tried to make with the world.

Wanting to squeeze as much time with her baby as possible, Signe leaned over the Moses basket as she did her feet stretches. The feet are vital. A dancer's feet must be strong, supple, and as sensitive as her hands. When standing, a dancer's foot holds her weight at three points: the back of the heel, the big toe, and the little toe. Each is vital to the proper stance. To be steady, the dancer must get her foundations right. This is all that really matters.

Signe finished her stretches and leaned over to kiss Bee goodbye. His forehead was as soft as feathers and he breathed as fast and light as a mouse. On her way out of the door, she paused. She reached up and carefully patted the highest shelf. Sure enough, there was a pair of open scissors. She started to take them down, then stopped. She'd leave them be. Let Peter have his superstitions. It hadn't done the girls any harm to believe in a little magic.

Thrawn

Mara and Pearl were ankle-deep in the loch at the middle of the island, contemplating their next step. Their fingers were intertwined like weaving. The water in the deep centre was black with secrets, and the rest reflected the silvery clouds. But the shallows were clear enough for them to see their own numb feet.

'We could try this in summer instead,' said Pearl. 'When it's not, you know, utterly fucking freezing.'

'You'll be gone by summer. And if I'm ever going to learn to go underwater, I have to start somewhere. Maybe someday the sea, but –'

'Mara, you don't have to go in the sea if you don't want to.'

'I know. But I don't want to be forever unable to. You know?'

'I know,' said Pearl. 'I know, crazy lady.' The water was cold, but Pearl wasn't shivering. Her underwear was black and lacy, pushed out taut with honeyed flesh, and Mara was trying hard not to stare. Her own body felt meagre in its skintight wetsuit, but she could feel Pearl snatching glances at her, and that made her warm. She took another step, and the water chilled up her calves.

'It's better to do it fast,' said Pearl. 'If you creep into cold water slowly, it hurts. But if you dunk yourself all at once, body and head and all, your temperature adjusts.'

'I don't think I can –' Mara could hardly speak for shivering. The cold was so cold that it felt hot, burning her from the feet up.

'That's fine,' soothed Pearl, stroking her thumb across Mara's palm. As her hand stretched, Mara could feel the soft scarring between Pearl's fingers. 'You don't have to do anything you don't want to.' Pearl led Mara deeper into the water, their steps skittering on the stones.

'Is your name really –' Mara chittered through her teeth. The water was creeping up her thighs now. 'Is your name really Pearl?'

'Ah, now that's a secret.'

'So it's not Pearl?'

'We should never give away all our secrets, Mara. You have to keep some here.' Pearl touched her first two fingers to her forehead, then to Mara's lips. Without thinking, Mara kissed them.

The water was past Mara's waist now, and she stumbled on a loose pebble and the water would have swallowed her up but Pearl had hold of her hand, so although she pulled Pearl with her when she slipped they both were only devoured to the shoulders. The cold sucked Mara in and her breath tightened and her heart raced and her skin burned and she wasn't even cold any more, she wasn't anything, she couldn't feel a thing.

'Now, Mara. It has to be now. I'm here, I've got you. Take a deep breath. We're going under now. One, two –'

'Wait! Wait. Have you –' Mara's words came out in gasps. 'Have you – done this – before? With others?'

Mara thought of Pearl's past lovers, all their different textures and shapes and tastes. She imagined Pearl wearing them like a string of coloured beads. Mara's own throat, still dry above the freezing water, felt cold. She wanted to pull Pearl close and hurt her, mark her: teeth dimpling blood to her wrist, a bruise blooming on her arm. Some evidence that Pearl was real, that Mara had really touched her, that they had really waded into a loch in the middle of January.

'No,' said Pearl. Under the water, she got a better grip on Mara's wrists, shifting her feet on the unsteady stones. 'Only you.'

'How did you know that this was what you were? What if someone is struggling and working, hoping someday it will come together – how can they know if the struggle is just the process, or the struggle means it's not right?'

'If it's right, then you know,' said Pearl. 'You feel it.' And she reached out and placed her hand on Mara's wetsuit just below her collarbones, where her breasts began their swell, where her heart beat fast. 'Here. Now stop playing for time. We can get out of this freezing water and wrap ourselves up in all those towels and go back inside, or we can dive. But we can't stay in between forever.'

'Will you show me?'

Pearl sighed. 'For you, yes. Though I don't know how much you'll be able to see from above the water.'

And Pearl let go of Mara, and took several steady breaths, and dipped her head under the water, and swam away. Mara could see the shape of her, the blur of her body as she swam and swam and swam, turning circles around Mara, disappearing into the darkness at the centre of the loch, slipping shallow through the silvery edges, and still she swam, and shouldn't she have come up by now? Shouldn't she be breathing? Mara began to panic – but she could see the flip and angle of Pearl's body, still swimming. Finally, she emerged in front of Mara, so slowly the water barely made a sound. Her dark hair was flat to her head, her eyes bright, her cheeks round and smiling.

'How do you stay under for so long?' asked Mara.

'I've worked my whole life, and you know what I have to show for it? Nothing but this. My breath, and my control of it. You understand?' She reached out and took Mara's hand.

Mara nodded. She breathed in, breathed out, breathed in. She was ready.

But then – the weight of a small body under her arm. Kicking for shore. Eyes rolled back, all white. Skin clammy. Blood clotted black. Her breath caught in her throat and she panicked, limbs flailing, the water fighting against her. The pulse she'd felt had only been her own. But what if it wasn't? What if he was still – and she had left him – and – and –

'I can't,' gasped Mara, unbalanced, feet skiffling on the rocks, arms cuffing the water. She clenched her back teeth hard, trying to keep her jaw from chittering. Her feet felt warm, and she wondered if they were bleeding. 'I'm sorry. The water – I wanted – but I can't, I –'

'Shh,' said Pearl. 'Shhhh, it's okay. Stop fighting.' The water was unsettled, moving a quop-quop around them from Mara's struggles. Pearl held Mara still until she and the water calmed. Then she tugged on Mara's wrists, pulling her feet out from under her, letting her float in the water. She began to draw Mara towards the shore.

Mara's face hadn't gone under the water, but it was wet. 'I can't,' she said. 'I'm sorry.' Her breath hitched in sobs.

Pearl kept her grip on Mara's wrists, kept pulling her ashore. 'You can want something,' she said, her voice soft, 'and also be terrified that it will hurt you. And maybe knowing it could hurt you –' She kissed Mara on the forehead as they reached the shallows. 'Maybe that just makes you want it more.'

Divertissement

W hen her daughters were little, Signe entertained them by pretending to be a bird. She strutted around their old house, hands on hips and elbows cocked out gawkily, squawking 'bu-uuu-uuuuk', knocking apples to the floor and picking them up with her feet. She hadn't danced, or properly trained for years, but her feet could still bend into the curve of a C, toes halfway to heels. The tips of her toes, if she wanted them to, could still support her entire weight. Bee, newly made and still unknown, was the size of a kidney bean, and added no extra struggles to the feat. After so many years of dancing, Signe had no toenails on her big toes. Her girls didn't find this strange; it was just a thing that happened to mothers, some lack or injury that they never thought to question. All grown-ups had scars, and there was no reason to ask about them. Their mother was a bird, and that was that.

All of the Ross children had delighted in collecting up the small remains of birds and making things from them. Things that need small hands to make and small eyes to see.

Once Mara spent the whole summer making a diorama of a dead baby bird sailing in a boat made of mussel shells, spackled blue and grey with their pearlescent innards. The boat had oars made of fishbone and a flag made from a scrap of rabbit fur she'd found in a hollow, its surface so soft her fingers could barely feel it. Signe exclaimed with delight when Mara fanfared it into the kitchen, even though she was on her knees scrubbing under the cooker and couldn't see what her daughter held. Together they put the diorama on the windowsill of the front hall, so that it could greet any visitors to the house. After summer, when the Ross family schedule of home-schooling started up again, the diorama got in the way of the autumnal wax-paper leaves they wanted to put in the window. It was moved to the dresser in the kitchen, where Signe felt it wasn't quite hygienic, what with it containing dead things; then to the coffee table in the living room, where it kept getting knocked over by accident; then to Mara's bedside table, where she got sick of it and moved it somewhere else, just temporarily. Where it ended up, no one was sure. For all any of them knew, it lurked still in some forgotten corner of the house, the mussel shells fuzzed grey, the bird's ball-bearing eyes watching, watching.

Islay preferred feathers. Long white-grey ones with barbs rough enough to skelf into your fingertips and pull out drops of blood. Tiny blue-black-green ones, with a shimmer to them like oil on water. White ones so soft you could stroke them across your cheek and use them as a powder-puff for your make-up, probably, if you wanted to. She mingled them all together in a heart-shaped pillowcase from which she'd removed the cushion. It had a little satiny pocket on the front, which was meant to be where you put your tooth for the tooth fairy, who would take the tooth and leave a coin in its place. It was years since Islay had lost a tooth, but still she kept the pillowcase, and still she collected the feathers from wherever she found them. When she left, she took the pillowcase. Sometimes, in the night, in the dark, she unfastened the pearl buttons and slid her hand inside the pillowcase to feel the soft barbs and jagging shafts of the feathers. She fell asleep easier like that, being soothed and hurt at the same time.

Bee had liked to scoop up the bird bones and bird beaks left by the foxes and make a collection of them. On his bedside table he laid them out, neat as a museum exhibit – it was the only neat thing he ever did in his life – and wouldn't let anyone else touch them or look at them or breathe on them. He said goodnight to them as if they were his pets.

Peter was less enamoured by birds. He hated their beady black eyes, their cruel beaks; but he could sit for hours and watch them. He knew that birds were not to be toyed with, close as they were to any gods who might exist up there. Owls seen in daytime mean a death. Six crows together mean a death. Three seagulls flying overhead mean a death. Any bird calling from the north means a death. An albatross near a ship means a death. Doves around a mineshaft mean a death.

Peter crept into Bee's old room and knelt on his windowsill to watch the birds swoop and rise and roller-coaster-dive against the clouds. He checked that the windows were latched; a bird flying into the house means a death. On the bedside table Bee's collection of bones and beaks still sat, now wearing a winter jacket of dust, though still perfectly arranged, ready to be bid goodnight.

Every Sunday, still, Signe roasted a chicken. Every Monday she made soup from the carcass. As there were only three of them in the house now, they had to have chicken sandwiches every lunch-time for the rest of the week to use up the leftovers. Signe always saved the wishbone to split with Mara. Sometimes it was the only time they spoke to one another all week. The bone waited for them on the kitchen worktop, a translucent angle of a thing made jagged with scraps of chickenflesh. Then Signe and Mara stood there in the ramshackle kitchen, the bone gripped in the hooks of their pinkie fingers, and wished in silence.

Scunnered

'Shit,' said Pearl. She flicked the light switch again, but again, nothing happened.

Mara stood outside the front door, shivering in three layers of towels. 'What is it?' she said. Each shiver cascaded drips to the peeled-off wetsuit by her feet. She was numb from the thighs down.

'The bulb in the hall's gone. Wait.' Pearl disappeared into her dark house. Night fell fast in winter, and though it was still afternoon the sky was blue-black. Mara heard the click of another switch. 'Shit, shit! It's not the bulb, it's the fuse.'

'Can I help?' Mara took a step into the dark house, which felt like stepping into nothing, as she couldn't feel her feet and she couldn't see the ground.

'Hang on!' Pearl's voice came from far away, as if she were underground. 'I'm trying to find the ...' Her voice faded.

'Pearl? Pearl, are you okay?' Mara shuffled into the black hallway, hunched in her towels.

Thud-thud-thud of feet, the sudden heat of another body, and there was Pearl beside her.

'I can't see a thing,' said Pearl. 'I was trying to find a new fuse, and then I was trying to find a torch so I could see to find the fuse. But it's darker than a – I don't know, a very dark thing.'

Mara remembered her first visit here: the candles, the wood-burning stove. 'Do you have matches?'

'Can't bloody remember where I bloody put them. And you're so cold, Mara, and I want to get you inside and warm by the fire.'

'Let's just wait.'

'For what?'

'Just wait,' said Mara, taking her turn to soothe.

In the darkness, she could hear Pearl breathing. She moved closer, opening the sides of her towels like wings to enfold Pearl. Her body was warm and soft and good. Mara was still cold, but parts of her were heating up. While they'd been in the water, she was helpless and Pearl was in charge. She liked that now she could take her turn. They stood together in the dark, staring blind into the house. Slowly, edges began to emerge from the darkness. With each blink, shapes resolved. Soon they could see how the dark house was peopled with grey shapes.

'There,' said Mara. 'See?'

'Yes,' said Pearl. 'Yes, I can see. Good thing I ate all those carrots when I was a kid. Just wait here, okay? I'm going to get a fuse.'

Mara didn't want to wait. She went inside, moving slowly through the shadowed rooms, letting her eyes adjust as she went.

'Pearl?' She didn't know why she was whispering, but it felt logical at the time. She heard a metallic creak and the tumble of water.

'In here!' called Pearl. 'Just running the bath.'

'Aren't we damp enough already?'

'Ha bloody ha. Now get in here and put your feet in the water. It's the best way to warm them.'

Still wrapped in her towels, Mara felt her way towards the bath. In the darkness Pearl's breath was loud. She helped Mara step into the bath. The warm water prickled, then it soothed.

'You okay?' said Pearl. Mara nodded, their bodies so close it didn't matter that it was too dark for Pearl to see her. 'Good. Sit tight, and I'll fix the lights.'

Mara sat on the edge of the bath, leaning back so she could peer out of the doorway. The shadow of Pearl opened the shadow that was the fuse box. Mara heard the heavy thunk of a switch, a click, a scrape of metal. The room was lit with a distant light. Mara blinked; it was coming from the bulb in the hall. Coming into the bathroom, Pearl flicked the light switch. Nothing.

'Shit,' said Pearl. 'The bulb in here must have tripped the fuse. Hang on.' She disappeared into another cupboard, and emerged with a stepladder and a light bulb.

'Let me help,' said Mara. 'I'm warm enough now.' She stepped out of the bath and dried her feet. Her body would look ridiculous next to Pearl's: ghostly, insufficient. She made sure the towel covered as much of her as possible and stepped into the hall.

She couldn't deny that she found it sexy, watching Pearl being practical, as if digging through cupboards in her underwear was no big deal, as if she spent all day every day fixing things. Mara wanted to be practical too. She wanted Pearl to look at her the way she looked at Pearl.

Mara unfolded the ladder and took the bulb from Pearl's hand. She climbed the ladder, unscrewed the dead bulb, and swapped it for the new one.

'I'm sorry about this,' said Pearl. 'I wouldn't have let you go in the water if I'd known this would happen.'

'I'm not cold,' said Mara. 'Not any more.'

In the dimness of the room, details were lost. The shape of a hand, the contours of a face. The dark made Mara bold. She stepped down from the ladder and into Pearl's arms, the dead bulb still held gentle in her hand. Pearl reached for her, their hands meeting. Mara could hear a tiny clicking, and it took her a moment to realise it was the broken filament inside the bulb. She looked down at where they both held it.

'Your hands,' said Mara. 'They're shaking.'

'I know!' Pearl put the dead bulb on the top step of the ladder. 'Don't make me feel like a dickhead.'

'Why?'

'Because I don't like to feel like a dickhead?'

'No.' Mara reached for Pearl's hands, feeling her own grow steadier. 'Why are they shaking?'

'Because. You.'

And, then – Pearl was nervous, and so it was okay for Mara to be nervous, and so suddenly she wasn't. She pressed her lips to Pearl's, pressed her body against Pearl's. Her underwear was still cold and damp from the loch, but her skin was hot as fever.

'I didn't know,' said Pearl, 'if you wanted to.'

'I did,' said Mara. 'I do.'

Pearl pulled away, keeping Mara's hands in her own. Through the kitchen, across the dark hall, into the mystery of Pearl's bedroom. The sofa, piled with duvets, soft with years of sleep and smelling of Pearl's skin.

Mara's entire body became heartbeat and breath. She could not open her eyes wide enough. Pearl's body was like the island covered in snow: familiar as a memory, as her own self; but still mysterious, her curves and hollows still to be discovered.

Pearl pulled off her underwear, then Mara's. She pressed her body full length against Mara's. The silk of her skin, the heat between her legs. Mara felt her body turn to liquid. Her fingers moved across Pearl's body; slid down, down.

Mara hesitated. Pearl placed her hands on Mara's jaw, wrists touching at her chin, and looked her eye to eye in the darkness. 'You don't have to,' she said.

'I know. But I want to.' Mara took Pearl's hand and kissed her palm. Her mouth lingered, open, tasting salt. She kissed Pearl's forehead, the tip of her nose, her bottom lip. She didn't know what she was doing, her hands and mouth so clumsy, so unsure - and it didn't matter, not at all, because with Pearl everything was the way that it was, not right or wrong, not a test she could pass or fail, not a way of being she had to strive for or fight against. It just was, and they just were. Together.

Pearl made snacks. She arranged them on a copper tray, each tiny dish a different colour. Rough oatcakes spread with butter and flakes of sea salt, smoked salmon arranged in slim curls, radishes and shaved carrots, peeled apples and hard cheese. And for dessert, winter berries on a dollop of cream.

Mara padded naked around the kitchen, picking things up and putting them down. She was no longer shy about her body. She'd felt meagre and pallid beside Pearl, but now she felt strong, northern, mythical: like a figure carved in ivory. She picked up an apple and bit into it, keeping it held in her teeth as she reached both hands out to lift the tray. Pearl bit the other side of the apple, trapping it between them. Their eyes locked as they each silently dared the other to be the first to bite. Mara raised her eyebrows, challenging. They both bit at the same time, and the apple thudded to the tray, an equal bite taken from each side. Still chewing, they took the tray to the bedroom and settled among the hillocks of duvet, made warm from their bodies.

'Couldn't you stay?' Mara popped a brambleberry between her lips, rolling it between her tongue and the roof of her mouth. She could taste Pearl. She tried to be playful, not to show her sadness, her desperation to make Pearl stay. 'I think it would be fun. I think you'd like it.'

'You see this place,' said Pearl. 'There's no bed. Barely any furniture. There aren't even any bloody windows. It's a weird little den, a cave meant for hiding out. You can take shelter in it for a while when you need to. But it's not a home, and I can't stay here. I've already stayed too long. I get ...' Pearl rubbed the back of her hand. For the first time, Mara saw how the skin was starting to flake. 'I get restless.'

'But you could stay for a little bit, couldn't you?'

'Mara. I'd need a reason to stay.'

She knew that she could try to give Pearl a reason. She knew – she hoped – that she could be a reason. She barely knew Pearl, but she knew enough that she didn't want her to leave yet. And so she would do it. She would ask to be with her.

But what if. Pearl might say no. Pearl might tip back her head and laugh at the very suggestion. Pearl might say she had a hundred girls just like Mara, quaint island girls whose locations she marked on a map in case she ever wanted to visit them again, though she probably wouldn't.

And now it was too late, she'd left it too late, Pearl was dropping her gaze and stretching her body away to reach for something on the tray, her skin not touching any part of Mara's skin.

'Okay,' said Pearl, her smile small and sad. 'That's okay.'

'Let's ...' But Mara couldn't say it, she couldn't say anything, she didn't even know what she wanted to say.

Finally she said: 'I have to go back.'

'Okay,' said Pearl again.

'Pearl, don't –' Mara could feel the air in the room tipping, souring, becoming cold. She couldn't make it better again, but she could make it slightly better than it was. 'Maybe next week,' she said, 'if you want, you could come round for dinner, and you can meet my parents – but not in a big meet-my-parents way, just that they'll be there too.'

Pearl turned to Mara, her smile wide. The room was warm and sweet and light again. She stroked her thumb along Mara's bottom lip, and Mara had meant to say something else but now she'd forgotten what it was.

'I'd love to meet your parents,' said Pearl. She kissed Mara on the tip of her nose. 'I'm good at parents.'

They turned back to their feast and ate until the plates were empty.

Mara woke close to midnight with her body on fire. Pain burned through the centre of her: belly, hips, thighs. She hadn't been paying attention to the date – of course it would come now, when she was in the bed of a beautiful woman. Of course.

She slid out of bed, back hunched, arms crossed over her middle. She closed the bedroom door silently so that Pearl wouldn't wake. In the bathroom she folded toilet paper into her underwear. She padded around the twilit house, searching for something to ease the pain. A hot-water bottle, a cup of warm milk, paracetamol. All the silly things that are supposed to help. But they were silly, and they didn't help.

She slid back into bed beside the warmth of Pearl and tried to sleep. There would be no pain in sleep. But the world shrank to the size of her body. The deep ache between her hip bones. Inside her was a pepper grinder, a rusted vice turning tighter and tighter. She could feel the too-big teeth of the gear, dark with oil but still scraping. She fidgeted in bed, stretching out her legs to relieve the ache, tensing her toes until the bones cracked.

'You okay?' Pearl's voice was thick with sleep.

'Sorry, I didn't mean to wake you.'

'Can't sleep?'

'I've got cramps. They won't go.'

Pearl pressed her body against Mara's back, sliding her arm around Mara's waist, holding her close. 'Let me help.'

Mara cringed. 'No, don't come close to me. It's not nice.'

Pearl slid her hand to Mara's lower belly, pressing her palm flat against the centre of the pain. She spoke in velvet. Calm and soft and insistent. 'Why would you think that I would only like you when you're nice? I like you like this,' she said, 'and I like you not like this, and I like you every way you can possibly be.'

Mara tried again: 'I don't want you to be disgusted by –'

'Shhhhh,' said Pearl, sliding her hand lower. 'Let me help.' She pressed her kisses to the side of Mara's neck, her breasts against Mara's back. The closeness of Pearl's body tripped a switch inside Mara, and all she wanted was the softness of Pearl's body, the heat of Pearl's tongue in her mouth. She rolled onto her back and wrapped both arms around Pearl, pulling closer to her kiss.

Firmly, steadily, Pearl's fingers stroked, slick against her own slickness. She closed her eyes and the world was pinkish, veins in her eyelids, squeezing to red as she reached higher, higher, almost peaking, almost tipping over. Her breath came in gasps. The flesh between her hips clenching, releasing. She opened her eyes wide to the dark. She bit her lip, hard, catching Pearl's hands between her thighs, feeling the bones grind. Eyes closed, she waited out the throbs. Through it all, Pearl held her close.

'Does it hurt?' asked Pearl.

'It doesn't,' she said, smiling, her breath slowing, her eyes closing, as Pearl kissed her nose, her forehead. 'It doesn't hurt.'

Besom

In the whispering dark, Pearl told Mara stories. Mermaids: those sinister, shifting fish-girls who want to sing you to your death. Who want to drown you in salt water. Who have shark-teeth and fingernails like claws. Breasts hard and cold as carved ice, a belt of sharpened shells slung over hips more scales than skin.

Forget that. For a woman, there's no living to be made in death and glory. Think instead of pretty little sea-maids. Think sweet smiles and beckoning fingers. Think crowns of starfish and combs of clamshell in hair the colour of childhood.

To be a mermaid, you need three things.

You need hair.

You need a tail.

And you need to know how to breathe.

Pearl had many wigs as part of her mermaid show. All of them were long and all of them were beautiful, made specially and at great cost so that they could be attached with water-proof tape to her temples and nape, the long lengths flowing and twisting perfectly under the water. Sea green, sky blue, shell pink. Of course they were bright. Of course they were

136

beautiful. What would be the point of a mermaid who looked like any other girl? Why would you pay to see her if you'd already seen someone just like her out in the street? The hair was such a vital part of the mermaid that, ten minutes after a performance, Pearl could whip off her wig and her tail and walk anonymous among a crowd who had been staring wide-eyed at her moments before.

The tail takes some getting used to, but everyone is so eager to believe that they're easy to please. To make a tail, lie on a large piece of wetsuit material while wearing a diver's monofin and have someone trace your shape. Your tail must be tight to your skin, because it's not skin, and so water can get inside and slow you down. Don't forget the zip, so you can get in and out – a very strong stainless steel is best, one that won't rust or break, the sort used to make garden awnings. You'll need scales, of course, and for that you need screen-printing paint. And why not some sequins too? You must be pretty. Sew it all shut, or use waterproof glue. We know that the real swimming fins are on the inside, but you should add some decorative ones too. Flexible plastics are best, the sort used for floor matting.

Breathing is hardest of all. No amount of sequins or pink hair will help you here. You'll need to practise yoga and breath-holding, as well as exercise to strengthen and expand your lungs. Start by blowing up a large balloon every day. When you're ready to try in the water, slow down your breathing so your heart slows. Deep-breathe for one minute, keeping your exhalation slow. One, two, three long breaths – and you're ready. Of course, it's easy to run out of breath. It's easy to black out and drown. It's easier than – well, than breathing.

Waterproof tape, steel zips, flexible plastic: it's not so glamorous when you know how the magic trick is done, is it? Perhaps it's best only the magician knows.

Unless – Pearl grinned in the dark. Unless the magician only pretends it's a trick, so you won't know that the magic is real.

Fash

Mara was in the utility room – which was a kind name for the freezing, spider-infested triangle of brick cemented onto the side of the house – transferring a load of sheets from the washer to the dryer, when she heard Signe cry out. Mara's hands were waxy and numb from the cold, and it took a few tries to turn the door handle. Her leg muscles twitched with her need to move faster, to get to her mother. She finally flung open the door, catching her shoulder on the door frame as she ran.

'I'm coming!' she called. 'Where are you?'

'I'm – Mara, I'm okay.' Signe's voice was tiny and shaking, but Mara could hear that it came from the kitchen. She ran in to see Signe, bent double by the back door, both hands clutched to her belly. For one awful moment Mara thought her mother was giving birth. The thought lasted less than a second – ridiculous, illogical – and she was across the room and easing Signe's hands away from her body, up where Mara could see them. Signe's right hand clutched her left, both smeared with bright blood.

'I hurt myself,' said Signe, her voice awed, as if she had just witnessed an unlikely miracle.

'What were you doing?'

'Fixing the latch. You know it doesn't catch properly. I thought if I unfastened it and screwed it back to the door again at a better angle, then it would work. But my hand slipped, and the screwdriver, and I – I ...'

The blood on the floor was starting to clot in the cold air, its surface puckering. Mara couldn't look at it. Her scar twinged. She grabbed a clean cloth from the oven handle, folded it, and wrapped it around Signe's still-bleeding hand.

'I'll get Dad,' said Mara. She hoped that Signe couldn't hear how her voice was shaking.

'No! Don't.' Signe reached her hand to touch her daughter's face, then noticed that it was blood-smeared and withdrew it. 'It's fine. We can sort it.'

'You're bleeding.' Mara pressed the cloth into Signe's hand, making her hold it tight. She turned her head towards the inner door and shouted: 'Dad?'

Signe and Mara stood together in the kitchen, breathing too fast, feeling the pressure of Signe's slowing blood.

'Please, Mara,' whispered Signe.

Mara let go of Signe's hand and walked away. She ducked her head into the living room, the hall, the front garden. Nothing.

'Dad! Dad, where are you?' She heard her own voice echoing back at her. She waited. If she stayed very still, she could hear the sea.

She gave up. Back in the kitchen, she dragged a dining chair across the tiles and stood on it to reach up to the cupboard above the cooker. The cupboard was a graveyard for everything that had no other home: plastic bags full of other plastic bags; boxes of nails, matches, bin bags, saw blades, a cluster of keys that had never opened anything. Mara pulled down a green plastic box and opened it on the table. She selected bandages, antiseptic ointment, and paper tape. She laid a bowl of cold water beside it.

'Come on.' She took Signe's elbow and led her over to the table. 'Sit here. Put your hand out on the table – straight out, like that.'

Signe hesitated. 'I'll get blood on the table.'

Mara eased the cloth away from Signe's hand and folded it, so that the bloody part was on the inside and she could use it as a pad. Old memories nudged at her, though she refused to look directly at them: the feel of her sister's hands on her blood-slick face, the fast whine of her panic, the soothing voice of the 999 operator.

'Stay calm,' said Mara in the voice from her memory. 'It's all okay.' When she wiped the blood away with a wet cloth, she could see that the cut wasn't as bad as it looked – shallow and clean, its open edges easily pressing together. Nothing visible, no fat or sinew or bone. Mara spoke as she worked, explaining everything she was doing, even though Signe could see it perfectly well. 'I'm rinsing out this cloth so I can wipe your hand again. I'm putting on antiseptic. I'm sticking on these butterfly stitches. I'm wrapping this bandage.'

Signe slumped in her chair, eyes wide, watching as her hand disappeared beneath layers of white bandages.

'Mara,' she said, when her daughter was finally tucking in the end of the bandage. 'Thank you.'

Mara smiled. 'It's okay. If it was me, then you would've done –'

The broken latch clicked, the back door opened, and Peter walked into the kitchen. He moved slowly, jerkily, like a marionette. His feet scraped on the tiles. It seemed he might tip over at any moment.

'I'm here, Mara,' he said. 'What's wrong?'

Distracted, Mara dropped the roll of bandage. It unwound itself as it rolled off the end of the table. 'Where were you?'

'In the garden,' said Peter. 'Just by the trees. I heard you shout. I came right away.'

'But that was ten minutes –' Mara stopped. She looked at her father. She saw the slow-motion tremble of his hands. She saw his tentative steps. She saw the way his chest rose and fell slowly, so slowly, one breath to every ten of hers. Finally, properly, she saw him. And then she could not bear to see, so she looked back down instead. She picked up the bandage and wound it into a tight roll. She packed it into the first-aid box and clicked the lid shut and put the box in the cupboard above the cooker. When she pulled away the chair, the oven door fell open with a crash. She made herself take three deep breaths before easing the oven door closed.

'Thanks, Dad,' she said. 'Thanks for helping.'

Later, when Signe and Peter had gone to bed, Mara picked up the phone. She knew that everything she was doing with Pearl was leading her to one place: away. But the thought of her parents, clattering around alone in this huge empty house, tightened her throat. If she was ever going to leave the island, she needed someone to take her place.

She paused, finger hovering over the numbers. Against her ear, the phone held its breath. She imagined explaining about all that had happened in the past few months. That she loved a mermaid, that she wanted to run away with a mermaid, that she wanted to *be* a mermaid. Clunky, awkward Mara, with her scarred face and her gawky limbs, who would never have a boat named after her.

She imagined saying the word *mermaid*, imagined confusion turning to understanding turning to pity. She hung up the phone and walked away.

But it didn't matter if she was a joke. It didn't matter if she was mocked or pitied or scorned. There was only one person who'd be willing to come to this strange little island and help a man who was turning to stone. She walked back to the phone and dialled.

'Islay?' she whispered into the receiver.

Greet

Islay spent her days in empty beds and full baths, in soft-lit restaurants and Formica-tabled cafes. In Paris and Chicago and Sydney. She leeched from men who liked old wine and young women. She talked too much, drank too much, danced too much. Too much hair tumbled down her back. The milky skin of her back showed too much in her dress. Her dress sparkled too much in the coloured lights. The lights reflected too much in her eyes.

She didn't like to hold anything in her hands for long. She hated clutch bags. If she had to bring shopping home from the market, she'd carry it in a backpack. When driving, she kept only one hand on the wheel. She had to be ready to grab things – something, anything, whatever happened to come along. She didn't want to miss it. Sometimes she woke in the night and her palms felt clammy, smeared with something reddish and hot, and her sister's split-open face flickered in the dark, and she heard the steady lash of the waves, and she had to get up and rinse her wrists under the cold tap until her blood cooled.

When she had first left the island, she cut her hair. 'Short,' she said to the hairdresser. 'I want it all gone.' The hairdresser trimmed it close to her head, cutting out her curls to a smooth cap. He called it a pixie cut, and at first that irritated Islay. She was a city girl now; she'd left behind her childhood island world, magic and fairy tales and fucking pixies everywhere. She thought of her hair as a crop, as something that grew like a plant and had to be removed for practical reasons. But as time passed, and she kept her hair short, she began to ask hairdressers for a pixie cut instead of a crop. Maybe it wasn't so bad to be brought closer to that other world, even only in name. No matter how much she tried to cut herself off from the island, it was still there. The further away she got, the closer she grew to it – its narrow edge of reality, its flirtation with the other side. Its attempt to build bridges. There was no use pretending that it was not there.

Islay had always known she would have to go home eventually. This wasn't a fairy tale, and home wasn't an enchanted tower: one girl taking another's place to break a curse. But the days passed, and passed, and passed, and still she didn't go – until the phone rang, and she heard her little sister say *please*.

Canny

Every night that she fell asleep beside Pearl, Mara woke convinced that she wouldn't be there. That she was wrong about the ending of the selkie story: that her love would have found her true skin and slipped back into the sea. But every night she reached out her hand and Pearl's hands were there, waiting. In sleep, her skin was cool and still as stone. Mara waited to make sure Pearl wouldn't wake, then pressed her fingertips to the pulse in Pearl's throat. Just to check, gently, just once.

The next night she woke, sure she was alone, and reached out for Pearl's hand. There it was – but it wasn't enough. Before she knew what she was doing, her hands had moved to Pearl's throat, searching out her pulse. There it was. She felt it throb, steady, sleep-slow.

She pulled her hands away and lay back down. But was she sure? Had she checked for long enough? Was that really Pearl's pulse, or Mara's own heartbeat in her fingers? She put her hands back to the vein and pressed harder. Just to check. Just once more. And again the next night, and the one after, again and again, pressing harder and harder, pressing so hard she felt the gristle and sinew shift in Pearl's throat, pressing so hard her hand shook, stopping the blood so she could make sure it started again, and again, and again.

One night, Mara reached for Pearl's throat as usual, and glanced up. Moonlight caught Pearl's eyes as she blinked. Mara snatched her hand away. She fumbled, pretended she was reaching for the clock, a glass of water, anything.

'It's okay,' said Pearl.

She took Mara's hand and put it back on her throat. She pressed on the throb.

'I trust you,' said Pearl. 'Do what you need to do.'

And Mara kissed her, softly, gently, and she kept her hand on her throat, and pressed.

Cannae

The sea at night was cold as death, full of secrets, nothing but a mass grave that can't be marked. Mara and Pearl stood on the shore. Under her wetsuit, Mara's skin prickled with goosebumps. The water was so still that the moon's reflection made a road, leading far out to sea.

'Mara, are you sure about this? When you called, I thought you wanted to - come over, you know. I didn't think you wanted to crawl into the sea in the middle of the night.'

'I'm sure,' said Mara.

'But it's late. It's dark. I can't see a bloody thing.'

'We don't need to see. We only need to breathe.'

'It's not that simple! The sea is dark, and I - I don't know if I can keep you safe.'

Pearl took Mara's hand, ready to lead her back to the house. Mara pulled her the other way, into the water.

'No,' said Mara. 'You don't understand. I want to do it now. It has to be now.' She took another step into the water, letting it chill up her calves. 'When I spoke to Islay again, it reminded me - when we were younger, we used to do this thing, and I'd forgotten. It used to make me feel better. I can't explain. Just let me try.'

'Fine,' said Pearl, matching Mara's pace into the shallow waves. 'But I want my objection – my strong objection – to be noted for the record.'

'Noted,' said Mara. Another step, and she disappeared off the edge of the sandbank. She dropped into nothing, the water rushed up to her throat, and her body spasmed in the cold water, and she was breathing water, and she was drowning – and then Pearl's arms were around her, pulling her to the surface. Mara emerged with a gasp, held safe in Pearl's arms.

'Is this part of your big plan?' Pearl's voice was sharp through the darkness. 'Thank fuck I'm here, Mara, or you'd be at the bottom of the sea.'

'I forgot,' choked Mara through a mouth of seawater. 'I forgot it was like that.'

'Fine,' said Pearl. 'Fine. But I don't like this at all. Just so you know.'

Pearl trod water until Mara had caught her breath. Freezing water lapped at their shoulders. Mara felt the undertow tug at her feet, grasping for her. Sharp things skittered around her ankles; she was sure she could feel the slippery grasp of seaweed around her thighs. She pulled Pearl close and kissed her. Pearl hesitated, but kissed Mara back. Mara took all the strength she could from that kiss before speaking.

'I lied,' she said, her voice shivering in gasps. 'I lied – I told my mum I had tried to fix the latch – on the back door but I – just didn't want to. And then she hurt herself – and I felt bad but I – was still glad it wasn't me. Let the sea – take it!'

They waited, Pearl holding them both afloat in the cold night sea. Silence. It began to rain, a light skiff pattering the sea's surface. With each falling drop, seawater splashed up into Mara's face. She tried to blink the salt away, her eyes burning. She didn't feel any better.

'I don't understand this,' said Pearl. Mara felt something burn through Pearl: impatience, confusion. 'Are you done? You're freezing. Can we please go back now?'

'No, it – just let me try again.' Mara's shivering had settled to a deep shudder, low in her body. She could only feel her hands and feet when she moved them. 'Sometimes,' she said, 'sometimes ...' And she didn't want to say it, not in front of Pearl, but there was no way to say it to the sea and not to Pearl. She had to say it, and she had to say it loud. She turned her back to the island and faced the endless sea. 'I think it's better,' she shouted into the dark, 'that Bee is gone. It's better that he's gone from this world because it wasn't right for him. It was too big and too loud and too cruel. I think it's better, but I still want him to come back.' Her words fell heavy on the water. 'Let the sea –' Mara's throat ached tight, and her eyes were sore and wet from the salt water, and her breath came in hitches. She tried again. 'Let the sea take it!'

Silence. Rain. The black and endless sea.

'Mara. Seriously. What are we doing here?' Pearl's voice had turned velvet, warm. She kissed the tears from Mara's cheek. 'You gave it a shot. But let's go back, okay?' Pearl held Mara close, ready to pull them both ashore.

'No!' Mara stretched out her limbs in the water, stopping Pearl from pulling her. 'The sea is still against me. I need to give it more.'

'The sea isn't against you. And no matter what you do, it will never be for you, either. The sea just is.'

'But it wants –'

'It doesn't want anything! You can't bargain with it and you can't convince it and you can't show it that you're worthy.'

The rain slowed, then stopped. The waves calmed. The undertow stopped tugging at Mara's feet.

'You see?' said Mara, her voice triumphant, even though she was half drowned and red-eyed. 'You see!'

The clouds slipped away, revealing the bright moon and a sky full of stars. The air seemed warmer. Behind them, the island sighed.

'Mara, that's not why.' Pearl's grip on Mara relaxed; now they could both float without effort. The stars reflected on the black sea, and they were swimming between the constellations. 'The sea does what it wants.'

'You're wrong. I made this happen. Now you can show me again.'

'Show you what?'

'How to breathe.'

In the calm and sleeping sea, Pearl pulled Mara underwater. It wasn't as easy as they hoped: no matter how much Mara tried to relax, her body rebelled. As soon as the water closed over her head, she thrashed her limbs, kicking out at Pearl in an effort to get back to the air. Each time, Pearl pulled her to the surface, her hands hooked under Mara's arms so her head was clear of the surface, seawater streaming down her chin. Pearl could go down into the dark, strong under the water's pressure, and come back up. But Mara knew if she went down there, she would never come back.

'Mara! Calm, calm. Don't fight. You have to let go and trust me. If you try to save yourself, we'll both drown.'

Mara tried her best. She forced her limbs to relax. She counted her breaths, deep into her belly. She let Pearl pull her into the dark of the sea.

Down under the water, she didn't dare open her eyes. What if she saw a distant gleam, hair twisting in the current? What if she saw a tiny hand reaching out to her?

Instead she let the sea soothe her: the dark behind her eyes, the pressure of Pearl's hands on her forearms, the slow pound of water against her ears. It was okay. She was okay.

And just when she ran out of breath, when her lungs began to burn, when she felt the cold trickles of panic behind her eyes - there was Pearl, pressing her lips to Mara's, breathing into her mouth. Mara inhaled Pearl's breath and pushed bubbles out through her nose. Pearl waited a moment, then pressed their lips together again, breathing into Mara's mouth. She squeezed Mara's hand to check she was okay, and Mara squeezed back.

They surfaced, and Pearl taught Mara how to swim: not to kick the feet, but to flex the legs from the hips. Think seal, think otter. Think mermaid. Back down they went, and Pearl breathed for both of them, and Mara flexed her legs from the hips. She grinned into the darkness, teeth cold against the sea. She was blind and freezing, but she could do it. She could stay underwater.

She emerged triumphant: body numb, eyes burning, lungs aching. Together they swam to the sandbank and staggered ashore, water sheeting from their bodies. The clouds were back and the rain had started again, but they didn't notice. With the water still licking at her ankles, Mara took hold of Pearl's waist and lifted her into the air. Pearl laughing, kicking, their wet skin slipping, and Mara lowered her back down into a kiss.

Balançoire

From the trees, in the shadows, Signe watched. She didn't mean to spy on her child. Sleepless, restless, skin itching from paint flakes, Signe just wanted to be outside. To put her feet in the sea. To breathe air that moved. A day spent in a room with painted-over windows was barely a day at all. What bird could live without seeing the sky? She slipped from her bed, leaving Peter snoring like a giant. She pulled rain boots and a woollen coat on over her nightdress. Through the crumbling house and the grasping trees.

But there, at the edge of the trees, she stopped. Voices. For one wonderful, terrible moment a voice struck familiar and she was sure it was her child, her little Bee, come magically back to her. She peered out from behind a tree, heart in her throat. And it was her child, but it was not Bee.

The moonlight caught Mara's back, casting the rest of the world into shadow. Who goes for a swim in the middle of the night, in the middle of winter? Signe, motherly, frowned at her child, standing at the edge of the sea. What was she thinking, the silly girl? She must be freezing! She'd catch her death! And how out of character. Mara had never been one for such things, adventures and dangers and joy. She was the sensible one, the calm one, the – Signe let herself think the treacherous thought, but only for a moment – dull one. What on earth could she be doing, alone on the beach in the middle of the night?

Perhaps she was – Signe's heart rushed up her throat again. Perhaps she was going to do harm to herself. Perhaps it was all too much for her. Her missing brother, her absent sister, her distant father, her ...

Signe faltered. What was she to her younger daughter? She was a good mother, she was sure. But how good could any mother be? Do any of us really get it right? She'd lost almost all of her children, to the grave or to the sea. Was that what a mother was supposed to do? She would run to her child and scoop her up and take her home and save her, like all little girls want to be saved.

Mara stepped towards the water, and the beam of moonlight shifted, lighting up something else. Signe stopped. Mara was not alone. Someone else was there. Someone with hair like a shadow and skin like burnished gold.

A selkie. A creature from the sea. Webbed fingers and secret hidden gills. A scuttering, shifting, inconstant thing you could never truly catch. Signe knew how that story ended.

Before she could cry out, her daughter took the selkie's hand and stepped into the sea. One, two, three – and they both disappeared under the water. Signe's feet rushed forward and her hands flew up, a cry pulled from her throat. The selkie was taking her daughter, was drowning her, her bones would disappear under the silt and Signe would never see her child again. The wind slapped at the waves, layering lace.

Then two heads broke the silvered sea. Mara coughed and gasped, and that meant she was breathing, and so Signe could breathe again. She was having no more of this. She readied herself to march into the sea and push the selkie back beneath the waves and save her baby.

Signe blinked from the darkness, trying to discern shapes. Mara and the selkie, slick and tangled in the water. Mara and the selkie, leaning closer. Mara and the selkie - kissing.

In Signe's mind, Mara stretched and grew, upwards and outwards, from pixie to giant, from baby to adult. She put her hands to her temples, trying to sort her thoughts, trying to calm the beating wings. She was getting confused. Mara was not a little girl now. If she wanted to leap into the night sea and freeze herself half to death and kiss strange girls, then Signe couldn't stop her. Couldn't save her.

Bee was the one - Bee needed her. He needed a home to come home to. If she wasn't going to sleep, she should work. There was still so much to do. The rain began, a shiver on Signe's cheeks. She got ready to slip back to the house before Mara saw her.

'I think it's better that Bee is gone.' Mara's voice was thin and shaky, but the wind brought it right to Signe's ears. She paused, listening. 'It's better that he's gone from this world. Let the sea take it!'

At the sound of Bee's name, Signe felt her body turn as heavy as stone. Mara's words leadened through her. Such weight inside her. She watched mutely as the two girls disappeared beneath the water. She told her legs to move. They didn't.

The girls stayed under for so long that the sea's surface stilled. The waves lapped steady over them, as if there was nothing there at all. The black sea reflected the constellations, the world folded in two. Distantly, she noted that the rain had stopped and the waves had calmed. The air felt warmer. She wondered when that had happened. She wondered when any of this had happened.

When Signe had first come to the island, she brought many things with her: furniture, children, hopes. And belief. Signe had a good Swedish upbringing, but even the most modern family has its share of ritual. For Signe's mother, it was confession. We all sin, Signe's mother told her, but we don't have to let the after-taste of that sin sit in our mouths forever. Why let it ruin the good food that the Lord provided? God doesn't want that. He will forgive us, but only if we tell Him true. And so confession, every Saturday.

The cedarwood scent of the confession box. The priest's soft voice. The patterns of light through the mesh. Every week, Signe had given her confession.

She had grown, and she had married, and she had birthed girls, and she had made a new home for them all. There was no church service on the island. There was a church – or rather, the remains of a church. By the time Signe got to it, it was mostly walls. A caved-in ceiling, pews layered in old leaves. Puddles fuzzing green in each corner. Signe had tried to give her confession there – had even climbed into the confession box and hovered over the broken seat, water-warped and thick with grime. She tried a few times, but felt silly confessing with no one to hear it. Even the birds had no interest in her sins; they were happy enough to convene chattering on the pews when Signe was outside, but as soon as she creaked open the door they exploded towards the sky in a thrashing, shrieking cloud. She couldn't shout her confession fast enough.

For weeks she held her sins inside. They were small sins: resentment at the tantrums and whims of her growing daughters;

fear that even though she was giving every part of herself to her tiny son, it was still not enough to help him; worry that she'd made the wrong decision in coming to the island; the flash of anger when Peter interrupted her mid-sentence, or answered a question different to the one she'd asked; being less than ecstatic about the constant motherly treadmill of cleaning-washing-cooking-cleaning-soothing-mending-cleaning-cleaning-cleaning.

Small sins. But even the tiniest splinter can poison our blood if we don't pull it out.

On the first full moon on the first summer on the island, she walked through the sleeping house and through the garden and past the trees. She stood on the shore and gave her confession to the sea. Her resentment, her anger, the razing ache of the small lives she'd lost inside her: she gave it all away. She felt instantly lighter, ready to take flight. Her darkest thoughts were the heaviest: tiny blackened stones that she did not need to carry with her.

Every month when the moon was full, she escaped from the house and unburdened herself to the sea. She did not expect anything in return. That was not the point of confession. It was not a fair deal; her sins were not meant to provide nourishment or joy. It was a selfish act, meant only to lighten her soul, to cleanse her palate.

What Signe didn't know was that the sea was not the only one to hear her confession. Once her words were out in the world, the wind could snatch them and take them anywhere it wanted.

Islay always slept with their window open. Even in winter, even in snow, she needed the taste of clean air. And that is how she heard her mother's words, snatched and carried by the wind, seeping into her sleep.

The first time she crept along to the night sea and decided to let it take her sins, she thought she was enacting something she'd first done in a dream. And perhaps she had. The midnight sneaking, the water-wading, the shouting out of all the nasty petty cruel daily things that little girls delight in doing and then later, secretly, regret.

Islay never told her mother that she was doing this. It wasn't a secret, exactly. She didn't think she was doing anything wrong: it wasn't shameful or dangerous. It was just playing. But what girl does not want to keep something from her parents? A small thing, sweet and spiked, a stealth held close.

It did not take long for Mara, always trying to tag along, always watching her sister from the shore, to want to play too. The girls, unlike Signe, did expect something in return. Why give something for nothing? They never had. Lost teeth could be exchanged for coins, chores for freedom, playing quietly for new toys. They gave something to the sea, and because they expected it, they got something back. Sometimes the waves calmed or the rain paused. Sometimes the seals sang. Sometimes the sea kicked up something for them: a spiralled shell in shades of dusky pink, a cluster of crabs still twitching, shards of blue-patterned pottery. Sometimes, jellyfish.

And so each of the Ross women confessed their small sins, each thinking that the sea gave them what they wanted.

Signe wrenched herself out of the trap of memories. She was heavy, every part of her body so heavy. Hiding in the shadows, she watched as Mara and the selkie emerged, shook and shivered on the shore, then leaned their bodies close and made their giddy way back into the trees. Signe had never said that she didn't blame Mara for losing Bee. Saying it out loud would name the fear, make it real. It would suggest that she actually did blame her.

Signe crept from the shadows and walked to the water's edge. The tide was going out; as the sea retreated it cut channels for itself, but sometimes it lingered too long and became trapped, a tiny pool among the stones. Signe faced the sea, letting the waves tug at her feet, and whispered her confession.

'I would have given one away,' she said. The words scraped up her throat, but came out as a whisper. She tried again, louder this time, her throat already raw.

'I would have traded one of them – any one – for Bee.'

It was true, and it hurt, and she gave it away gladly.

'I would have traded one,' she said. 'I still would.'

Détourné

Signe was alone in the studio, rehearsing a role she already knew by heart: Odile, the wicked black-costumed witch of *Swan Lake*, the contrast to the good white-costumed Odette. She'd been playing the dual role for three months in this particular production; there was another month to go. It was hard not to measure time in months now. Ever since she'd met Peter – his knuckles big and knotted like they were carved from wood, his shoulders curving round her like the walls of a house – she knew she wanted to make new life with him.

Signe brought her foot up to the barre and bent to touch her raised toe, feeling the pull in her inner thigh, in her obliques, through each finger as she stretched – and there, suddenly, another pull where there shouldn't be one. A flutter, an insect-wing flicker deep inside her. She straightened and stretched her arms above her head until it went away.

Love had already begun to fill her out. A ballet dancer's clothing is tiny and tight, but the practical thinness of her figure makes the skimpiness elegant, classic, rather than sultry. In the streets, in her coat and ankle boots, Signe was still a slim woman. But at the barre she was fleshly, an embarrassment of curves. Her shiny black leotard seemed more to oil her body than cover it.

After her performance the night before, she'd run straight from the stage to a theatre two streets over to see Peter fight. They'd spent every night that week with his bent and swollen hands resting in a salad bowl of ice, his body hunched over the kitchen table. His knuckles were salted white with scars.

'There are two ways out of a life like this,' Peter had said. His voice was thickened and drowsy, treacle-slow. Signe turned from the sink where she was tipping more ice into a cloth. 'One way is to fail. The other is to die.'

Signe brought him a new bowl of ice and lightly kissed his forehead and slid her heavying body onto his lap. She distracted him with her love and herself – but she knew that he was right.

Most dancers, if they're lucky, will perform as prima ballerina throughout their twenties. Then, when their thirties roll around, they can no longer play the princess or the young lover. There are still plenty of good roles to play – some may argue that these roles are better. The wicked godmother in *Sleeping Beauty*, the grotesque fortune-telling witch in *La Sylphide*. By the time the dancer is in her late thirties, even mothers and witches are too young, and the only choice left is to train others. That's assuming you've hung in there that long: it's possible you'd have snapped your Achilles tendon, dislocated your knees during a spin, or had a hip replacement after too many leg extensions. But whenever you go, it's rare that anyone will notice you've gone. As soon as you stop dancing, there's another dancer already prepped to step into your place. She'd snatch the shoes off your feet, too, if you hadn't already danced them to rags.

Signe had soaked Peter's hands, and the next day he'd got up again and gone to the gym and prepared for that night's fight. He was hurting, but that wasn't enough reason to stop. Signe watched from the crowd as he threw a punch, blinking as it landed. According to the rules of boxing, a boxer cannot hit a man when he's down. But when he is still on his feet, half senseless, reeling, both eyes blood-blind – then you can and should hit him as hard as you can to bring him down. Hit hard and you're a champion; show mercy and you're nothing but a fool. And so down he goes, and out comes another boxer. Another strong, ignorant, innocent boy. But why blame the gloved opponent or the cheering crowd? We don't blame a ballet's audience for the dancers' bleeding feet.

There was a time that Signe had loved to watch Peter work. He had nothing except his own body, and still the crowd wanted it, and he happily gave it away. The bell rang, and Signe clambered into the ring, her small nervous hands slippery on the ropes. She was still wearing her swan costume, the white leotard patched with nervous sweat. A scatter of crumpled white feathers from her tutu floated across the heads of the crowd, and surely they must be thinking that her appearance was a planned – though melodramatic – part of the show.

Peter looked up at her, and it took a full three seconds for recognition to spark in his eyes.

'You're not here,' he said, but he reached for her anyway.

'Peter,' said Signe. 'Peter.'

There was a time that Peter had nothing except his own body. But didn't he have something else, now? Wasn't she something? His slick, hot forehead pressed to her smooth, cool one. He was as strong as stone. He would never break. The roar of the crowd fell away. They both watched as a dark glob of blood spattered onto the diamond of floor between their feet. Peter looked up at her in surprise, one nostril ringed red.

'But he didn't get a head hit,' said Peter. 'He didn't ...'

The problem is not the impact of the fist and the face. The problem is that a punch makes the head snap back and then forward, causing the brain to thud repeatedly against the hard inside of the skull. It's a concussive blow. A car crash, over and over. It's common for two boxers to bump heads while sparring. But just because something is common, that doesn't mean it's not devastating. The worst collision is when the soft circle near one man's temple collides with the tough band on the top of the other man's head. It's not just about how sturdy a man is, not if the softest part of you hits the hardest part of someone else. Detached retinas, blood clots, cauliflower ears, broken thumbs, obstructed nostrils. And that's just the damage you can see. Signe had watched as Peter's other nostril darkened, a trickle of blood on his top lip.

Now, standing at the barre in the silent white studio, she remembered that blood. She thought of her suddenly too-tight clothes, the fluttering low in her belly, and the world shifted. That falling drop of blood – it was a sign. It was a warning.

That night, Signe was ready for the pinnacle of her performance: to whip herself around thirty-two times on the same standing leg, using the force of her other leg to propel her around, the whole thing done on the tip of one toe.

But she didn't get that far. First came a leap. She dropped her body, ready. Her feet tensed. Her calves, her thighs. Her body poised to spring – and she let it go.

An audible bang, like a stone thrown to the ground.

Pain exploded in her right ankle.

She fell to her knees, too shocked to cry out. She felt like she'd been kicked with a dozen booted feet all at once, like she'd been shot – not that she knew what either of those things felt like, but it couldn't be much worse than this. The music carried on, but Signe did not.

Later that night in her hospital bed, to explain why she'd refused sedatives, to explain why she kept saying that the days of dancing and boxing were over, to explain why she was crying with happiness when she should be crying with pain, she told the doctor and Peter and anyone else who would listen that she was pregnant, she was pregnant, a baby was coming, and now that she had this life she did not need any other.

Bidie-in

Mara watched from her bedroom window, waiting for Pearl. The sun was beginning to set, and all the puddles gleamed liquid gold. Mara still had Pearl's copy of *Mine*, the black-covered book with its silver title. She kept it under her pillow, feeling the solidity of it every night as she fell asleep, and now she slid her hand beneath the pillow to comfort herself with its sharp edges. She stood like that, thumbing blindly through the book's pages, waiting.

Earlier, Signe had told Mara that Peter was sleeping in. But when he had emerged from his bedroom, his shirt wasn't buttoned and he wasn't wearing shoes. 'Your mother,' he said, his words running together. 'I don't want her to see.' As Mara helped him, she tried to keep her smile steady. She spoke in a low voice, like she was soothing a horse. Under her buttoning fingers, his skin felt solid and cold, like meat from the fridge.

Finally, Pearl appeared, swaying up the path like she was moving underwater. Mara felt her heart stutter. She'd wanted to stay there as Pearl approached. She'd wanted to make Pearl wait downstairs for her, to make a grand entrance, to be the heroine of the story. To be someone else.

But with Pearl, she didn't need to be someone else. She ran down the stairs and out of the house to meet her on the path.

'Hey,' said Pearl.

'Hey,' said Mara, a little out of breath. She didn't know what to do with her hands.

Understanding, Pearl took Mara's hand. She stroked her thumb along the soft, scarred curve between Pearl's thumb and first finger. Her hands felt cool and rough. Useful hands.

'Is this really your house?' said Pearl.

Mara turned and squinted at it, even though she doubted the house could have changed while she wasn't looking. 'Of course it is.'

'Serious?' Pearl looked like she was trying not to laugh. 'I didn't realise it was ...'

'I told you we were fixing it up. I know it's a mess. There's still lots to do, but every time we fix something it seems like something else breaks, and I don't know why it –'

'Mara. That's not what I'm saying. I mean – this house. Look at it.' Mara looked at it. Then she looked back at Pearl.

'It looks like a birthday cake,' said Pearl.

'What? It's a house. It looks like a house.'

'It's *pink*! It's a castle, and it's pink. It's got bloody turrets and everything. It must have a thousand rooms.' Pearl made a sound halfway between a gasp and a laugh. 'Seriously, I feel like I'm hallucinating. Did I make you up? Did I make this all up?'

'It's not a castle! It is pink-ish, and it does have turrets, but only little ones. You can't go in them. And there aren't a thousand rooms. There aren't even a hundred. Maybe fifty, if you count the shed and the utility room and the bigger cupboards, but most of the bedrooms have been shut up for years.'

Pearl shook her head, still staring up at the house. 'If fairy tales were real,' she said, 'this is where they would happen.'

'That's not – don't say that, okay? Let's just go in.' Mara started walking, tugging Pearl along after her, up the path and into the house.

'Curiouser and curiouser!' Pearl was staring back at the doorway. 'This house is unreal. Did we just walk through a shark jaw? You're just full of mysteries.'

Mara couldn't help grinning, even though it tugged her scar tight. She squeezed both of Pearl's hands in her own.

The click of a door closing. The shush of footsteps in the upstairs hall. Right at the last minute, just before Signe appeared at the top of the stairs, Mara let go of Pearl's hands. In the space of a second Pearl looked surprised, then sad. Then she composed herself and tilted her politest smile up at Signe.

'This is my mum,' said Mara. 'Oh, but you don't have to call her mum. Signe.'

'Nice to meet you,' said Pearl. Signe came down the stairs and put out her hand. Pearl hesitated, as if unsure whether Signe wanted her to shake it or kiss the back of it. She shook it. Signe extricated her hand a little too hastily.

'Excuse me,' she said. 'I just have to get ...' And she disappeared back up the stairs.

'And this' – here Mara led Pearl into the front room, where Peter was sitting in his old leather chair, apparently lost in thought – 'is my dad, Peter.'

'Nice to meet you,' said Pearl, and held out her hand. Peter turned his head slowly, slowly, but did not move his hand. Pearl stood for a moment, hand outstretched, before reaching for the nearest object, which happened to be a photo frame.

'What's this?' she asked, before she'd looked at it. She held it out to Mara.

'It's us,' said Mara. 'All of us.'

In the centre of the photo was birthday boy Bee, newly five, solid and blond and grinning to show all his teeth. A girl leaned grinning over him, willowy and knowing with her blood-red curls. And off to the side, Mara, square-bodied and unscarred. Their faces were lit below by the birthday cake candles. It was the last photo of their last summer together.

'Nice to meet you too,' said Peter from his chair. 'It really is a pleasure.'

Pearl glanced up at Mara in surprise. Mara held her gaze, pointedly not looking at her father. Pearl followed Mara's lead, though she couldn't help casting a polite smile in Peter's direction. She looked down at the photo in her hand.

'Your sister has great hair,' she said.

'Islay doesn't live here any more,' said Mara. 'She moves around. But she's coming – I think she's coming. Soon. Maybe.'

Now Pearl was looking properly at the photo, and a frown furrowed. She caught Mara looking and smoothed her brow. Mara knew it must be obvious to Pearl that Bee was much younger than his sisters. It must be obvious that he was too young to be out in the world alone, and he should be in his house. And it must be obvious that he was not.

'Your brother,' said Pearl carefully. 'He looks like a wee heartbreaker.'

'Yes,' said Mara, because she couldn't think of anything else to say.

'Sit down on the sofa, Mara,' said Signe, who'd appeared behind them. 'And you too, ah … Just sit yourselves there out of the way, and I'll get started on dinner.'

'I was hoping,' said Pearl to Signe, and while she was distracted Mara eased the photo from her hands and placed it back on the table, 'that you'd let me cook dinner for you.'

'I got the ingredients,' added Mara. 'I walked to the shop earlier.'

Signe hesitated.

'Don't argue,' said Mara.

'I'll just pop into the kitchen and warm some cream for Peter's whisky. I don't usually, but – well, why not?'

'I will,' said Mara. 'Let me. And I'll make one for you too. You and Dad can talk.'

'I ... no, I don't ...'

Peter turned his head and looked at Signe then.

'Yes,' said Signe, and her smile spread quick and then stayed. 'Thank you, Mara.' She sat on the chair beside Peter and put her hands beside his, not quite touching.

'I'll get the drinks,' said Mara, 'and then Pearl and I will cook.'

Before Signe could argue she took hold of Pearl's elbow and led her out.

Ecarté

All those days that Signe watched her girls from the kitchen window. Her hands resting idle in the soapsuds, dishes forgotten as she warmed her fingers. In those early years on the island, she could never get warm. Strange, really, as she came from a much colder country; but it was different here. The way the wind raged, the way it snatched the hair up off the back of your neck just to drip icicles down your back. The way it would wait until the sun had warmed the air, until you had decided to be brave and go out without a jumper, to let the clouds pillow thick across the sky and the rain drip sharp on your scalp. Even now, deep into a slow summer, you couldn't always trust the sun to stay. Signe shifted her hands in the water, watching as her knuckles turned red from the heat.

Out in the garden, her girls in their pastel pants and vests. Islay with her burning red hair. Mara with her face scrunched up in concentration. The pair of them, knees bent, heads bowed, hunched over in the middle of the garden. Little witches making potions with petals and insects and spit. Speaking in magic spells, combinations of words that sounded made up - but the more you listened, the more a sense emerged. They were making something real from the unreal: a glamour made of grammar.

It was at those times that Signe worried she'd made a mistake in naming Mara for the sea between two islands. In stories it was always three: three little pigs, three billy goats gruff, three bears in three beds. Three brothers off to find wives, three princesses in three beautiful dresses made of stars and moon and sun. It was always meant to be three. But Mara was not really the third child.

And then came Barra. Her little Bee. Cradling his red, wrinkled body, so long a part of her own body, she counted. Fingers, toes. Bee's eyes looked past her at something she couldn't see. He had been in this world for minutes, and he was still stuck half in another. What Signe didn't realise then was that he would never fully emerge from it – and then, too soon, he would be back in it. That other place, the barrier between the worlds membrane-thin and yet a thousand miles away. The land of dreams and magic and terrible, awful beauty. Was that where Bee lived now? Was that where all her lost children lived?

When Mara was first born, the scent from the crown of her head was the most delicious thing Signe had ever smelled. It was a miracle, a strange magic, to think that this creature she had made inside her body was now outside it. She'd have to touch and smell her over and over just to make sure she was real. Her little ghost baby, her lost child, come back to her.

That milky cotton scent of her – could it be real? The winter sun catching her gingery hair, lighting strands pink as rose petals. Her cheeks sculpted from porcelain, turning in the light as she snuffled and mewled. Her grasping fists, her restless pink tongue, the moth wings of her eyelashes. Signe held her closer, breathing her in. She pinched the velvet flesh of Mara's arm – harder, harder – just to make sure she was real. And when she cried, she couldn't be sure that it was the sound of a real child, or the sound of a thing pretending to be a child: a ghost in the shape of a girl.

Signe shifted her hands in the dishwater. She watched the witchery of girlhood, the casting of spells. She watched this Mara who was not that Mara. Her misnamed girl, her changeling.

Tatties

I n the kitchen, Mara and Pearl moved around one another like a dance. Pearl refilled Mara's wine glass just before she noticed it was empty. Mara handed Pearl a chopping knife at the moment she needed it for the onions. The fridge door opened and closed, the flame on the hob flared and was lowered. Pearl bubbled butter in a cast-iron pan. Mara pulled back her hair and tied it in a knot. She busied herself taking peas from the pod, slipping the odd one into her mouth and letting it pop between her molars.

With a grin and a glance to make sure that Mara was looking, Pearl tossed the chopping knife up, let it arc a loop, and caught it.

Mara laughed. 'Did you practise that?'

'Yep. It's my trick to impress pretty ladies.' Pearl put down the knife and held her open hands out to Mara, palms exposed. 'You have no idea how many times I caught the sharp end before I got the hang of it.'

Mara lifted the proffered hands and studied them. 'They look fine to me.'

Pearl pressed their hands together and squeezed, pulling Mara closer. 'Okay, so that wasn't true. I don't have any tricks.' She pulled

Mara in for a kiss. Mara kept her eyes open, looking at the open doorway.

If Pearl noticed, she didn't show it. With a grin, she picked up the knife and got to work on the onions.

Twenty minutes later, the fisherman's pie was in the oven and the prep dishes were soaking in the sink.

Pearl raised the half-full bottle of wine. 'Shall we –' She was interrupted by the back door swinging open. In the gap, a rectangle of dark garden. It slammed shut, the latch shuddering. Seconds ticked. The wind was silent for once; the only sound was the drip of the leaky tap and the distant lull of the sea. Mara turned to speak and the door swung in again, still revealing nothing. Pearl frowned at the door, then walked over to close it.

'Don't touch it!' called out Mara, louder than she'd meant.

Pearl took a step back, hands raised in surrender.

'Sorry,' said Mara. 'Sorry. The latch is broken, and I didn't want you to hurt yourself. Mum already cut her hand on it.'

'Okay,' said Pearl. 'Thank you for looking out for my hands.'

'I need your hands,' said Mara, and then felt her cheeks flame.

'If it's broken,' she said, 'then let's fix it.'

Mara retrieved the toolbox – one of many stashed throughout the house – from under the stairs, then dug through it for a screwdriver and a packet of screws. She went to toss the screwdriver in the air, to copy Pearl's trick. But mid-flight, she felt her heart jolt as she recognised a smear of her mother's blood on the handle. She snatched back her hand and the screwdriver clattered to the floor. It rolled across the tiles, revealing that the plastic handle was daubed with black paint that looked, Mara realised, nothing at all like blood.

Pearl headed for the door, pausing to pick up the screwdriver and peer through the oven's window at the pie. Her arm brushed the oven door, which fell open with a crash. She jumped.

'Did I do that?'

'No,' said Mara. 'It's fine, I broke it last week. I told you, nothing works here.'

Heat blasted out of the open oven door. Mara eased it closed, holding it longer than she needed to, willing it to stay closed.

'I've already got the screwdriver out,' said Pearl. 'We might as well fix that too.'

'There's too much. You don't understand.'

'Well, you can't just leave it broken, can you? Speaking of which...' Pearl knelt on the floor and examined the latch. Mara brought over the toolbox in case there was anything else they needed. She reached out and tucked a strand of Pearl's hair behind her ear.

'Your brother,' said Pearl, her gaze on the latch.

Mara was glad of the tools, as she could keep her eyes fixed on them. 'His name is Bee. Was Bee.'

'And he's gone.'

'Yes,' said Mara.

'And,' said Pearl, 'you think it's better that he's gone.'

'Sometimes.'

'But you still want him to come back.'

'Yes,' said Mara. 'All the time.'

In the silence, Mara could hear the metal scraping together as Pearl tightened the screws.

'It's okay. It's not a question. I just needed to make sure I was putting the pieces together right.' Pearl put down the screwdriver and rocked back on her heels. She thumbed the latch, letting it click open and shut. 'There,' she said. 'Fixed.'

The oven door crashed open, scattering baking trays across the floor.

Mara and Pearl repeated their synchronised dance as they laid out the dishes, filled the wine glasses, served the dinner: mashed tatties on top of creamy fish, honeyed carrots, garden peas. It felt strange at first for Mara to see Pearl sitting where Islay used to sit, wrists resting on the edge of the kitchen table, back taut against the rickety chair. It felt strange to see Pearl do anything normal: sneeze, yawn, misunderstand. Mara still sometimes felt that she was only dreaming Pearl.

The kitchen was cosy in the candlelight. The heat from the oven brought colour to Signe's cheeks, and Peter did all his worst jokes. They laughed. Really laughed. And they loved Pearl. Mara was sure that they did. She couldn't imagine how anyone could be less than bewitched.

But, but. Signe ate three bites of her dinner before pushing the rest to the side of her plate. Peter's laugh was always a little behind everyone else's. Pearl glanced up at Mara after every sentence to check that she had said the right thing. Looking around the table, Mara felt joy and shame and disgust and grief and compassion and anger and love, all of it, all at once.

Afterwards, clearing the plates, Signe asked: 'Was everything all right with the toolbox?'

'What do you mean?' replied Mara.

'I heard you clattering it around.'

'We were fixing the latch. On the back door.' Mara nodded unnecessarily towards the door. 'Dad, do you want me to make you another whisky with cream?'

'Signe,' said Pearl at the same time, 'are you pleased about the bridge? I imagine it will be good for the guest house. More tourists.'

'You must let me fix things.' Signe's voice grew quiet and tight. 'I don't want you touching the latch, and I don't want – her either. It all has to be a certain way. I need it to be just right, and only I can ...' Signe stopped, her face tight.

'Yes, thank you, Mara,' said Peter. To Signe he said: 'My dove, would you like to join me in a whisky?'

'I'll need to just wash the cream pan,' said Mara. 'Mum, do you want one?'

Signe was not listening. Balancing the stack of plates in one hand, she reached out for the latch with the other. She thumbed it, feeling its smooth movement. It was good as new. It was better than new. Since they'd moved in, nothing in the house had worked as invisibly, as effortlessly as this latch. What was different? Why did it work?

She remembered Mara and Pearl in the sea. She remembered Mara's confession, the way the sea seemed to calm straight after, the way the island had been soothed. She remembered what she had given to the sea. Her hand fell away from the latch.

'I'm going to walk Pearl out,' said Mara.

'Thank you for having me,' said Pearl.

'Yes,' said Signe, to no one in particular.

Mara led Pearl out of the kitchen and along the hallway and through the shark jaws. She closed the front door behind them.

'Where are you going?' asked Pearl.

'I'm walking you home.'

'You don't need to do that. It's far, and it's late.'

'I want to.'

'But I don't need you to.'

'Halfway,' said Mara.

Pearl smiled. 'Okay. Halfway.'

When they got to the bottom of the drive, out of sight of the house, Mara slipped her hand into Pearl's.

Swither

Every night, Mara crept out to the beach with Pearl. They slid into the cold sea together, lips full of confession, and breathed for hours; then afterwards they slid into Mara's warm bed. With a kiss on Mara's forehead, Pearl slipped out and back to her house before dawn. Her footsteps were as light as sand.

Every day, Mara worked on the house. Slowly, surely, she changed. Her hands grew strong and rough. Her lungs stretched. Her legs developed muscles, lean and long, and she push-pulled her body through the water without having to think. Sometimes she forgot to come up for air, only surfacing when black blurs sparked in front of her eyes. She never again fought against Pearl's presence under the water, trusting that breath would be there when she needed it.

One night, emerging from the moonlit waves, Pearl held Mara until they caught their breath. 'I can't stay here much longer, Mara,' she said. 'But maybe you could come with me?' Seawater sheened Pearl's skin, diamonded her eyelashes. 'Join the show, perform, travel with me.'

Mara couldn't help but laugh. 'You know I want to. But I'm not – mermaids have to be – and I'm not …'

'Not what?'

'Not beautiful.'

Now it was Pearl's turn to laugh. 'Oh, forget beauty! Why would that matter? Under the water it's all hair and tits and tail.' She held her wet hands over Mara's eyes. 'Picture it,' she said. 'Flowing, curling wigs the colour of sweeties. Couple of seashells glued on to your chest. And the tails – you've never seen anything shimmer like those tails in the water. With all that, who's even looking at the rest? Who'd ever notice whatever flaws you think you have? Because trust me, no one else sees them.'

Mara felt tears prick hot in her eyes. She blinked hard. 'I know people see. You can't tell me people don't see.' She looked into Pearl's eyes, daring her to drop her gaze, to look at Mara's scar.

Pearl didn't. She leaned in and kissed from the outer corner of Mara's left eye, down her cheek, to the corner of her mouth; from one end of the scar to the other. What a strange way we are expected to heal: stitch the wound shut and hope that underneath, hidden away, the flesh will knit back together.

'I could,' whispered Mara. 'I could try to get rid of it. See about surgery, maybe, or –'

'Don't you dare,' said Pearl, her voice a little too loud in the closeness. 'Why would you want to get rid of any part of yourself?'

'But I'm not beautiful.'

'Beauty is boring. The best lives leave a mark.'

Mara remembered the sealskin-shine of a boy in the water. The burn in her lungs and the jag of small stones against her shins. Eyes rolled back, blood clotted black. He was gone long before she reached him. She'd made a choice that day. Years had passed, and she still wasn't sure.

Mara felt the flicker of a fish against her ankle. Pearl's hands were warm and her fingers were strong. From far across the water, the lights of distant ships caught in the corner of her eye.

Wheesht

Islay had been in many depressing places in her life, but this pub was surely the worst. It wasn't the fuzzy brown velour on the seats. It wasn't the pervasive smell of beer and cleaning fluid. It was the look in her sister's eyes.

Islay sipped her gin and watched over the lip of her fizzing glass. There Mara stood behind the bar, pulling pints and counting out change. She was grinning like an absolute loon. What the hell did she have to look so cheerful about? This shitty pub hadn't made Mara happy, and that crumbling house hadn't made Mara happy, and their grieving parents certainly hadn't made Mara happy. Which meant that it was something from off the island, and that did not bode well. Yes, Islay had obeyed Mara's summons – but it was not a permanent state of affairs.

Her stomach was still unsettled from the trip over. It had been a long time since she was on a fishing boat, and her muscles ached from trying to stay upright. She drained her glass and took it to the bar.

'Same again?' said Mara with a grin. 'It's nice having you back, Islay.'

Islay opened her mouth to say that she wasn't back, not like that – and before she could, the fruit machine in the corner spat out a clatter of coins. She remembered a story that Signe used to tell them about two sisters, a good one and a bad one. Every time the good one spoke, gold coins fell from her mouth; but every time the bad one spoke, slugs and snakes fell from her mouth.

While Mara pressed a clean glass to the optic, Islay filled the silence. She tried to be good. She tried to care about the island – or at least to seem like she cared.

'What's with all the stuff at the harbour? Concrete and diggers and that? The boat didn't go close and it was hard to see what was going on.'

'They're building a bridge to the mainland. Good, right?'

Islay shrugged. 'Do you like working here?'

'It's not forever.' Mara pushed a full glass across the bar to her sister and smiled.

Islay resisted the urge to drain her glass in one go. 'Cheers,' she said bitterly.

A chubby mixed-race girl with a blunt-cut bob walked in, pausing by the door to scan the room. She spotted Islay and Mara, and her face split into a smile as she headed over. Excellent: another tourist who thought they would be immediate friends just because they were the only females in the building.

'Hello,' said the chubby girl.

'Hello,' replied Islay, which meant *go away*.

'Pearl!' Mara practically leapt over the bar. 'You came! Let me get you a drink. What do you want? I'll get it.'

The girl smiled, and Mara smiled, and Islay, unnoticed, grimaced.

She didn't enjoy hating people on sight, but it seemed pretty obvious that this girl was the reason for Mara's happiness. From the moment that she walked in, Mara was weird. Well, Mara had always been weird, but this was ridiculous. Her eyes were too wide and she moved her mouth too much when she spoke. She was gesturing so much with her hands that she'd hit herself in the face if she wasn't careful. Islay wished she would; maybe then she'd shut up for a minute.

'So,' said Islay to the chubby girl as Mara went to pour a pint. 'What do you do?'

'Pearl is a mermaid!' Mara interrupted, calling back over her shoulder before Pearl had a chance to speak. Her eyes gleamed, and that was not a good sign. Not at all.

'Is that right,' said Islay, eyebrows raised.

'She travels all around the world, and performs underwater in different shows. Don't you think that's amazing?' Mara's eyes were wide, wide. If she wasn't careful they'd pop right out of her head. 'There are lots of girls, with all different skills, from all different places. Anyone can do it, you just have to learn how to stay under without panicking. Most people do, you know.'

'But not Pearl, I suppose?' Islay knew she hadn't managed to keep the sarcasm out of her voice, but it didn't matter. Neither of those googly-eyed girls was really listening to her anyway.

'Oh no,' said Mara, 'not at all. But Pearl isn't like most people.'

'Well, shit,' said Islay. 'Isn't that just something? Excuse me.' She made an effort to keep her face expressionless as she got up. She didn't need to go to the toilet, but she did need to go somewhere she wouldn't laugh or slap her sister in the face or drop to her knees and beg her to please please please never leave the island because Islay wasn't staying in her place, not now and not ever.

Later, after her seventh G&T and during her third unnecessary trip to the ladies, she thought she might as well pee, since she was there. By then the lights had a halo and the walls weren't quite upright. Her breathing was too loud; she could feel the heat of it in her nostrils. She was getting annoyed now. She rolled the toilet paper roll round and round and round and round and the end wasn't there, it was a perfect circle, no break to be found. Her breathing was annoying. The paper was annoying. The fucking cold toilet seat on her fucking thighs was annoying. She would not stay here. She would not give up her life for a crumbling house and a needy family. And the paper, the stupid fucking paper. Finally she gave up and scraped at the unending roll with her fingernails, ripping a section of ragged sheets from the middle.

After leaving the island Islay had lived in many homes, and they all had one thing in common: they were small. She had often dreamed that her tiny rented spaces opened out to reveal secret rooms, corridors, entire wings that she'd never seen before. In the dream she was never surprised, only excited. She'd always known that she was entitled to more than she'd been given in the world, and now here was her reward. She began planning what she would do with all that extra space. How her life would expand within familiar bounds. Even after waking and seeing that it was only a dream, the expansive feeling lingered. She felt both immense, and safe-small.

And now that she was back on the island, the dream was real. The house with its endless rooms full of hulking furniture from people long gone, their loose hairs tangled in every corner, their abandoned belongings in every cupboard. It was a house full of mysteries. Islay was sure, in fact, that the house had expanded in her absence, grown extra rooms like a nautilus shell getting bigger with each passing year. So why didn't she feel immense? The house was as huge as the ocean, but as confined as a submarine.

Islay stood at the sink in the pub toilet, hands still held under the tap though the water had long ago gone cold, practising her smile in the mirror until it looked convincing.

Glaikit

Once, when Islay was littler and Mara was littler still and Bee was non-existent, their mum took Islay down to the harbour to get some shopping and catch up with the local chat. Islay couldn't fasten her shoes fast enough, and every step was a skip. It was exciting, to be out without her sister. Having a little sister was fun, mostly – but it was more fun to have her mum's attention to herself.

Summer was her favourite time. The air breathed warm and the sun painted everything bright. The days lasted forever. The sea came close to sleeping. You could lie in the grass and roll and roll and roll until you were dizzy, and wherever you stopped you were still lying on a carpet of daisies. At first Islay held her mum's hand, but their palms were sweaty and her mum didn't walk fast enough. Why walk when you could dance?

At the shop, her mum went inside to do boring things, popping out only to hand Islay an ice cream from the freezer.

Islay, obedient, said thank you and put the wrapper in the bin. The ice cream was already starting to melt down her hand. She explored the harbour, hopscotching along the stones and peering inside the empty lobster pots. They were made from rope that was bright blue like a doll's dress, but it felt rough enough to cut and smelled like old fish.

Islay found the best bench and got to work on the remains of her ice cream. Above her, seagulls scribbled across the sky. Ladybirds tickled her sandalled toes. The sun was as hot as a wool blanket on her bare arms.

She heard a splash and looked up. A dog, helter-skeltering into the waves. It would be okay, wouldn't it? The sea was at its sleepiest. Islay forgot her ice cream and watched, wide-eyed, as the dog paddled further and further out. Where was it going? She climbed up on the back of the bench and strained her eyes. A yellow ball floating, far off where the current liked to pull things under. Already the dog looked tiny, almost lost under the waves.

'Mum,' she said. 'Mum!'

She wanted her mum to grow to a giant and lean over and pluck the dog free from the waves. She wanted her to turn into a mermaid and swim to shore with the dog safe on her back. Her mum came out of the shop with a bag in each hand, and she did not do any of the things that Islay wanted. She took a long look at the sea, then she took Islay's hand and led her away so that she couldn't see the space where the dog had been.

It was only later, after dinner, after bath, after bed, that Islay realised she had dropped most of her ice cream.

'Mum,' she said, just as her mum reached to turn off the light.

What Islay wanted to say was: *Why did the dog go in the sea? Why, when it was an island dog? It had always lived here. It was old enough to know that the sea takes everything – why didn't it know?*

She knew that the dog had gone into the sea, and it hadn't come out. When something was gone, it was gone.

'It doesn't matter,' said Islay. 'Night, Mum.'

And her mum switched off the light and closed the door.

Gallus

earl came round for dinner, like Pearl had come round for dinner every other bloody night this week. Islay knew that Pearl came over for more than dinner, but Mara made a big fuss about walking Pearl to the end of the path and saying goodbye in a big loud voice. Mara thought she was being ever so clever, but if she was actually clever she wouldn't give Pearl massive wet lesbian kisses right on the front path where anyone could see. Luckily, Islay wasn't quite as dense as Mara. She kept it to herself, though; no need to break their poor mother's heart.

After they'd finished the cottage pie and vegetables boiled to within an inch of their lives – seriously, was Signe still cooking like this? They might as well be eating baby food – Islay stacked the empty dishes in the sink and joined Signe and Peter in the front room. Mara and Pearl stayed in the kitchen to make the tea.

In the front room, Peter sat stiffly in his leather chair, his palm pressed over the white ring stained on the arm. Signe pottered, her back to the room, rearranging the photo frames on the mantelpiece, patting Peter's hand every time she got near him. He was so much worse than the last time Islay had seen him. He was practically a statue already, hardly different from the ones up on the cliff. Islay could see that Mara had helped dress him; he had a polka-dot handkerchief folded in his top pocket, and he'd never have chosen that himself. Islay wondered about the mechanics of putting someone's socks on for them. Did you make them sit on a chair first? Or did they stay standing and rest their hands on your shoulders? Did you get them to lean up against a wall and lift one foot at a time?

She wished Mara had called her sooner – but then, she also wished that Mara hadn't called her at all. Did it mean she loved her family less if she wasn't strong enough to carry them all? From the kitchen, Islay heard the clatter of the bin lid, the sucking gasp as the bin bag was lifted, the click of the back-door latch.

'I'll just go and ...' she said, but no one was listening. She slipped away to the kitchen, which contained only Pearl. She nudged the kitchen door shut behind her and leaned on the worktop, casual-like, as if she'd just come in to help with the tea.

'Listen, Pearl. I just wanted to say thanks.'

Pearl smiled, cups clustered in her hands, and Islay tried hard to smile back. What on earth did Mara see in her? She was chubby and her teeth weren't straight and she always wore black like a witch. Didn't that use to be one of the signs of a witch, having your eyes two different colours? Then again, Mara had been no great beauty even before she got that bloody great scar across her face. Islay loved her sister, obviously, because she had to love her. But why had Pearl chosen her? Why would anyone choose Mara if they didn't have to? She must be up to something.

'You don't have to thank me,' said Pearl. 'I haven't even made it yet.'

Islay tried not to roll her eyes. She put all her effort into smiling without clenching her teeth. 'Not for the tea. I mean thanks for keeping Mara company. You're a good friend to her, and she needs a friend here.'

'Right,' said Pearl, half smiling, half frowning. 'A friend.'

'It can get lonely on the island. It's good that she doesn't have to be lonely now.'

How far could she push it? Fuck it. A little bit further. If Pearl called her on it she could deny, deny, deny. She had been practising her innocent face.

'I never asked, where do you stay?'

'Not far,' said Pearl. 'It's not a house, exactly, not like this one. But it will do for a little while.'

'Oh? So you're leaving?'

'We might be.'

'We?'

'Look, Islay, you should talk to your sister about this. It's not my place.'

Islay's stomach lurched. Fuck the teasing tone. Fuck all of it. She didn't have the energy to be coy and cutesy so she was just going to ask, she was going to make this chubby annoyance tell her exactly what –

Mara was a little smarter than Islay thought. She'd taken the bin out, yes; but on the way back in, she'd heard her sister's voice from the kitchen. She crept to the back door and slid up the latch. She held her breath and pressed her ear to the gap.

'Do you intend to stay on this island with my sister or not? It's a yes or no answer.'

'Yes,' said Pearl. 'And no.'

Islay snorted with impatience.

'Yes, I intend to stay with your sister. And no, I don't intend to stay on this island.'

'This is bullshit! You're bullshit. I don't give a fly's fuck what you do with your life, but you're not taking my sister with you. You can't just come here and spin some stupid story about mermaids and travel and whatever-the-fuck else. Mara's not like you. I can see that you like girls, and –'

'Islay,' said Pearl, in a tone that Mara had never heard her use before. She spoke with care, as if each word might explode. 'I don't *like girls*. I love a woman. And she loves me.'

Mara felt the tension building in her bones. Should she clear her throat? No, that's stupid. Whistle a tune? No, she couldn't whistle. Scuff her feet or rattle the latch or … and it didn't matter, it was all the same, she just needed to get in there and stop them arguing. She pushed open the door. Islay had already stormed out, leaving Pearl alone in the kitchen.

'I heard that,' said Mara.

'She's just looking out for you. She wants to keep you safe.'

'Trust me, Pearl. That's not what she wants.'

'Then what does she want?'

'I don't know. But whatever it is, it's about her, not me.'

The kettle rocked in its base, steam billowing, then clicked off. Pearl poured water into the teapot.

'Don't worry,' she said, her voice soft. 'It's fine. Your sister will love me and your mum and dad will love me and everything will be fine. We just need to give them a little time.'

'But she –'

'Look. Me and Islay, we're just having a negotiation. In negotiations, you always start with the things you can agree on.'

'How do you even know that?' Mara, distracted, picked at the splintering edge of the worktop.

Pearl grinned. 'I read books. Now, there are a few things that your sister and I agree on: one, Mara is a person we like. Two, we want Mara to be happy.'

'Is that it?'

'It's enough.'

'It's only two things! And they're basically the same thing. What about the rest? You think you can win her over, but I know her. I'm not holding my breath.'

'Well. We don't need to agree on everything. We just need to be in the same house for a little while, until … well, just until.' Pearl arranged the tea things on the tray: the pot, the cups, the milk in the silver jug. Mara hadn't told her how she used to carry the warm cream for her dad's whisky in that jug, and later it slipped her mind, and after that it didn't seem important, and in the end she never told Pearl at all. Everyone has secrets, even if they don't matter.

'The thing you should have realised about me by now, Mara –' And here Pearl circled her arms around Mara's hips and pulled her close, pecking a kiss to the tip of her nose. 'The thing is, I am very' – *kiss* – 'very' – *kiss* – 'very good at holding my breath.'

Shadow-boxer

Peter dreamed he was standing on the beach, dressed in pyjamas, watching the sea. Even in his dreams his limbs were heavy. Everything looked as it should, as it had the first day he'd arrived on the island, as it had every day since then. The night sky above him. The stony beach below him. The sea between, relentless.

But then the waves slowed, stuttered, stopped – and began to turn backwards, the front edge of the water curling in on itself. As Peter watched, the heavy sea rolled back like a carpet. Left behind on the exposed sand lay bones and shipwrecks, gasping fish and beached sharks, seaweed laid out thick as velvet.

And Bee.

Bee was there. His boy was so tiny, so distant – but the moon lit him silver among the dead and dying things. Peter set off at a run, his feet skiffling up sand, his muscles cramping, his bones shrieking. He skitted across the carpeted seaweed and leapt over the vast schools of gasping, flip-flopping fish. He was a runner, a sprinter, his lungs huge as airships. He'd never moved so fast in his life. His feet pounded the seabed, kicking up huge gouts of wet sand. He felt that if he ran any faster his skin would peel away where the wind whipped it, his limbs would stutter off his body, he'd topple apart like an old car driven too fast. He stayed whole – but no matter how hard he pushed, how fast he ran, he could never quite reach Bee.

He glanced up. Slowly, slowly, the sea was rolling back. It was as high as a skyscraper and utterly silent. On its underside, Peter could see endless shimmering layers of jellyfish, pale and pulsing. And on the seabed, still, stood Bee, his little Bee, so far away. Just as Peter thought his heart would break, Bee reached out for him, and then it did break. The sea was coming for his boy, and there was nothing he could do.

He ran harder, a cry pushing out of his throat. He reached for Bee, and his fingertips just brushed Bee's hair as the wave crashed in. He tumbled, blind, deaf, dying, his body prickled freezing from the water and stinging hot from the jellyfish. The sea flipped him and choked him and turned him end over end before depositing him, finally, on the cliff.

Peter gasped into the wind, but there was no wind. The cliff was still and silent. His body and clothes were dry. Above him, the stars twinkled. Below him, the grass was as soft as his bed. Behind him, the mass of statues. And in his arms, smiling in his sleep, was Bee.

Peter woke. He lay for a long time, listening to his wife breathe by his side. Now he knew: this was the deal he had to make. There was one way to get his son back with Signe and Mara and Islay. He would have to trade, one life for another. He would have to give himself. His failing body, his lagging mind – he didn't know if it would be enough to get his boy back, but he had to try.

And if it didn't work? If he gave himself, and Bee didn't come back? Well, at least they would be together.

Peter was used to bargaining with the world. He'd inherited plenty of superstition from other fighters: never shave the day of a fight, never sign a fight agreement on a Friday, never do thirteen reps when training, always wrap your left hand first and put your left boot on first. Over the years he'd added his own, to do with rusty nails and blades of grass from graves and swilling out his mouth three times with salt water. Perhaps they didn't help, but they certainly didn't hurt, considering how lucky he'd been: how much he'd worked, how many punches he'd taken and thrown to earn his savings, enough over the years for a ramshackle island house and its devouring upkeep. The charms he believed, the bargains he struck with his own body.

At a weigh-in, the boxers' weights must be evenly matched. A few pounds could move a fighter up or down a class. Drying out – no liquid for forty-eight hours before a weigh-in – was no rarity, though that didn't make it any easier to bear the results. The glazed eyes, the sores cracking at the corners of the mouth. Still, it's better than it was, in the days of bare knuckles and cudgel fights. Peter had heard stories from the old-timers. For cauliflower ear, a freshly roasted whole mouse was bound to the head. Cuts over the eye were treated with cow dung, spiderwebs, mud. Surprisingly effective, the old-timers said; spiderwebs stop bleeding, speed healing and reduce scarring.

When Peter was a young boy in Ireland, his family lived at the north end of the street, in the very smallest house, number 1. Every night his father sat in his chair and stared at the TV. It took Peter a long time to realise that his father wasn't looking at the TV at all, but out of the window, to the biggest house at the top of the street. The next year, Peter's father got a promotion and they moved to number 5. By the time Peter started secondary school, they were in number 20. By the time Peter was turning eighteen, his family had made it right to the south end of the street, to the very biggest house. Peter had made his own way from that big house, to the boxing ring, to Signe's bed – and eventually to his own big house, the biggest on the island. What had he wanted then, other than her? The stories his mother had told him as a child, fairy brides and how to catch them; the way they valued courtesy and independence above all things, except for shelter. Signe was his fairy bride, and he still couldn't quite believe he'd made her stay. Stay or leave: that was the choice. But losing Bee showed him that it wasn't that simple for either of them. They never meant to lie to one another.

Boxing had taught him that belief mattered. He'd needed his beliefs the way they all did, all those bold and beaten men. What else did they have to believe in, other than their own bodies? It wasn't hard for Peter to imagine the house without him in it. He was barely there at all, just a slab halfway between meat and stone. What good was his body now? What good was he to his girls? Without him, the whole house would be lighter. Stronger. Better.

Once, many years ago, Peter was knocked out and couldn't remember anyone's name for three days. It had felt like hot water was being poured into his skull, flowing over his eyes, leaving a boiling film over his brain. His opponent was smart; he knew to hit a groggy man on his body, so he will lower his hands from his head. His opponent knew something that Peter did not. To save ourselves pain, we forget about the things that matter.

Palooka

Peter knew his final walk would be slow. He started before midnight to give himself enough hours until dawn. He knew he would stagger and he knew it would hurt and he knew he would want to turn back and he knew it would be ugly and cold and dark.

But it was, as it happened, far too quick. The island helped him along, seeming to agree with his decision. The stars came out to light his way, a thousand-thousand bright pinpricks above his head, a treat just for his eyes. For his ears he was given the waves, steady like the applause of some distant crowd. And for his skin, the warm night breeze behind him, urging him on.

Stage one of dementia pugilistica can happen within seconds of a boxer taking a punch. Effects include respiratory arrest, drop in blood pressure, loss of corneal reflex, and loss of consciousness. When consciousness returns, it brings with it drowsiness, dizziness, disorientation, double vision and vomiting. If the fighter is unconscious for several hours, these after-effects can last for days or weeks. When the fighter awakes, he may not remember anyone's name. He may not be able to orientate himself. He may not be able to speak in sentences.

Peter reached the base of the hill and began the trek upwards, the breeze encouraging him, a gentle stroke to his limbs. The moon blinked bright above him, silvering the island.

Stage two of dementia pugilistica can begin months after a boxer's last fight. Effects include dysphasia, agnosia, and apraxia. Which basically means a fighter who can't speak, at least not in words that anyone else would recognise. It means a fighter who can't interpret sensations and so can't recognise things, like the sight of his son's face or the scent of his wife's skin or the sound of his daughter calling his name. It means a fighter who can't perform everyday actions like getting dressed, brushing his teeth, or, one day, wiping his own arse.

Peter emerged at the top of the hill. The wind was stronger up here, tugging at his clothes, pulling him closer to the edge. The heaviness in his limbs was almost too much to bear. With each step his toes dragged along the ground. Around him, like ghosts from the breathing night, the statues emerged. Each stood facing the sea. Peter approached their backs, hearing his knees creak over the static of the wind. He recognised many of the people. Elinor, who illustrated books. Caleb the shepherd. Eilidh the doctor. Peter had been there to light so many of them up to the cliff. He knew that he shouldn't be going up this way, alone in the night. He should have made his intentions clear, let everyone get ready, bring everyone together with their candles and their neighbourly whispers. Well. He had the stars.

Stage three of dementia pugilistica can appear without warning, years after a boxer's last fight; when he hasn't thrown or taken a punch since before his children were born. Medically, it's degeneration of the substantia nigra, neuronal loss in the cortex and cerebellum, cortical neurofibrillary tangle formation and cortical diffuse beta-amyloid plaques. Casually, it's called getting punch-drunk. Physical effects include tremor, rigidity and slowness of movement. Mental effects include memory loss, confusion and mood swings. The most fortunate boxer, in the end, is one who received a significant punch early in the fight, was knocked unconscious and so spared further punishment. But no boxer can do that in every fight. What kind of career is that? What legacy is left by a healthy, safe fighter? Never a fan favourite, never loved by your agent, never earning a decent living. A boxer is more likely to sustain extensive brain damage if he is a 'good' fighter. Good fighters are esteemed by fans and promoters, and have long and successful careers during which they stay upright to take hits to the head over and over and over, and they do not fall. This is the reward for putting on a good show.

Peter made his steady way through the statues, closer to the edge of the cliff. It took all his strength to hold up his heavy head. He couldn't bend his toes or his knees, and he staggered like a giant, weighty hands swinging. Finally he made it right to the edge of the cliff. It was too late to turn back now.

He dragged his toes to the edge so that nothing stood between him and the sea. At the last moment, before his muscles ground to stone, before the whites of his eyes turned grey, Peter raised his hands to the sky.

Sucker punch

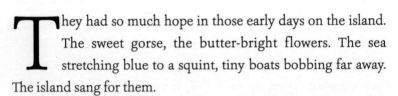

They had so much hope in those early days on the island. The sweet gorse, the butter-bright flowers. The sea stretching blue to a squint, tiny boats bobbing far away. The island sang for them.

It wasn't always friendly. Let's not pretend it was sunshine and rainbows every day. If Peter tried to hang the wet sheets on the drying line, the wind snatched them before he could peg them down. And if he chased the sheet across the garden, brambles scratched his calves bloody. And if he caught them, there would be some buzzing stinging insect tangled in the damp folds, and it raised a welt on his arm. And if he actually did manage to hang the sheets, then the second he fastened the last peg the rain started. No, snow. Hail. It wasn't always good. But when it wasn't bad, it was glorious.

And that day, as Peter ambled across the island to the shop with his wee boy on his hip, and the sun on his face, it was wall-to-wall glorious. To celebrate – it didn't matter what, the lack of clouds or the fact that they were all alive and healthy – he wanted to get something special for dinner.

Bee fidgeted in his arms. So new, his boy, so fresh and bright in this world. Peter wanted to make a cage of his body and hunch over Bee to keep him safe inside. How had he helped to make something so perfect? He wanted to drop to his knees in thanks for each one of his healthy children. Signe didn't like him to talk about what the girls would be one day – she said a child is already all it needs to be, perfect in each day. But he liked to dream of the future.

Islay, sprouting up weed-fast, still a child to him but already haughty and perfect like she'd been carved from marble. She'd be off the island the second she could, he knew. All he could hope was that she'd get her adventures out and want to come back. Perhaps the island was no fun for a teenager, but a grown girl could make a life here if she wanted.

Mara, his awkward dreamer. How she'd whined and tantrummed about coming to the island. She'd probably leave too, as all the growing kids did, but he knew she'd be back. Hopefully before too long; the guest house would have to be left to someone one day, when he and Signe were gone.

Under the burr of the wind and the distant waves, the island was silence. He still missed the rumbled lullaby of traffic; the roads on the island were no good for cars, so there were only bikes and motorbikes and a few battered Land Rovers owned by crofters. The island was so small; why drive around and around pointlessly? Your own feet would do.

Peter pushed open the door of the shop with his non-Bee hand.

'Morning, Mr Pettersen!' He resisted the urge to lift Bee and present him for applause.

'It is,' said Mr Pettersen, and went back to his newspaper.

Peter surveyed the shelves. 'Anything special in today?'

'Since you said. Good lobster down at the harbour. Big ones.'

Peter thought of blue rubber bands, peppercorn eyes, the crack of bodies. He thought of holding the lid on the pot, the rush of it, the thrill. His stomach clenched.

'No.' Peter held his boy tighter, then forced himself to relax; he had squeezed too tight, shocking Bee into a wail. 'No, not that.'

Mr Pettersen shrugged. His *suit yourself* was implied rather than said.

'Right,' said Peter, jiggling a now-grizzling Bee. 'Special.'

He bought pork-and-apple sausages and some sturdy-looking vegetables; it was only later when they were all sitting down to eat, and he saw the cut-up sausages and neeps and tatties all mashed together, that he realised it was exactly what his mother used to make for him when he was a child.

Skelp

Mara was the first to notice that Peter was gone. Why did she always have to miss the missing first? She hadn't chosen that role, and she was no good at it. And yet, there it was.

She'd stumbled half asleep from her bed. On her way downstairs she'd glanced through the open door of her sister's room – still sleeping in a duvet mound – and her parents' room – empty. She thought nothing of it, assuming they would be downstairs. Standing in the kitchen, watching her tea steep, still blinking sleep-blurry, she felt the hollow gasp of empty rooms all around her. There was no reason to worry. Her parents were both grown-ups; they were allowed to get up without telling her. It wasn't as if the house was going to eat her. She left her tea on the worktop and climbed to the top corner of the house. She wasn't searching. She was just looking.

One by one, she pushed open every door and peeped inside the room. Dust sheets, half-painted walls, pasting tables. In one room, a spiderweb of piled-up dining chairs. Mattresses stacked to the ceiling. A floor that was more hole than floor. If a door was locked, she pressed her ear to it; no paintbrush rasp or tinny shrill of a radio, and she moved on.

During her second sweep of the house, when her tea was stone cold and steeped the colour of mahogany, she realised that she wasn't alone after all. Signe's sandy hair was just visible over the back of the couch. Mara stepped into the front room. Signe didn't turn round. Mara, holding her breath, stepped so close that she could see the light catching the silver strands through her mother's hair, could hear the catch of her breath in her throat, could smell the floral sawdusty scent from her skin.

She wanted to say: Mum.

She wanted to say: Where is Dad?

She wanted to say: I'm sorry I can't be the child you want.

Mara turned and crept out of the room. It's not that she knew for sure where Peter was. It's that she knew where he definitely wasn't. He wasn't in the house, and he never went to the beach. Really, there was only one more place.

At the top of the hill, breath coming faster now, she emerged. She walked to the edge of the cliff through the forest of statues, looking at each stone face. Despite the wind and the hail and the constant damp breath of the sea, none of the faces looked worn. They were still every bit as beautiful or as ugly as the day they'd come up to the cliff. Every face was familiar. And not a single one was her father's.

Mara's smile was part relief and part worry: he wasn't here – but where was he? She glanced up at the cliff, knowing she wouldn't be able to identify the patch of flattened grass where she'd first shared wine with Pearl, but wanting to look anyway. She stepped closer, and her smile dropped.

She had found him.

He was set apart from the rest, less than a step from the jagged fall to the ocean. Mara crept closer. She didn't want to see. If she didn't look, maybe it wasn't real.

The thing she couldn't bear was his position. He wasn't standing to attention, noble and serene, arms at his sides like all the other statues. Instead his arms were raised, his hands flat, palms to the sky as if trying to catch rain. He looked unready. Unfinished. Ridiculous.

Her fingers were numb from cold. She reached her hand up and rested it on his upraised arm. Then she pulled down as hard as she could. Only when her muscles spasmed did she stop. Even if she were to put her full weight on his arm, pile every rock she could find on his hands, tie ropes around his wrists and tug, she knew it would be no good. He couldn't be changed now.

Up close, she could see the tiny stones that made up her father's skin. His always-red hair, thick as pelt, was the colour of clouds. His shoulders were as wide as a bear's. She walked around him, but no matter where she stood, she could not see his face. Was it twisted in pain? Was he crying? Were his eyes closed? If she were to step off the edge of the cliff, only then – for a split second before she fell – would she be able to see him, and to know.

Mara raised up on her tiptoes, one hand resting on her father's stone shoulder, leaning in to the stone curl of his ear. 'I love you,' she said. She blinked and swallowed. Words congealed in her chest. For years all she'd wanted was to come up to the cliff, and instead she'd stayed and helped. She hadn't let herself give up. And for what? The grey of him there on the cliff, an eternity of being blown by the wind and pecked by gulls. Silent, still.

She stepped away from him. Another step. Another. 'I hate you,' she said. She turned from what her father used to be, and she didn't look back.

Ken

We can't carry our whole lives with us everywhere we go. Memories have weight, and no one can lift them all at once. We have to leave some of them behind.

But Bee was so tiny. Perhaps Mara didn't have to leave him behind. She could tuck him in soft and carry him with her. And everything else, all the other parts of her life, the memories and the love and the responsibilities, the weight of that future up on the cliff? Well, she couldn't be expected to carry all those things. She would drop them to the ground, and she would walk away.

Mara said nothing and saw no one. She found Pearl. They left the island together, with no bags and no baggage.

PART 2½

Gloam

For almost two years, Mara and Pearl travelled the world as performing mermaids called the Dreamings. They lived in dozens of different homes: windowless internal cabins on cruise ships that throbbed with the sound of the engine, trailers with bunk beds and fibreglass walls, penthouse hotel suites with silk bed sheets and carpets thick as summer grass. Every home was a shell, and they lived inside them like hermit crabs. They owned only what was necessary - and Mara, coming from a house of endless rooms full of other people's junk, was surprised to find just how little that was. A toothbrush each, a few books, spare underwear. Their costumes and wigs for performing. And each other.

They weren't the only mermaids in the show. There was Céline, and Katinka, and Stephanie, and Mary Elizabeth. But Pearl and Mara were the Dreamings, and they could stay underwater for longer than anyone.

Every night Pearl listened to the shipping report. She didn't need to: they always performed in pools, enclosed, artificially heated. Their very own climate, unaffected by the outside world. But still. It was good to know where the storms were, even if you weren't caught in them.

Mara read maps like books, making a story of everywhere they went. She folded in the top and bottom of the map, tucking away the poles, and fingertipped their route. So many places to lose. To be lost.

The seasons were constant and never; always on the move, they sailed through summer and into winter and straight to autumn and back. One week a sundress; the next two layers of coats. They spent a lot of time above the clouds. They crossed time zones, flew from one night into the next. Mara always gave Pearl the middle seat, let her stretch out across the aisle and rest her head in Mara's lap. She didn't want to miss the take-off or the landing, where she could look out and see the fallen constellations of the city lights, a world so utterly unlike the island. Mara knew Pearl's face so well that when she looked in the mirror, she was surprised to see her own face looking back. She never stopped seeing her scar, but in public she learned to keep her face still so it didn't show as much. The only time she didn't think about it was when she was alone with Pearl in the dark.

Once, glancing at faces in a crowd, Mara saw Signe and Peter. They were young again. They were happy, free, light as birds: Signe slinging her arm around Peter's shoulders, Peter pulling her in for a kiss. Mara blinked, and her parents' faces were strangers. They always had been; she knew they couldn't be there. Peter was a stone figure on an isolated island cliff, the petulant sea stroking his stone face. Signe was stuck between the walls of a pink house, a crumbling castle slowly consumed by trees, waiting.

At every church, every temple, every shrine, Mara paused. She lit a candle, she burned joss paper, she sent a bright paper lantern floating candlelit down a river. She made up her own acts too: collected rainwater in a copper bowl, wove a shiny sewing needle into the corner of her bed sheets. She wasn't sure if these were acts of remembrance or of atonement. She knew she should feel guilty about what she had left behind.

The nights were wide and endless. Every morning Mara got up and looked at the wrinkled sheets of the bed she shared with Pearl, and felt content in a simple, deep, animal way.

What Mara didn't see was that this time with Pearl was the gloaming: that space between day and night, that lowering of the sky, when the light pales to blue and everything is outlined in gold. It's the most beautiful part of the day – the golden hour, the photographer's favourite. But it can't last.

To stay in the gloaming is to hold off the night. But if the night never comes, then neither can the day.

Fouter

Mara and Islay spoke every month or so. Awkwardly, politely. Sometimes jokily, but not often. Islay's resentment at being on the island was so familiar to Mara that it made her feel sick. She could taste the bitterness on her tongue. At the end of every call, Islay asked Mara when she was coming back to the island. 'Soon,' she'd say. 'Soon.'

But one day, Islay called, and Mara knew something was wrong. It wasn't that Islay sounded unhappy. It was that she sounded content. She didn't ask Mara when she was coming home. She didn't ask Mara anything at all.

'It's so nice here now that summer is coming,' said Islay, her voice dreamy, sing-songing. 'Perfect, really. The quick clouds, the flowers. The late light. I don't know why I stayed away for all those years. I should never have left at all. When I first came back, I never meant to stay. You wanted me to help with Dad, and then he went to the cliff, and I was going to leave then. Lucky I didn't.'

'How's Mum?' asked Mara, half listening, phone cradled against her shoulder as she washed her make-up brushes. The mermaid make-up all had to be waterproof, so you had to scrub to clean it off the bristles. It might not seem important, but there would be no good in trying to paint your eyelids blue and the brush staining them with yesterday's bronze.

'Oh, she's wonderful,' said Islay, 'just wonderful,' and it was only then that Mara started listening. She dropped the brushes into the soapy sink.

'Wonderful? Really?'

'Oh yes. I've never seen her happier. The house is perfect, Mara. And Signe has slowed right down. She doesn't rush around like she used to. And there's none of that hectic high colour in her cheeks, that brightness in her hair. Remember she used to be scared of going grey? And it suits her, it really does. Even on her hands.'

Mara barely heard her goodbyes. She was calling Pearl's name before she'd even hung up the phone.

PART 3

Tae

There are many legends of mythical islands. Hy-Brazil, Ysole Brazir, Hy Braesail: a Celtic land of copper-roofed towers and gleaming mountains, where faerie queens lived alongside magicians and healers. Or there's Tir fo-Thuin, the Land Under the Wave; Magh Mell, the Land of Truth; Hu Na-Beatha, the Isle of Life; Tir Tairngiri, the Land of Promise; Mael ruin, a submarine country with roofed forts, psalm-singing birds, and magic fountains that spouted wine; the Isle of Eynhallow, which once belonged to the fairies, who can make it vanish or appear as they wish.

The thing about these islands is that you can never find them when you want to. If you're lucky – if the wind is blowing right, and you've made the correct sacrifices, and the world is tilting just so – then the island will emerge from the mist, waiting for you. But if you go in search of it, it will sink down beneath the waves, and all you will see is the distant wink of those bright towers.

There is plenty of wonder in the real world too. Every place has its own small magic. Perhaps you've heard stories of rental hearts, or girls with giraffe horns, or smoke-ghosts, or mushroom houses. Perhaps you've heard of an island where the inhabitants slowly turn to stone. They're always stories from distant lands – but everywhere is home to someone, and no land is distant from itself.

So what happens if you make it to an island, whether mythical or real? Well. Whatever it is, it's rarely what you expect – and it's never what you want.

Volé

It took Signe a while to realise that her work on the house was getting slower because her body was getting slower. As far as she was concerned she was moving at the same speed as ever, and yet everything around her seemed to be moving faster. How could it be that the radio played three songs in the time it took her to screw on one doorknob? How could the sun travel halfway across the sky while she crossed a single room?

One bright morning Signe went into a room to sand the old paint off a window frame. Her fingertips were so rough that she couldn't feel the sandpaper she was gripping. On the other side of the windowpane crawled a bee. Signe could see its slender black legs, its questing antennae, its golden fuzz catching the sunlight.

When she blinked, the bee had gone. The windowpane was black with night. It took her a long time to walk out of the room; as she bent and stretched, her spine felt like it was wrapped in gravel. Sometimes she stayed so still that she'd look down at her hands and see the silky powder left by moths' wings.

That night, the same as every lonely night, Signe dreamed. In her dreams she found everyone she had loved and lost, only to lose them all over again.

There was Bee, her golden boy, curled sleepy in her arms again. But then, as quick as she found him, she lost him. She lost him in sand dunes and shopping centres and between the puffy ribs of bouncy castles. She mislaid him in the shadowed hollows of her own body. She failed to fight off a bear, which proceeded to eat him. She cut the wrong colour of wire on the bomb strapped to his midriff.

There was Peter, her loving fighter, with his scarred knuckles and easy smile. She lost him in rainforests and deserts and mountain ranges. She tapped him affectionately on the head, only to realise too late that he was made of glass, and he shattered. She gripped a metal pole in a thunderstorm, willing the lightning to strike her, then watched helpless as the lightning chose him instead.

There was Mara, her strange changeling girl. She lost Mara when everything else in the world became suddenly enormous, and she slipped through the cracks. She lost her when everything else shrank microscopic, and she was too huge to see. She watched as the space shuttle containing her exploded moments after take-off. She couldn't convince her not to enlist in a strange foreign army fighting a war in a strange foreign country, from which she never returned.

She lost them all every night, and every morning when she awoke, she lost them again. And then she got up to start breakfast. As she walked past Islay's bedroom, she pushed open the door to hear the soft sleeping sounds of her. She stayed there for a long time, sure that her presence was the only thing that kept her daughter breathing.

Haar

It takes a skilled sailor to approach the island, to navigate the channel between the rocks on one side and the cliffs on the other. Neither Pearl nor Mara was such a sailor, so all they could do was cling to the side of a stranger's fishing boat, trying to keep their bodies upright and their breakfasts in their stomachs. Mara held Pearl's hand so tight that their knuckles were white.

She didn't think the island would be happy to see them – though she wasn't happy to see it either, so that seemed fair. Her cheeks felt damp from the slaps of salt-spray, burning hot from the icy wind. Things had changed in their absence – the bridge seemed almost complete, its wide grey pillars doubled like legs between the shore and the mainland, ready for the road. The fisherman wasn't the same fisherman who'd sailed them off the island. He didn't even look similar – not a son, not a cousin. Another change, in what Mara had thought was an unchanging place. When they boarded the boat, she let Pearl do all the talking. She kept her own face still so she could be unscarred, normal. Standing there on that deck crowded with bright blue creels and slimy coils of rope and water-proof postbags and plastic crates of food for the shop, trying to keep her balance as the boat rode high on the waves and dropped into the swells, Mara made the same mistake as the readers of books. The last part of a story is where we think we know exactly what will happen. But, inevitably, we are wrong.

The fishing boat emerged from the channel and into the bay. The world dropped to an eerie calm. The wind and waves silenced. On the rocks by the shore, fat seals lolled. The air smelled of salt and soil and the coconut scent of gorse.

The boat pulled into the island, neat and sudden as the end of a dance. Mara waited for the fisherman to tie up the boat, to catch his breath, to reach his steadying hand out to her - anything to have another moment before she had to step onto the island. But it had to happen, and so she took a breath and leapt for shore. When she'd found her feet she turned to help Pearl off the boat, feeling the wobble in Pearl's knees as she found her balance on the land.

'Home,' said Mara, and was surprised to hear it come out as a question.

As they approached the house, they could see only trees. The house was in a dip, a rounded hollow like a giant had pressed his thumb into the land. The trees had grown up and out, closing over the house so only a few chipped chimney pots emerged. Either that, or the house had sunk deeper into the belly of the island.

Signe was pleased to see them, though surprised. Perhaps not as surprised as she should have been, considering that Islay had neglected to tell her that they were coming. Islay would have been pleased and unsurprised, but she was at work.

'Coffee?' asked Signe, not waiting for an answer. She swayed out of the front room, and her years of dance gave her excellent control over her body. You would have to look closely to see that her gait was not quite as elegant as it was, that her steps fell heavy and her hips were held stiff.

In the minutes that Mara and Pearl were alone in the room, they said nothing. Pearl wanted to say something. She wanted to talk about calling an estate agent. She wanted to talk about how long it would take to shut up the house. She wanted to see whether they could do it all remotely, because she was beginning to suspect that it wasn't doing any of them any good to be on this island. She'd never quite figured out how it worked, but she knew its magic was a dark one.

Mara did not talk about any of these things, because she was too busy straining her ears over the sounds of the kitchen - the boiling kettle, the clatter of cups - to hear the creaks and cracks of her mother's crumbling body. She couldn't stay here. She didn't want to be stone. She wanted to fix the house, and fix her mother, and fix her sister. And then she wanted to leave. Perhaps she didn't even need to be here for long. It wasn't all or nothing: live on the island forever or leave it forever. Maybe if she phoned home more, or sent more money, or visited every few months, then perhaps her mother - perhaps her sister ... but she knew that wasn't enough.

Signe wasn't thinking about her crumbling body, or whether her daughter was discussing plans with her mermaid lover. She wasn't thinking much of anything. Or rather, she was thinking too much of everything. This grey flutter in her mind, these endless wingbeats. To have so many children with so many needs - three mouths to feed, six hands to wipe clean, so many tiny white teeth to preserve. How any mother got anything else done. Well, why would they have to do anything else? What else was there?

Signe carried a tray back into the silent room. A cafetière of dark roast espresso, a jug of warm milk, and three bone china cups so fine you could see through them when you held them up to the light. Mara always hated those cups, the way they were thin as fingernails.

'It's so nice to see you,' said Signe. She drank her coffee black and unsweetened, as ever.

'We came to help you with the house, Mum. Getting it finished. You've worked so hard on it, we thought it must be almost ready.'

'We'll just help with a few finishing touches,' said Pearl, 'to get it ready for –' She put her cup down in the saucer too hard, and both shattered. Coffee pooled across the table. 'Oh shit, I'm sorry! And I'm sorry, I didn't mean to say shit. I'll get a cloth.'

'It's fine.' Signe's voice was calm. She sipped her coffee, her back straight, her head high. 'A cloth won't fix my grandmother's china, now will it? A cloth won't make it so that the ghosts can use it.'

'The what?' Mara, assuming Signe was joking, laughed.

'The guests.' Signe's smile was as tight as string. 'The guests who will stay here. They will have to have their coffee in something sturdier.'

For the first time since they'd come to the house, Pearl and Mara looked at one another. Mara didn't want to laugh now. She wanted to cry. She wanted to shout. She wanted to run upstairs to her bedroom and leave a grown-up to deal with this. Her mother was confused, and she was confused about what she should do with that.

'I'll go,' said Pearl. 'To get a cloth.' She picked up the biggest shards of china and carried them out of the room, gentle and slow though they were already broken.

'Don't use the sink in there,' called Signe.

'Is the tap broken?' Pearl's voice came back from the kitchen. 'That's okay, I'll just get the toolbox. I can fix it for you.'

'Leave it, please. It's not the tap, it's the water.'

'What's wrong with the water?' asked Mara.

'It's just salt,' said Signe.

'It's what?'

'Sorry again. I'll replace the cup.' Pearl reappeared in the doorway with a damp cloth. She knelt by the table and dabbed at the spilled coffee, the needles of broken china.

'The water from the taps,' said Signe, 'is seawater. It's the pipes. A crack somewhere. It's fine, we'll get it fixed. But for now you must use the outside sink for fresh water.'

'Mum,' said Mara, 'what's that noise?'

Signe sipped at her coffee, watching Pearl clean up over the rim of her cup. 'It's the generator. It kicks in every now and then.'

'For what? For electricity?'

'It's fine, Mara. Don't fuss. It's just that some seawater got into the cables, and sometimes it shorts out. It's not dangerous.'

'How do you know? Did you get an electrician out?'

'It's fine. Electricians are expensive and we don't need one. When the power has a hiccup, I start the generator. It's fine.'

Pearl stood up, cradling the wet cloth so she wouldn't jag her hands on the broken shards. She looked at Mara, tried to catch her eye, tried to speak in silence over the burr of the generator. Mara did not catch Pearl's eye. She did not say anything, in words or in silence. She reached for the coffee pot and refilled Signe's cup.

Haver

I slay hated daytime shifts. The pub slouched. Everything was grey and brown. She wiped non-existent fluff off the optics and slid into her seat behind the bar, resting her head on her hands.

She could only have the chair when Ida wasn't there to take it away. It was all part of the new regime: best behaviour at all times, not like the lazy old days of flipping through books behind the bar. When Islay was on shift she wasn't to drink or read or sit. She just had to be ready. Islay cast an eye around the pub. Regulars sat in clusters, talking in murmurs, turning pints round and round, tearing beer mats into layers. Oh yes, it was a hotbed of activity. Good thing she was on high alert. Good thing she could be ready while also sitting.

When she was travelling, she'd loved to talk about the island. It seemed so glamorous then, at a distance. She held court in tropical beachside bars and city-street coffee shops and the post-club living rooms of friends-of-friends. They loved the stories, or at least they listened enough to make Islay think they did. The bright blue lobster creels, the nodding daisies, the suck and crash of the sea, the sprint of storm clouds across a summer sky. What a perfect childhood. What an exotic life. She'd never wondered what they said about her back on the island. What did she care? She wasn't there.

Now that she spent half of her time answering questions about what Mara was up to these days, she felt for her sister. Had Mara spent all Islay's travelling years answering questions about her? Islay had been someone about whom stories were told. A cautionary tale, a dream of escape. While she was away, the island hadn't felt real; just a charming first chapter for her life story. And now she was back, nothing else was real.

Sunbeams caught golden motes. Islay breathed deep to pull the glint inside her.

After her shift, Islay went up to the cliff to visit Peter. She lay on her back at his feet, knees bent, hands resting on her belly, toying with the collection of tiny petals she'd tugged from nearby flowers. She closed her eyes, heavy beneath the hot sun. Sea breezes lifted strands of her hair and let them tickle her cheeks. The grass was soft, the ground held her steady.

'Mara's visiting,' she said. 'She's due today, I think. She'll be there when I get back to the house.' Peter couldn't hear her, and wouldn't say anything back. Islay wished she'd said things to him more before he turned to stone. But it was easier to talk like this: to the sky, the grass, a distant stone ear.

On Islay's first few visits to Peter, she hadn't said anything. She could barely approach him. His pose was so embarrassing. Palms raised to the sky, facing the sea, right at the edge of the cliff as if he might topple over. Why couldn't he be standing properly like the others? But she kept coming, and soon familiarity dampened her emotions. Soon she realised that Peter didn't look embarrassing.

He didn't look anything; he just was. That's when she crept closer. That's when she spoke.

'I guess,' she said, 'if Mara's back, that means she can look after Mum and I can go ...'

Back to Paris or Chicago or Sydney. Or somewhere new, if she wanted. Cape Town. Reykjavik. Tokyo. Or all of them – why not? She had time. She could pack up and go anywhere, every-where. She thought about how it would feel to leave. She tried taking the first step: lifting her feet, just to see how it felt. But her legs were so heavy, and the sun was so warm, and the grass soothed with tickles. Would the breeze stroke her skin any more softly in Tokyo? Was the ground any steadier in Reykjavik?

She leaned over and tugged free a dandelion without looking, plucking its bright petals and adding them to the pile on her stomach. She'd been lying still for so long that her elbow creaked with the movement. A tiny forest of dandelions and daisies had sprouted all around Peter's feet; no matter how many Islay plucked, on her next visit there were more.

'I can't wait,' she said. Pressed against the grass, her body felt as warm and as steady as the ground. Her hair stroked her cheek, soft as grass. She licked her lips and tasted salt. 'I can't wait to come up here for real.'

Coorie

The island was sleeping, the night closing velvet around them. Mara crept through the moonless dark and into Pearl's room. She slid under the covers and felt Pearl's warmth, the hidden curves of her. She breathed in deep to fill her lungs with the scent of Pearl's skin: salt and spice and home.

'I missed you,' she said.

'I missed you too. You know I can't sleep without you.'

'Well, in that case,' said Mara, 'I'll just have to creep in here every night and sing you lullabies, won't I?'

'Or we could share a bedroom like grown-ups.'

Mara hadn't argued when they found that Signe had made up a spare bedroom for Pearl. She felt exhausted at the thought of the conversations still to come.

'Let's not fight. Please, Pearl.'

The house creaked and sighed like a seagoing ship. Mara curled close to Pearl, wrapping her arm around Pearl's waist, tucking her knees into the curve of Pearl's knees. Everything was okay now. As long as she could stay here, everything was okay.

'What happened earlier? That conversation over coffee.'

'With the cup? Don't worry, it'll be okay. Mum will get over it.'

'Not the cup. What's going on with the house? I thought it would be almost ready by now. You've been sending money home, haven't you?'

'You know I have.'

'So why is the house in worse shape than when we left? Haven't your mum and Islay been working on it?'

Mara thought of Signe's stiff hips, her heavy steps. Her silvery hair, the colour of stone.

'I don't know,' she said. 'But, look, it doesn't matter. We just need to get the house sorted, and then we can take Mum and leave.'

'Okay,' said Pearl, though she didn't think it was okay at all. Mara seemed to think they'd get everything fixed up quick-smart and be back on a boat before they could blink. Or did she think that, really? Pearl knew the lure of the island, its desire to make people stay. She had felt its tarry magic too.

'We left because that's what you wanted,' she said. 'We came back because that's what you wanted.'

'I –' Mara sighed, stroking a lock of Pearl's hair behind her ear. 'I know that. It's just – being home. It's hard to see things clearly here. It all looks so different. So much the same. You said once, about homesickness, remember? The soldiers in the American Civil War. The way you kept coming back to the island – I thought you understood.'

'I don't get homesick any more, Mara. You are my home.' Pearl pulled Mara close. They lay slotted like spoons.

In Mara's bed it had been far too cold, her feet numb, the sheets so chilled they felt damp; now, the heat of another body made it too hot. Mara put her arm outside the covers. The tartan blanket was scratchy under her armpit, the wool as thick as a door, heavy and waxen with age. She didn't like to think of the blanket touching Pearl. It was too rough, too real for Pearl's cool coppery skin.

From outside, the generator throbbed to life. Mara was sure she could feel it vibrating the house, juddering her bones. The cobwebs in the corners breathed. Somewhere in the chimney was the fidgeting of mice.

'I don't care what we do,' said Pearl, 'as long as we can leave. We'll sort your mum, get her settled somewhere more manageable. A house for one person, not fifty. And then we can find our own place.'

'How can we? We'll never be able to settle – being the Dreamings means travelling.'

'It's easy if you want it to be,' said Pearl. 'Work isn't everything. We'll figure it out.'

'Don't you want to be a mermaid any more?'

'It's not the only job in the world. The Dreamings – we made them up, and we can unmake them just as easily. I can do something else. A swimming instructor. An underwater welder. A pearl diver. Wouldn't people love that, a pearl diver called Pearl? Maybe it's okay to grow up, you know? A house and a dog. A baby one day.'

There was a lump in Mara's throat, a threatening twinge at the corners of her eyes. 'What will we call it?'

'We'll call him Cal.'

'Callum or Calvin?'

'You're asking the wrong question,' said Pearl, turning in Mara's arms to press a smiling kiss to her lips. 'You didn't ask whether Cal was the dog or the baby.'

Mara remembered the drag of her father's heavy steps. The weight of his hands on her shoulders as she eased socks over his unyielding toes. His cold-meat flesh against the graze of her knuckles. She couldn't live that life again. She'd fought for this new life, and she would not let it slip away.

Shoogle

Early evening, and Pearl was cooking dinner. Mara was meant to be helping, but every time she picked up a peeler or a wooden spoon Pearl shooed her away, saying she had a system and Mara would only mess it up, and she should just pour some wine and sit at the table and relax and keep her company.

'Tell me a story or something,' said Pearl. 'One I haven't heard.'

'You already know all my stories,' said Mara. 'Two years together, all day together, all night together. I don't think there's much left that you don't know.' This wasn't true. Every couple has secrets, even when they say they don't. We can't ever really know ourselves – so how can we expect to really know another person? Mara knew it was a tiny lie, and Pearl knew it was a tiny lie, but they still let it sit there between them.

'I have to tell you something,' said Pearl, putting down her knife and fixing Mara with a serious look. 'This might come as a surprise. There are these marvellous new things called *books*. They've got stories inside them – hundreds, thousands of stories. I can't believe you haven't heard of them. You'll love them!'

These last few words had to be said louder, as Mara had already left the room, sticking out her tongue and holding two fingers up at Pearl as she left. She returned with a leather-bound book, its cover soft as fingertips, its bronze letters almost worn away.

'How about one of these?' Mara lifted the book for Pearl to see. 'They're fairy tales. My mum used to read from it. She read from it so much that we all knew the stories by heart.'

Pearl slid the chopped onions off the board and started on the carrots. 'What are they about?'

'They're about ...' Mara thought of the stories that made her childhood. Snow White, beautiful and dead. Rapunzel, waiting in her tower. The swan sister, silent for years, hands swollen and bleeding from knitting her brothers' nettle shirts. 'They're about love,' she said.

Pearl glanced at the cover. 'Oh, I know those sorts of stories. Mermaids and sirens and swan maidens. All sorts of faithless, miserable women. Those stories just exist to soothe men who stole foreign women. The town starts talking about your mysterious wife, her spun-sun hair and lips like coral, salt glistening on her cheeks, her breasts proud as the prow of a ship, blah bloody blah. And of course she leaves, because why would she stay? So you say she was never a real woman anyway, she was always a thing from the sea, and now she's gone back. Not your fault, right? She could never belong here.'

'It's not like that! They're love stories. I always wanted to be like those women. So beautiful. So desired.'

'They're not love stories,' said Pearl. 'Love isn't about lying and making yourself into something you're not. Anyway, who wants a woman all wispy and sad? I'd prefer a woman who's sturdy and happy.'

'Sturdy,' said Mara, flicking through the book, past illustrations of wispy sad-faced women – but beautiful, so beautiful. 'Happy,' she said. 'What about ...?' She paused. 'I think I've got one.'

Pearl, head down, chopped, chopped, chopped.

'There was once a handsome young fisherman,' read Mara, 'who could not find himself a wife. The island girls were pretty enough, but he felt something missing. Every day he took out his boat and set his lobster pots, and every night he sat alone in his cottage and watched the peat fire rise and fall.'

Mara couldn't help stroking the paper as she read. It was strange to read the words from the page when she'd heard them so many times from her mother's mouth. She could have closed her eyes and recited the story from memory. This story. It was everything she'd thought she wanted. She'd wanted to be the selkie, not the fisherman – and yet here she was with her sea-love. Still, perhaps it didn't matter. There didn't have to be a fisherman at all; two selkies could love one another just fine.

And so she read the story to her mermaid, her selkie, her sea-love. The fisherman seeing the woman, stealing her skin, hiding it away so she would marry him.

'One day,' said Mara, reading from the last page of the story. 'One day their youngest son was exploring the house, and found the sealskin under the bed. He brought it to his mother and asked her, what was this strange thing, so soft and smelling of the sea? The boy knew nothing of his mother's history; he was simply curious. The selkie ... The selkie ...'

'Mara, what is it?' Pearl paused in her chopping.

'Nothing. It's nothing.'

This story was wrong. At the end, the selkie was meant to stay. Love was enough, and so she stayed. That was the story that Signe had always told them.

'Mara? Can I hear the end of the story?'

Mara moved her eyes to the next sentence and began to read aloud, her words stumbling, each sentence unfamiliar. 'The selkie kissed her children goodbye, slid on her true skin, and went home. When the fisherman came back to the cottage, his children were fast asleep and stew bubbled on the fire – but his wife was gone. Fear shivered through him and he threw open the wooden box. It was empty, and with it his heart emptied too. In time he learned to live a good life with his home and his children. But sometimes, late at night, he slid from his bed to gaze out at the water and mourn his lost love.'

Around Mara the kitchen was noisy with activity. The hum of the cooker hood. The shuffle of Pearl's feet. The rattle of the glass in the window frame. The chop of the knife. Mara heard none of it.

'She leaves,' said Mara.

'What?' Pearl tipped onions into a pan, and their hiss hid Mara's words.

'The selkie leaves,' she said. 'And the fisherman is left alone forever with his empty heart.'

'It's a story, Mara. It's about women as other. Men's fear of giving away power.'

But Mara wasn't listening. 'She always left,' she said. 'That's the end of the story. She'll always leave.'

Sleekit

It took a long time for Pearl to tell Mara the whole truth about how she learned to breathe underwater. She told part of it when they lay in bed sleepless at 7 a.m., fingertips puckered and ears muzzy with water after an all-night Vegas show; part of it during a night flight between Amsterdam and Tokyo; part of it in a Toronto emergency room at midnight after Mara had cut her mouth on a poorly installed breathing tube, Pearl speaking because Mara couldn't, laying sentence upon sentence without pausing to try to distract Mara from worrying about damage to her teeth, to stop her from saying 'another scar for the collection', because she'd only just managed to stop her from thinking constantly about her other scars.

Pearl did all her storytelling at night, when they were supposed to be sleeping. Stolen hours, half-dream time. Pearl didn't notice this, not consciously – and yet she never told her story in the everyday parts of life, and never all at once. It came out in fits and starts: an ending one day, a beginning the next.

'Here it is,' Pearl would have said, if she'd told it all together. 'Here's how I learned to breathe.

'I lost my family one by one. My grandparents before I was born. My parents together in an accident. My sister and uncles to disease – a lung thing, hereditary. It doesn't matter how, really. I just lost them. Stupid phrase, that. As if I'd put them down some-where and forgotten to pick them up, and if I only looked hard enough then I'd find them again. If something is lost then it can be found, or it's not lost at all. So I'll say – my family were gone. Are gone.

'I came back to the island because there was nowhere else. It's an old house and it's been with us forever, even though we never lived there together. It's just a place to visit. My family is from all over – bits from Romania, New Zealand, South Africa. Some from pieces of land that have changed names a dozen times. I think of those lands sometimes: the eastern sun, village squares, white crosses, a heavy snow lying full of stones, people with my blood speaking in a language that's as foreign to me as it would be to any foreigner. Some of them might be there still, for all I know. I was never told which of us stayed.

'When I lost the last of them, I came back to the island. The house was the only thing I'd been left with. A house, and a body, and a name that was no good for the person I had become. I crept onto the island and I was silent, invisible. No one knew I was there, and no one would know if I wasn't there. When I was a child, sadness was the islands – rocky, yes, but small and containable, easy to leave. Now sadness was the sea. So in I went. I knew the water was cold, but to me it felt warm. No, that's not right – it felt like nothing.

'I swam. Small strokes at first because my muscles were numb and my limbs were shaking, but bigger strokes as I swam further. It was night, I think, that midnight summer gloaming where it never really gets dark. I swam out past where the seaweed tangled around me, until my legs kicked free. I swam past the breakers. I swam out among the pulsing purple jellyfish, their bodies making the water gelatinous. If they stung me, I didn't feel it. I turned to look back and I could barely see land. But I kept going. I swam until my whole body shook, until I saw black spots throbbing in time with my blood. I swam out so far that I knew I wouldn't be able to get back.

'And then I stopped. I turned my face to the sky and let the sea hold me. The water covered my ears. Above me the sky was empty, and below me the sea was silent. I rolled my body into a ball so that I would sink quickly. Life is heavy, and it's hard work to stay afloat. Drowning is easier than breathing. So I closed my eyes and opened my mouth, and I gave myself up.

'The next thing I knew I was on the beach, dripping wet and shaking, coughing up lungfuls of salt water. It was morning, the sun creeping silver across the sky. Seagulls shrieked in my ear. I managed to walk back to the house and light the fire, and I wrapped myself in all the blankets I could find and I sat there until I knew I was alive.'

'Oh, my mermaid,' said Mara in that sleepless Vegas bed, on that night flight over snowy mountains, through a mouthful of bloodied gauze. 'My mermaid, my mystery, my selkie.' She punctuated her words with kisses. 'My creature from the sea. I always knew you were from another world.'

'No,' said Pearl. 'No, listen. That's not what I'm telling you. The other world didn't want me.'

But she spoke in murmurs, and Mara wasn't listening, and they were both half in a dream, and perhaps she didn't really want Mara to hear anyway. Perhaps she wanted Mara to say she was a mermaid, just for a moment, even though she knew it wasn't real.

Mauchit

The next morning, Mara was up with the dawn and straight into the attic. She was starting from the top and working her way down, making a census of the house – seeing what would need to be cleared out and what could be left for the new owners.

Had the house always been this damp? When Mara stared at the ceilings, they seemed to sag. The plaster on the walls was clammy. She imagined underground gullies whispering beneath the floor, the sea around and under the house, seeping in. On the outer walls, rain had eaten away the mortar between the bricks. However hard Signe worked to pull the house one way, the island was pulling harder in the other direction. How could they ever expect people to stay here? All this damp would be no good for the ghosts. The guests.

Mara emerged in the afternoon, filthy and grumpy, to find Pearl hanging sheets in the garden. Summer was in full bloom, and it made Mara's skin itch. The buzz of hidden insects, the sun in her eyes. The white dandelions looked odd, too perfectly round like tiny snowballs, and she realised they were wrapped in spiderwebs.

'Let's go to the sea,' said Mara. 'I feel like my lungs are more dust than air. Take me into the water and help me breathe.'

'Not right now,' said Pearl. 'I have to finish this. The more we can get done, the quicker we can leave.'

'Okay. I'll help, and then we'll be done faster.'

'Are you kidding? Keep your grubby hands away from these sheets. I've spent all morning washing them – the bloody machine is broken so I had to wash them in a bath. Which, by the way, only pumps out salt water, so I had to haul fresh water in buckets from the outside tap. Who'd have thought I'd end up back here, like a housewife from a hundred years ago?'

'Why are you doing it then?' asked Mara. 'You were the one who said women shouldn't have to do all the housework. You said it should be equal.'

'And what men am I washing the fucking sheets for, Mara? Is the patriarchy hiding in the bushes? I'm doing this for you. For Signe.'

'So just stop. It doesn't matter to you anyway.'

'It does matter. It's important that Signe likes me. I want her to accept me and to accept our life together. I had a plan, do you remember? The negotiation with your family. It was going to take time, but then you – then we didn't stay. If Signe wants me to hang sheets, I'll hang sheets. If she wants me to cook dinner, I'll cook. If she wants me to put on a dress and marry you in a church, then I'll do that too. It's not about men and women and what we're supposed to do. I'll do whatever I have to do make her see that we're serious.'

Mara wandered away from the harbour of flapping sheets, over to the orchard. Which, actually, was a bit of a grand term for it now. It was barely set apart from the copse of taller trees; they'd encroached over the years, spreading their branches over the fruit trees so they were always in the shade. The drystone wall was now just dry stones, and Mara didn't have to climb over it so much as step among the wreckage. She kicked at a rotting pear. When she was a child, they spent every summer eating from these trees. Now the fruit all went to the wasps and the worms, mouldering sweetly in the dirt.

'We're leaving the island,' said Pearl, 'but you're not leaving your family. You never leave them, not really.'

'What would you know about family?'

Pearl let go of the sheet she was holding and stared at Mara, but Mara didn't notice. Even here in the shade it was too bright for her; she felt she was constantly scrunching up her eyes, constantly trying to focus on something the sun was blurring, constantly causing a headache to thud inside her skull. And the smell of the rotting fruit caught in the back of her throat, and she felt insects walking on the soft skin at the crook of her elbow. When Pearl finally spoke there was a catch in her voice, but Mara didn't notice that either.

'Someday we'll look back,' said Pearl. 'Someday this will be something we made it through.'

Mara rolled a pear under her foot, letting its curve press against her arch. 'You don't understand the island,' she said. 'You don't understand why anyone would want to stay.' She pressed her foot harder on the pear, feeling its flesh give and begin to split. 'You rescued me from all of this.'

'Are you joking? I can't tell with you any more.' Pearl bent, lifted, pegged up another sheet.

'You swooped in,' said Mara, her voice soft, half dreaming. 'You swept me up onto the back of your horse and you rescued me. But maybe you were the one I needed to be rescued from.'

'I didn't rescue you, Mara. You weren't in a burning building.'

Above them, the sky spread blue, the sun a blurred white fire. Whenever Mara moved she could feel the hot tight skin on her shoulders, on her chest, the redness where the sun had licked her.

'A person,' said Pearl, 'can't save another person. That's not how it works.'

'But it did,' said Mara. 'It did work. And now –'

A white butterfly landed on Mara's wrist. She couldn't help letting out a laugh. This tiny, perfect thing glowing white as dawn against her grubby arm. Its legs wavered, reaching. It took off and Mara followed its stuttering progress through the air, back towards Pearl. The butterfly landed on the sheet, right by Pearl's hand. Mara couldn't stop staring at it. Its wings thin as a breath. If Pearl just kept her hand still – if she didn't move or speak, then the butterfly would stay. Pearl let go of the line and reached down into the basket for the next damp sheet. The butterfly flickered away. Mara snatched out for it, her hand closing on nothing, her knuckles grazing the sheet.

'Seriously, Mara?' Pearl raised her eyes to the sky among the flapping sheets.

'Did you see it? It was so beautiful. It was like a painting, I wanted to show you.'

'All I can see is that bloody great smear you just left on the sheet.'

Mara looked at the space where the butterfly wasn't. There, on the clean sheet, was a greyish smut of knuckleprints.

'Now I'll have to wash it again,' said Pearl. 'Do you have any idea how much of a fucking faff it was to get it clean in the first place?'

Without thinking, Mara reached out to wipe it off, and succeeded only in adding more filth.

'I'm sorry,' she said. 'I didn't mean – I'm sorry. Let me do it. I'll wash it for you.'

'Just go away.' Pearl reached for the pegs and let the dirty sheet fall to the grass. 'I said, go!'

Without waiting for Mara to go anywhere, Pearl scooped up the dirty sheet and carried it inside.

Mara turned away from the sun and rubbed her aching eyes. In those early months, she had watched Pearl do everything. She watched Pearl stir sugar into her coffee. She watched Pearl squint up her mouth as she decided what to order in restaurants. She watched Pearl tip back her head and laugh at someone's joke. She watched Pearl read a novel and worry with her teeth at a sharp something caught in the pad of her thumb.

She had tried to remember everything, so that she could keep it when it was gone. She would lie back in bed, a book spread across her thighs, and pretend she wasn't watching Pearl pluck her eyebrows. The way she'd set each plucked hair down onto an unfolded tissue, all lined up like tiny fenceposts, before scrunching up the tissue and flushing it down the toilet. Every time she watched Pearl reach for the tweezers she thought: savour this, savour this. It can't last forever. But the thing was, no one can be a mermaid all the time. Eventually, the show ends, the performers go backstage, the costumes are discarded. In daylight, everyone gets blackheads. Everyone wakes up grumpy. Everyone has to pay their taxes and keep receipts in chronological order to send to the accountant. Everyone is just like everyone else.

And that was not what Pearl had promised her. Pearl had promised ...

She had said ...

Mara kicked out at a rotten pear, sending it smacking into the remains of the drystone wall. It exploded in the still summer air, its scent choking-strong, sweet as childhood. Pearl had promised nothing. She had taken from Mara the only home she'd ever known – and she'd given nothing in return.

Fouetté

For the first five years of Signe's dancing career, she played dead girls. Juliet, who stabs herself after finding her poisoned Romeo. La Bayadère bitten by a snake. Giselle, who dies of a broken heart.

Dancing Giselle almost broke her. It's a story based on fragility, both physical and emotional, and the dancer must look and act the part. She must become Giselle, a peasant girl with a weak heart and a passion for dancing. Giselle becomes engaged to a Duke disguised as a peasant, but the Duke is a faithless lover, already betrothed to another woman. In her grief, Giselle's heart fails, and she is summoned from her grave by ghost-women who want her to help them dance the faithless Duke to death. The ghost of Giselle dances with him until the morning, when the ghost-women must depart and the Duke is saved. The ballet ends with Giselle slowly disappearing into the dawn, leaving the Duke alone and heartbroken. The dancer, to become Giselle, must become a ghost. Fragile, ethereal – almost transparent. Mostly consumed by that other world, barely able to cling to this one. Years later, Signe was glad that Peter had not fallen in love with her when she was Giselle.

Signe needed two pairs of shoes every night because they wore away so fast. On the first day of rehearsals, Signe's feet were a size 5½. After a few weeks they were down to a size 5, and by opening night the arch of her foot was so pronounced that her shoes were a size 4½. She taped her toes before every show, but it wasn't enough. The skin on the knuckles of her toes was all sliced off, and she danced too often for it to heal. Most nights she bled right through her pointe shoes.

But Peter did not know her then, hollow and bleeding, transformed and transparent as Giselle. He fell in love with her at the dizzying height of her career, when she danced her greatest role as prima ballerina, when every night she was two women at once: the dual character of Odette and Odile, the good woman and the bad woman in *Swan Lake*.

Auditioning for *Swan Lake* started a whole new stage in Signe's life. No longer a dead girl, she became a bird. *Leda and the Swan, The Wild Swans, The Firebird, The Dying Swan*. Every costume she wore was feathered. She moulted a trail of white across the stage every night. There were constantly pieces of swan-down tickling the roof of her mouth. But always, no matter which bird-woman she pretended to be – always, she went back to *Swan Lake*.

Perhaps you already know the story of *Swan Lake*, but even if you don't it doesn't matter: what matters is that the role is so difficult because it includes the acrobatic feat of thirty-two fast, whipping turns on one leg, known as *fouettés*. During a *fouetté*, the dancer whips herself around on the same standing leg, using the force of her other leg to propel her around, the whole thing done on the tip of one toe. Just so you know, if you're ever watching this feat being performed, it's proper to start applauding after twelve *fouettés*. A dancer needs strong calves and thighs, as well as good spotting – meaning she must focus on one fixed point, whip her head around and return to that point, so she doesn't get dizzy. But the most important and most difficult part of the *fouetté* is for the dancer to keep that standing leg on the exact same point as she completes those thirty-two whipping turns. The real difficulty – the real skill – is in staying still.

Stour

'Why is the table,' asked Signe, 'set for three?'

'Islay's at her bridge-protest group,' replied Mara. 'Seems daft to me as it's almost finished, but she seems to think it's important. Symbolic. I don't know. She said she'd be out late and we shouldn't wait. They're making posters or something. She called it a peaceful protest. Are they seriously called the Landlubbers?'

'But it's dinnertime!' Signe paused halfway through pulling out her chair. 'Islay knows that. We always have dinner at this time.'

Mara shrugged. 'I don't know what to tell you, Mum. I'm just passing on a message.'

'Fine, fine. But that's still not enough.'

'If it's not enough, take it up with Islay. She's a pain when she gets back from these meetings anyway, always trying to convince us to join. I'll be glad if she's distracted.'

'I mean,' said Signe, 'that's still not enough place settings.'

Mara looked from Signe to Pearl and back again. A spiky, heavy feeling was growing in her belly.

Signe sighed. 'There are more than three people in this house, Mara.'

'Mum,' said Mara. In the silence, the island held its breath.

'No,' said Signe. 'No, I know.'

'I'll just get a corkscrew,' said Pearl. 'For the wine. I think I left it in ...' And out she went, though she hadn't left anything anywhere.

'Mum,' said Mara, 'it's okay.'

Signe pulled out her chair and sat down, placing her hands on the table on either side of her plate as if steadying herself. Her wrists were as beautiful and as frail as flower stems. 'I just got confused for a moment, Mara. There's so much coming and going in this house, so many people in and out all day. I can't keep track of everyone.'

Mara didn't think that she and Pearl and Islay constituted a lot of people, but the spiky feeling in her belly was back, and the smell of the rotten pear was caught in her nose, and she wanted to seize her mother and hoist her onto her shoulder and swim with her to the mainland before the island swallowed her up forever.

'I know it's hard,' said Mara, 'being here without Dad.'

'Don't be ridiculous. Peter is here.'

Mara couldn't help it: she looked around the empty room.

'Not *here* here! I'm not a crazy person, Mara. He's up on the cliff. He hasn't gone anywhere.'

To Pearl, listening outside the kitchen door, it seemed that those two things - he's up on the cliff; he hasn't gone anywhere - were opposites. In her mind, going up to the cliff meant going away forever. After you'd gone up to the cliff, you weren't actually on the cliff any more, because you weren't there. Your body was stone and your brain was stone and the rest of you was - well, she didn't know, but not there.

To Mara, though, Peter had been on the island, and he was still on the island, and he would be forever on the island. She didn't agree with Signe – she was afraid of what Signe was saying, because while her dad was still on the island he certainly didn't need a place set for him at dinner, and there weren't lots of people in the house, and anyway the house – the whole island – was a ramshackle pit of junk that was turning them all to stone.

'Silly me! I didn't leave the corkscrew anywhere after all.' Pearl, having heard several seconds of silence through the gap in the door, breezed back into the kitchen. 'It was here in the drawer all along!' She brandished it unnecessarily.

'Right,' said Mara. 'Right. Let's ...'

And Pearl poured the wine, and Mara served the dinner, and Signe pushed the food around on her plate, and they all said lots of things without saying anything, and after that Mara washed the dishes and Pearl dried them, and Signe sipped coffee and looked at the window without seeing through it, and later still they all went upstairs and lay sleepless in their cold beds, and the generator hummed and the trees crept closer and the mice scratched hectic in the walls and the persistent tide rolled in and in and in.

Pokey-hat

Their first summer on the island, Peter took Mara out for an ice-cream sundae. The harbour cafe didn't usually serve such exotic fare – it was pots of tea and tuna sandwiches, and perhaps a cherry scone if you were very lucky and Angela the owner was feeling flamboyant. But it was summer, and summer meant tourists, and tourists meant money – and tuna sandwiches weren't going to cut it with mainland folk. To avoid wasps, Peter and Mara took a table inside. Mara's elbows stuck to the plastic tablecloth and the chair back was broken, but Peter didn't care and Mara didn't notice. She only had eyes for the new picture menu propped between the salt and pepper: lusciously lit photos of plastic-looking sundaes, bright as new toys, unmelted as an iceberg.

After much deliberation Mara chose butterscotch with toasted nuts, whipped cream, and a glacé cherry on top. When the waitress brought it over, it was even better than she'd hoped: the perfect dream of a sundae, exactly like the photo. She beamed at Peter – who seemed happy with his cup of tea – and reached for her spoon. She could almost taste the ice cream melting on her tongue.

'Look, Mara!' Peter pointed out of the window. Mara forgot all about her spoon and felt her eyes open just as wide.

Trotting past the cafe, through the brightly scattered tourists, came the most beautiful horse that Mara had ever seen. Part of her recognised that it was only Peggy, Chris the carpenter's brown mare. Peggy spent her days snorting and whisking her tail up in the top field, kept company by a surly Shetland pony, both refusing to accept anything but the sweetest new grass no matter how flat you held your hand and how loud you clucked your tongue.

But the other part of her knew this was something more. It was Peggy the brown mare, but also it was not. This horse was perfect, like an illustration from the fairy-tale book, a picture framed in curlicues. Her braided mane shone like the sun on the sea. Her coat, instead of a chalky dirt-brown, was brushed to a glossy mahogany. Rows of tiny silver bells were set along her bridle, shivering a chime with each delicate trot. She even wore a crown of daisies – a touch which, when Mara thought about the event later, she must have imagined.

Tourist children flocked to the horse, their sticky hands holding up sugar cubes taken from the cafe tables. Chris the carpenter, who Mara had just noticed leading the horse by a black silk rope, brought her to a halt. The horse stretched her pink-brown lips and disappeared the sugar cubes.

Chris the carpenter led the horse in a neat dance, trotting figure eights between the children, the bells chiming. Horses couldn't smile, Mara knew, but this horse was definitely smiling. Finally the horse seemed to tire of her audience. Raising her gleaming head, she set her sights on the horizon. Off she trotted, and Chris the carpenter with her. The children turned back to their tasks of chase and hide-and-seek and ripping up daisies.

Mara turned back and reached for her spoon. But when she looked at her sundae, it was gone. In its place was a formless, liquid mess studded with pale flakes of nuts.

She knew that it was the same as before. When the waitress first brought it over, it had looked solid, but the ice cream would have melted in her mouth and ended up looking like this. She knew that if she just spooned it up, it would taste fine: the memory of a sundae rather than the dream, but still good. She pushed the bowl aside. It was not what she wanted. She would rather have nothing at all.

Dreich

Mara's bed no longer felt empty without Pearl. She liked the way that when she stretched out her legs, the sheets were so cold that they felt damp. Her toes were always numb, the tips white.

Midnight came, and with it Pearl. Mara opened her arms and let her in. This single bed was just big enough for Mara; now, with Pearl added, it felt claustrophobic, choking. Above them, the scrabble of birds' feet as they pecked at insects in the mossy roof. Every now and then came a screech, a scrape, as they tried to force their beaks into the edges of the windowpane to get at the wriggling things that lived in the decaying wood frames.

'I miss you, Mara.'

'I'm here. I'm with you every day.'

'You're not here. Ever since we came back, it's like we're never in the same place. Even when we're in the same room. Even when we're –' Pearl smoothed the covers down, pulling at a loose thread. 'Even when we're in bed together.'

Outside, the steady throb of the generator. In the hallway, the light flickered.

'We're not like we were,' said Pearl.

'We can't be,' said Mara. 'Because things aren't like they were. It's too complicated. We don't fit in the real world.'

'Why is this the real world? Why only the island, and not the rest of it?'

'We fight,' said Mara.

'Everyone fights. You think people shouldn't fight? It's normal, Mara. We're normal. We are a normal fucking couple who have fucking fights and fuck to make up after, okay?'

Pearl reached for her, and Mara let her. Her cheeks were damp and salty with tears.

Afterwards, Mara lay beside her, her whole body beating a fast pulse. Pearl, cradled in her arms, already drifting into the depths of sleep.

Pearl, her voice sleep-drowsy, said: 'I don't think we should stay here much longer. It's not good for you. There's magic here and it's dark as tar. It sticks.'

How strange Pearl was. How mythical. At first Mara had thought Pearl, with her one blue eye and one brown, was a mix of sea and land. But she saw now that that wasn't true. The blue-green veins twisting through her wrists. The cool, heavy silk of her hair. Each hand the complex movement of tiny bones. The salt of her kiss. Pearl was the sea, through and through. Always changing, never staying.

Since coming back to the island, Mara's sleep was light and fleeting. She was up with the dawn, shuffling downstairs to put the kettle on. She'd been reading more of the fairy-tale book. There were more stories about selkies, and ones about mermaids too. Some of the phrases and images felt familiar, like something she remembered from long ago. Signe must have read the stories when Mara was small, and although her conscious mind forgot it, the tiny beating heart of the tale stayed there inside her until she needed it. And she needed it now - she felt it throbbing inside her, louder each day.

One story was called 'The Mermaid's Revenge', and it went like this:

There was a grand house, and inside it lived a wealthy couple, and outside it was a large black rock. The rock was worn smooth by the generations of mermaids who slid up on it to sing every night. The last mermaid was as vengeful as she was beautiful, and every night as the moon rose, she'd slide up onto the rock and sing her lonely song. Though the sound was eerie, the couple grew to enjoy it as a lullaby. But that changed when they had a child.

The baby slept fine during the day, but as soon as the mermaid began to sing, the child opened its tiny pink mouth and cried loud enough to wake the whole island. All night the mermaid sang, and all night the baby wailed. Finally, the desperate father braved the dark and walked out along the shore to the mermaid's rock. He asked her, as politely as he could, to stop. The proud mermaid liked that not one bit. She turned her back and sang louder. Each time she was asked to stay quiet, she sang louder still.

The child's mother grew desperate and delirious from lack of sleep. One morning she gathered a pack of men and ordered them to smash the shining rock. They worked all day with pickaxes and hammers until there was nothing left but a pile of jagged black stones.

That night, the mermaid's fury was wild enough to sink ships. She opened her mouth - but instead of song, she shrieked a throatful of wild curses, prophesying the end of the family. Unseen in the nursery, the force of the sound began to rock the sleeping baby's cradle to and fro, to and fro, hard enough to shake the house. When the last note had died, the mother rushed upstairs – only to find the cradle upturned, and her child dead beneath it. Away swam the mermaid, her terrible curse made true.

Mara jolted to her feet, her left leg ablaze with pins and needles. Without realising, she'd been leaning on a splintery windowsill, lost in thought, the long-boiled kettle forgotten. The island was speaking to her, and she hadn't even heard. It was all around her: the shush of the sea, the whispering of the leaves in the wind, the gentle dunt-dunt of a bee buffeting against the window. And something had snapped her awake. She held her breath.

There – a quickening overhead, the light staccato of feet. Mara gasped for breath. It was a sound pulled straight from her memory. Bee, her little Bee, so excited about life that he couldn't bear to just walk through it. How long had the sounds been going on? How much had she lost in daydreaming about mermaids? How could she have let Pearl keep her away from here for so long? Pearl, always, dragging her to the bottom of the sea.

All the stories say that selkies will make you die of love. They'll flay you alive for loving them. Being in love with a selkie is like stepping on glass all day, every day. And it was true: Pearl did make her feel like she was dying. She felt dizzy at the thought of Pearl's desire, the abyss of her wanting. She was always asking and asking and asking. *I want to leave, I want to talk, I want this and that and everything*. No matter how much Mara gave, it would never be enough.

Couthie

'**M**um will be here soon,' said Islay as a farewell to Peter, her voice sing-songing. 'We all will, I think.'

She pulled in a sea-cool breath and held it in her lungs as she walked away down the cliff. At the bottom, she turned away from home and towards the loch. There was an old library bus there. Mr Pettersen in the shop had told her that he used to be the librarian and drive the bus around the island, delivering books to people's houses. But things change. Or, rather, things revert to how they were.

She took the long way home, wandering across the island from point to point and cove to cove, following generations of crofters and sailors and penitents, following those long-forgotten steps that made the veins and bones of the island. Bothies, cairns, burial mounds; old tombs, defences, gods. The island wasn't remote or empty at all. It was a city peopled by ghosts. It was so easy to get lost here, where you could never really be lost. It was so easy to be alone here, where you could never really be lonely.

In the lee of a grassy hill, a squat bothy with thick stone walls and a turf roof. Islay pressed her fingers to its mossy walls, feeling them come away damp. Perhaps once it had been a burial chamber, perhaps a jail cell. Perhaps a home. Now it was a shelter for shadow-dwelling flowers and stray sheep and ramblers caught out in storms.

Islay would never be a true child of the island the way that Bee was. Since Signe had brought him home from the hospital on the mainland, he'd never spent a night off it. They'd been over for day trips to cities, riding tour buses and traipsing round museums. But they'd never stayed overnight. Every night of his life Bee had been home in his own bed, the waves lulling him to sleep.

The island was inside him even before he was born. Islay remembered Signe telling her that when she was pregnant with Bee she wanted to eat soil. She'd said Islay and Mara were her little fishes, meant to have water all around them; that with her girls she'd believed that all babies were fishes until the moment they were born and their lungs choose air over liquid. But with Bee, it was not sea, it was soil. She'd said it was more than wanting. She needed it. Everything else tasted of air but she knew that the dirt would be the most delicious thing she'd ever eaten. Islay had read somewhere that pregnant women can crave coal, chalk, soap – all sorts of things. The books said it was to do with a lack of certain nutrients. But she liked to think that Signe's desire was because of Bee. It was because he was an island boy, through and through, and he wanted to get as close to the land as he could. He would always be a part of it. Sometimes, between the house and the cliff, Islay was sure she could feel the weight of his steady gaze, the tug of his insistent little hand in her own.

She slipped inside the bothy. It smelled of earth and cold stone. The murky light caught at her memory, and she was thrown back five years, smoking Signe's stolen cigarettes in the shed with her sister. She'd asked Mara about their first night on the island, creeping out of their beds and into the starlit sea. Mara had said she thought maybe this was what dying felt like; to let the sea keep lapping at you until you were only bones.

How strange Islay had found that. Dangerous even; morbid. Now she didn't think it was morbid at all. How could she not have understood what Mara meant? It wasn't about death at all. It was about belonging, being part of something bigger than yourself. It was about home.

At home Islay found Mara, making tea in the kitchen.

'Not hanging out with your *girlfriend*?' The words were out of her mouth, spiky and sour, before she knew what was happening, and why did she say it like that? Pearl wasn't so bad really. In other circumstances, Islay might even have been her friend.

Mara didn't deign to reply. Probably going for a high-and-mighty thing, trying for elegance like some woman in an old novel.

They stood together at the kitchen worktop, Mara waiting for her tea to steep, Islay staring into the cupboard she'd just opened so she could pretend she was looking for something. Her sister was a joke, but she was still her sister, and Islay didn't mean to be cruel. But apologies – ugh. It was easier to talk like this, not looking at each other. Islay was trying to shape her mouth to the word *sorry*, but Mara got in first.

'Who did you love?'

'Sorry,' said Islay, surprised. 'I mean, what?'

'When you were away, you must have been in love at some point. But you came back alone. How do people make it work?'

Islay slammed the cupboard and looked at her sister. 'Jesus, Mara, I don't know. Do I look like I know?'

'It's not like in books, is it? All those love stories – they weren't about love, really. Why did we never hear any stories about actual love? Then maybe we'd know what we were supposed to do. I just can't – I don't know – never mind.' Mara squashed her tea bag and threw it into the sink. 'Forget I said anything.'

Islay picked at the chipped paint on the cupboard door. 'Maybe there are other things besides loving another person.'

'Do you think that's true?'

'I don't know, Mara,' said Islay. 'I'm sorry.'

Ramassé

One Easter, newly pregnant with Bee, Signe got up early so she could lay out everything she needed to make painted eggs with her daughters. She set out the equipment: paints in pastel shades, chunky plastic brushes, cups of rinsing water. She put four eggs in a dish. With a sewing needle, she poked a hole in each end of the eggs and blew the wet insides out into a bowl. She'd whisk them all up and make an omelette for the girls' breakfast. No, not all of them: she'd set half aside, then add sausage and onions and red peppers and make a special omelette for Peter. She blew the last egg out into the bowl. A pinprick of blood in the centre of the yolk. Signe tried not to look at it. With a fork she reached for it, tried to lift it out. The yolk burst. The red threaded out, spreading, gelatinous, ruining.

Signe ran to the downstairs bathroom, vomited twice, flushed the toilet, then rinsed her mouth and went back into the kitchen. She tipped the bloodied eggs down the sink and turned on the tap as far as it would go. She placed a box of cereal and a pint of milk on the kitchen table.

'Girls,' she called up the stairs. 'Put your slippers on and come for breakfast.'

Later, Mara found one of the empty eggs left on the kitchen worktop. She knew that you had to crush eggshells before throwing them away, or witches would make boats from them. She raised the egg to her eye and looked into the hole pierced at one end. It was so light that she could barely feel it in her hands. She peered inside carefully, carefully; peered into the darkness, the shell's empty interior, which was all shadowed to black. Even after she crushed the eggshell in her small fist and pushed it down to the bottom of the bin, she could still feel that blackness, that emptiness, looking back at her.

Willnae

The cliff called to Mara. She went through the shark jaw and down the path. At the top of the hill, she slipped among the statues and thought of stone. The statues felt cool under her hand. A comfort. She should go and find Pearl. She should talk to her about – something. She'd felt that something was wrong between them, but it was hard to remember what, and why she had wanted to bother discussing it. And anyway, wasn't it nice up here? The salt-cool breeze, the held breath of the statues. No need to leave yet. She slipped off her shoes to feel the grass on her soles.

She approached the edge of the cliff, keeping her gaze down on her bare toes so she wouldn't have to see Peter with his palms raised to the sky. She settled close to the edge. The breeze stroked her skin. A bee hummed past her ear. The sun shone blinding in her eyes. Above her, clouds shifted from dragons to wolves to Swiss rolls to Italy to a sea monster – and she closed her eyes.

The grass was as soft as the seabed. Her limbs turned liquid. Sleep closed over her like water.

Those stories in the book held truth, she knew it. They described a dream she thought she'd forgotten. False love and pretending and the endless cold dark of the sea. Except it wasn't a dream at all. There was a reason that it sounded right, what those stories said. The vicious things from the sea and their untrustworthy beauty. She'd always known it was right.

'Mara.'

Mara snapped open her eyes to see Pearl standing over her, silhouetted against the clouds, her head blocking the sun.

'What? Why are you?' Which was all Mara, surprised, could manage.

'I was looking for you.' Behind Pearl, the clouds became rabbits. 'Were you asleep?'

'I was thinking,' said Mara. She was still waking up, her head punch-drunk, her mouth dry and heavy. 'I was thinking about a story. It was in a book and it had pictures and it's meant to be about love. But I think that's a trick to make it seem made up. I think it's really true.'

'Oh,' said Pearl, 'please, not that one about the selkie!'

Pearl laughed. Mara didn't.

'Seriously? I told you, that story is bullshit.' Pearl took a step back, and the sun blinked bright in Mara's eyes. 'It's not about love. Lying to trap someone – that's not love. Love isn't being forced. Love is choosing to stay.'

Mara closed her eyes. What could Pearl know about love? Selkies always leave.

'Can you come away from the edge?' said Pearl. 'You're making me nervous.'

'Don't be silly,' said Mara, 'I'm not that close,' and she put out her hand to prove it, but it met only air. She rolled the other way, a sudden choke of shock as the world fell away, and there was Pearl's hand on her elbow, helping her up. Under her feet, the ground felt steady again. She waited until her legs stopped shaking and pulled her shoes back on. She kept her head down as Pearl spoke.

'Do you remember I gave you a story once? The two concubines who escape the tower, remember? One of them worked in a diamond mine. The cover was black with silver letters. They each travel through the tower to get back to one another. Mara, do you remember it? Do you remember the end?'

'We should go,' said Mara, straightening. 'Let's go back to the house.'

'Wait, Mara.'

She waited, but whatever Pearl meant to say, whatever she wanted Mara to hear, she swallowed it back down. 'I found something,' she said, 'when I was walking. I don't know if you've seen inside, and I want to show you. Can I show you?'

Pearl led her down the cliff and between the fields and past the ancient brown horse gumming at the bracken and between crumbling stone walls and around patches of coconutty gorse, and as they walked Pearl said: 'I was thinking about Céline and Katinka, from the show in Vegas. Going by the dates they must be married by now.'

Mara shrugged. 'I guess.'

'Well,' said Pearl, 'I didn't know if you knew.'

Pearl led her past tiny red-roofed houses and over the remains of a summer-dry stream and on on on, right to the centre of the island.

There, in a cup of collapsed land that had once been a hill, lurked a church. It was long abandoned, its walls and windows still mostly intact. Its roof was entirely gone, a doll's house with its lid lifted. Islay used to sneak off there, Mara remembered, presumably to do things she wasn't supposed to, though now that she thought about it there wasn't much to be done on an island mostly devoid of boys or drugs or mischief of any appealing kind.

Pearl took Mara's hand and led her through the hole where the door used to be. The floor was carpeted with old leaves, ice-brittle, the colour of blood. The light was stained glass, colouring the air in thick brushstrokes.

'Listen,' said Pearl.

Mara listened. Shrill voices raging, hammers on steel, sobbing, whistling shrieks, soft whispers. An army of people, a city, a world. 'Who is that?' asked Mara. 'Who's down there?'

'No one. It's the sea.'

'But we're in the middle of the island.'

'There's an underground river running right through the middle of the island. Salt water, fast-flowing. It goes from one side to the other, and both sides are sea. It's underneath us. It's constantly eating away at the land, scooping it hollow.'

'Okay,' said Mara. 'Is that why you brought me here?'

'No,' said Pearl. 'That's not why. I didn't think you'd ever been inside here, and I wanted to bring you because – look, Mara. Look where we are.'

Mara looked. Without a roof, without a crucifix, without a confessional, without pews, there was only one place left to look: up. This was a church to the sky. A worship of birds, an adoration of the island. 'I'm looking,' said Mara, 'but I don't –'

There, among the ruined pews and the caved-in ceiling, the floating light coloured bright by the remnants of stained glass, before a congregation of ghosts. There, Pearl took Mara's hand. Mara saw Pearl's jaw clench as she swallowed.

'Yes,' she said. She smiled and held Mara's hand tight. 'Yes.'

And Mara knew what she needed to say. The closeness of Pearl's skin. The rustle of birds in the eaves. The slow painted light. She only had to say it, that reassurance, that promise, that one word.

She dropped Pearl's hand. 'It's not safe in here,' she said. 'The floor might cave in and there are probably rats. Let's leave. I want to go home.'

Brae

In the night, Mara rolled over in bed. She fell off the edge and into the claw-foot bath. It was full of seawater, salt in her eyes, seaweed tangling around her ankles. She choked instantly awake. She grasped out for the sides, tried to kneel, to raise her head above the water. The base of the bath fell away below her. She lost her grip on the slippery side. Her feet kicked down into nothing. It was as deep as the sea and she was sinking, she was drowning, she was dying.

She woke gasping in her bed, a caught fish. She breathed in-out-in-out until her hands stopped shaking. She reached out for familiar skin. Nothing. She stared into the dim light. The other half of the bed stretched, crumpled and cold. Her heart beat so hard she felt sick. She ran into Pearl's room and shook her awake.

'Did you do this?'

'What? Mara, are you okay?'

'Did. You. Do. This?'

Pearl, finally coming awake, dragged herself to a sitting position. The bedsprings squealed. 'Whatever you're talking about, the answer is no. I've been sleeping. Which is what you should be doing too.' She lifted the edge of the duvet. 'Come on. Come in.'

Mara breathed in the scent of Pearl's skin. Her half-dreaming smile. The soft hidden curves of her. The warmth. Mara's head swam.

'I know you did it,' she said. 'Don't do it again.'

Mara turned away and went back to her own cold bed. She kept her eyes open for the rest of the night, fingers pressed to the pulse in her throat, pressing harder and harder so that she would not drown.

Numpty

After Signe found a hole chewed in the corner of a box of cornflakes and a scatter of little black pellets on the floor, Mara spent a day taking all the food out of the kitchen cupboards and throwing most of it away. The small amount left over went into baskets, which she then attached to the laundry pulley and hoisted up to the ceiling. The rats, surely, couldn't climb walls. To get at any food, Mara had to unwind the rope from the hook in the wall, lower the pulley, retrieve the food, hoist the pulley back up, and rewind the rope. She already had a dozen tiny nicks on her fingers from the rope. She pulled down the basket, retrieved a packet of dry pasta, and pulled on the rope again. She'd found some mushrooms that weren't nibbled or shrivelled or covered in squishy patches, so it was mushroom pasta for dinner. The fluorescent lights flickered as the generator struggled.

She took down the salt to add some to the pasta water, then hesitated. Pearl always added too much salt. When they were away, Mara had done the same, putting extra salt in almost everything she ate, great white flakes of it, snowstorms on every meal. She'd been used to the island's salty air, to the taste of it in everything.

When they first came back to the island, she stuck to this habit, but now it was too much. All her meals tasted so strong, as if everything she'd eaten in the past two years was just a memory of food, a bland approximation, and this was the real thing.

She switched off the heat under the pasta water. She couldn't remember when she'd seen Pearl today. But what was time on the island anyway? What were days? Sunrise and stars and the taste of honey melting down your throat. The rasp of tongues. The soft butting of bumblebees against your hands. All the flower beds mattressed with clover. Dandelion seeds snowing onto your shoulders, sticking to your lips. The daisies open all day and all night, their watching eyes.

She opened the back door and stepped out to call Pearl's name. A light blinked from the warped door of the shed. Mara turned towards it. What the hell was Pearl doing in the shed? In the shadow of the trees, she pushed at the shed door. It wouldn't open.

'Pearl?' She felt silly calling through the keyhole, but any other option felt sillier still. 'Are you there?'

She straightened, then pushed her shoulder against the warped wood. It gave with a squeal and she stumbled into the shed. The air smelled stale and Mara tasted dust on her tongue. The window was dirty, the light inside the shed dim and yellowed.

'Pearl?' She forced the door shut and looked behind it, just in case Pearl was hiding, like the illogical weirdo that she was. But no. Nothing but a tangle of dead spiders.

Mara surveyed the shed in the feeble light. Chipped flowerpots stacked on a lumpy structure cast in shadow, cardboard files rotted to odd sculptures, pickling jars turned black with grime. The torn armchair, its floral pattern muddied grey from damp – there she'd slumped years ago, wishing that Islay would share her disgusting precious cigarettes, wishing that she could understand her disgusting precious thoughts.

She turned to leave. The door handle spun, catching on nothing. She pulled the useless handle – but the door was stuck.

'Shit,' she said to no one. She pulled again at the handle, jiggling it, trying to shake the locking mechanism loose.

'Hello?' She bent and shouted through the keyhole. 'Hello? Can you hear me? I'm stuck!'

She tried to jam her fingertips around the edge of the door to prise it open, but the gap was too small. She roamed the shed, feet shuffling in grit, trying to find something small enough to wedge into the space and force the door open. A chisel, a trowel. Anything.

Just as she was thinking about smashing one of the brown-rot jars and using a glass shard on the door, there was a voice at the keyhole.

'Mara?'

'Pearl! The door handle's broken on this side.'

Silence. Mara waited. In the dim light, the air tumbled silver. An itch threatened at the back of her throat.

'Are you still there? Just push the door.'

'No,' said Pearl.

'You have to push hard because the wood is warped. Are you pushing? Use your shoulder.'

'No,' said Pearl.

'What do you mean, no? Just push the fucking door!'

'So you can go back to avoiding me?'

'Fucksake, Pearl! Just let me out.'

'I'm not letting you out until we talk.'

'We've already talked. There's nothing left.'

'How,' said Pearl, her voice a rough whisper. 'How can you say that? Do you really think there's nothing left?'

'You know that's not what I mean.'

'I never know what you mean.'

'I'm doing my best here. I know that Signe and Islay would rather I wasn't here, and that whatever I do they'll never really like me. But that would be okay if things were okay with us.'

The shed wasn't well made in the first place, and the years had not been kind. Beneath the trees as it was, every rainfall meant days of slow drips. Now that Mara's eyes had adjusted to the dimness, she could see that each board had warped and shrunk, letting light seep in.

Words still buzzing through the keyhole: 'Mara, are you even listening? I asked you a question. Is that it then?'

'No,' said Mara. 'I don't ...'

She thought then of all the stories about people who fell in love with strangers. The selkie, so enchanting that you would lie and steal just to keep her. But how could you ever really trust her? She was just a thing from the sea.

Mara dropped to her knees by the shed wall, pressing her fingertips experimentally into the biggest gaps. Could she prise out a board? Should she smash a glass jar after all?

'So that's it? You want me to leave? To go back to the show and swim without you?'

'You managed it before.'

'That was before! Things have changed. Two years we've been together, Mara. Two years isn't nothing.'

'It was just a dream. It was an adventure. But we have to wake up sometime. Things off the island - they're not real. It's all just ...' Mara threw up her hands, though she knew that Pearl couldn't see.

'Do you know how insane you sound? Of course it's real. It wasn't just some madcap romp, something to do so you can tell a story about it. Don't pretend as if two years of your life didn't happen.'

Mara paused there in the shadows. All those hours under the water with Pearl. Their bright wigs and their shimmering tails making them so visible, the most eye-catching thing in a year of rooms – and also invisible, able to slough off their costumes and reveal their scars, anonymous in any crowd. But Mara knew now that they'd stayed under the water for too long.

Some days they stayed under for so long that Mara forgot what it was like to breathe from the air instead of from Pearl's lungs.

Some days they stayed under for so long that Pearl forgot to blink, and her eyes clouded silver like old mirrors.

Some days they stayed under for so long that Mara's hands grew as numb and white as fish-meat, and her fingertips were so wrinkled she couldn't pick anything up, and her ears were edged mauve, and when they got out of the water her body wouldn't stop shivering, and Pearl would get into bed with her and they'd lie together, Pearl giving Mara heat and Mara giving Pearl cold, until they equalised.

That time with Pearl was like being caught between sleeping and waking, between night and day.

It was enough. She was awake now.

'I don't even know why you're here,' said Mara. 'Why did you come back if you hate it so much? If you hate this house, and you hate my family, and it's all so horrible and difficult for you – why did you come?'

'Because. You asked me to.'

'You, Pearl, you –' Mara sat back on her heels in the shed, breathing deep in the dirty light. 'It's just too hard. It's too much. I don't want to drown.'

Without realising, Mara had crept across the floor and pressed her hand to the door. On the other side, though she couldn't see, Pearl was doing the same. Mara felt herself weaken. The familiar twin throbs, even now. In her throat, between her legs, the two heartbeats of her: speech and lust, everything she said and everything she wanted, everything for Pearl.

She shook her head. Why was this woman keeping her in here? Why was she trying to cast her spells, to play her tricks?

'Go away,' said Mara. 'I don't want you any more.'

'I don't believe you.'

But Pearl's voice was already fading, drowned out by Mara's thoughts. She remembered the window she'd broken, years ago. Creeping down to find Islay smoking in the shed, being so annoyed at being left out that she'd broken the window with an underripe pear, then pretended the pear had just fallen. She remembered the board Islay had put over the damaged part; the way they'd both pretended to believe that the pear had fallen through the window by accident, somehow, even though that was impossible.

She had to scrape moss away with her fingernails to dislodge the board. The wood had rotted over the years. She yanked and the board split. She pulled it with her nails, wooden skelfs scraping her hands, the muck of years caking her knuckles.

She wrenched the board away from the window and climbed over the ledge. Spiderwebs laced her hair and splinters scraped her legs but it didn't matter, she was through, she was free. Out of the corner of her eye, she saw the gleam of Pearl in the evening light.

'Mara, wait. Please.' Pearl's voice was cracking, the vowels strained, tears softening her edges.

And then Mara did the one thing she could think of that would make Pearl stop, that would burn up her tears, that would make her stand back and let Mara go. She said Pearl's name, the secret name, the one she'd given up long ago and never claimed again. The silence after Mara spoke was sticky and thick. She couldn't breathe.

'That's not my name, Mara.' Pearl's voice was low. There was a bang, a threatening shudder, and Mara turned to look as Pearl smacked her hand again on the closed door of the shed. 'I said that's not my fucking name.'

Her legs shaking, Mara walked away, and she did not look back.

Reverence

All Signe and Peter's children were perfect, but Barra – her little Bee – was somehow even more perfect. He was beautiful, of course he was. He was a pixie, an elf, a creature from a better world. His tiny upturned nose, his wide and restless lips, his doll-chin. And loveliest of all, his eyes: the icy snowflake in the blue iris, a starburst each time he blinked. His body was so delicate that he barely looked real. He was so much smaller than Signe's daughters had ever been. She remembered lying in her starched and weary hospital bed and wanting nothing more than to keep him inside her for just a little longer before he had to face the world.

First there was one nurse, then another. Then the doctor. The nosy neighbour and the health visitor and the snippy mother at the shop. 'Something is wrong,' they said. 'Something is wrong with your child.'

'What nonsense,' said Signe. 'What rot. Look at that child – have you ever seen a more perfect child?'

Yes, he flinched at loud noises and unfamiliar voices. Yes, he didn't move towards walking or pottying as quickly as her girls had. Yes, during a tantrum he sometimes got so hysterical that he stopped breathing. But what of it? Not all children were the same, just as not all adults were the same.

They could name it all they wanted, this thing they said was wrong with him. But Signe knew her child. They would just have to be patient, and everything would be fine. She never should have gone to the mainland to have him. It was no good for him there.

Signe knew that her boy just needed some quiet. Some space to himself. Some privacy away from prying eyes. Somewhere he could catch a glimpse of the other world he'd left to enter this one.

Répéter

igne was turning to stone. She had known for a long time that it was happening. At first it was a slowing, a stiffening. Normal enough for any woman of a certain age – and for an ex-dancer with a snapped Achilles tendon, inevitable. Her salted hair, now more grey than red. Her morning stretches making no difference to her sleep-stiff limbs. Her moving joints scraping like gravel underfoot.

There was one more thing that she had to try. One more way to make herself lighter. One more thing she had left to give.

She waited until the moon rose, then she walked through the sleeping house and through the garden and past the trees. She stood on the shore, ready to unburden herself to the sea.

'Take it,' she said, her hands held open to the waves. 'Take my loss.'

The sea did not.

'Take my sadness,' she said. 'Take all the hope I had for my son. Take all the love I have for my husband. Take the freedom and honesty I couldn't give to my daughters.'

The sea did not.

'Please,' she said. 'Take it from me. It's too heavy. I can't carry it any more.'

But the sea did not want her grief – or Signe did not want to give it away.

She turned and slowly, slowly made her way up the stony beach. Over the years, she read her children so many stories about that other world – and so many of the stories had lost children. Hansel and Gretel, following breadcrumbs, fattening for a witch. Seven cursed brothers, turned to swans, lost to their loving father. Rapunzel, locked in her tower. But the thing about the children in the stories is that they always came home. So where was her boy? Why wouldn't he come home?

However hard we try to make a deal with the world, the world hasn't agreed. Nature can't love us back.

Signe's progress up the beach was slow, and she was almost at the treeline. Usually she would stride right past this point, eyes already seeing through the trees to home. But her joints creaked so very loudly, and her bones were so very heavy. She just needed a moment to catch her breath. She dropped to her knees and rested on the stones at the high-tide mark. The steady lap of the sea. The silvery fuzz of insects overhead. The chill of the wind on her bare arms.

Idly, Signe stroked her hand along the stones, letting them click-clack together. Ready and rested, she glanced down to see where she could push with her hands to get back up. She paused.

'Bee,' she said, and she didn't know why.

Her eyes, adjusted to the moonlight, caught on something long and pale among the stones. Not driftwood. Not mussel shells.

She reached out her hand. And then, just like that, my mother found my bones. The bones were dirty from their time in the sea, caked in sand and wrapped in seaweed, their edges smoothed by the tumble of waves. But they were small, and real, and mine.

'Bee,' she said, and now she knew why.

Barra

So there it is. The sea had taken me, and now the sea was giving me back.

Remember right at the start of the story, when I told you about our last summer together? Me and my sisters on the beach, navigating a shore made squishy and silvered with jellyfish? Well, the thing about jellyfish is that they don't mean to sting. They don't have brains, so they can't have intention. They don't have eyes, so they can't plot a path. They drift, thoughtless, on their way nowhere. But it doesn't seem that way to us. Not if we're summer-sea-swimming, legs dangling down in the dark, and a jellyfish brushes past, the contact a sudden sharp burn in the cold water.

Because then we're stung. We're in pain. We're damaged.

We might think, *Why did this happen to me?* But we might as well ask, *Why did this happen to the jellyfish?* The answer is the same for us and for the jellyfish: it didn't happen to you. It just happened.

Back before I died, when I was little and golden and gorging myself on magic, the island never seemed small to me. Every day my sisters and I made the world anew. Every day was a world within a world. Perhaps if I hadn't been born right when I was, my sisters would have been different. I think they were almost ready to stop dreaming and see the world for what it was. But how could they shake off their dreams, when they had to dream them all afresh for me? How could that other world not be real, when there I was pulling them towards it?

The sea took me, and there I was all along. I was with my family, and not with them. I was close, and not close. Before I died I never really understood any of them. I never listened to them, and they wouldn't have told me what they were really thinking anyway. But afterwards - well, afterwards I could go wherever I wanted. And I chose to be with them. In their heads and in their hearts. I finally understood them, at least a little.

I had five years with them in their world, and I've had five years with them in this other world. My time is almost up.

Braw

Signe gathered up my bones and carried them through the trees and towards the house. She paused at the back door, where a figure stood in the shadows.

'Pearl,' said Signe.

'Oh,' said Pearl. 'Hello.'

'Are you going to the house?'

'Yes. I mean, no. I mean, I'm going to my house, because Mara, she thinks I've left the island, and – are those bones?'

Signe glanced down as if she didn't already know what she held. 'It's Bee,' she said. 'It's my baby. He came home.'

'Oh,' said Pearl. 'Oh.'

The night air was warm, the sea breeze tickling their arms and cheeks. In the darkness clouds of glossy insects flickered, reflecting the light, becoming night again.

'I can't take him inside,' said Signe. 'I don't want the girls to see him like this.'

'I understand,' said Pearl. 'Let me help.'

Together, Signe and Pearl took care of me. They unwrapped the seaweed and rinsed off the sand. From the outside sink they made up a soaking bucket of clean water. They scrubbed off the grime of the ocean, the muck of the land. The marks of the five years I spent away from my family, yet always with them.

'Near the house,' said Signe. 'In the orchard. He liked playing there.'

They did not need a big hole so they used their bare hands, scooping the damp soil of the garden with their fingernails, pushing the small stones aside with their palms. Then Pearl sat on the grass at a respectable distance, leaving Signe alone with her son.

Under the moon, Signe laid down my clean white bones. She kissed each one as she placed it in the ground. She pushed the soil back into place. She did not mark the grave.

'Now he's free,' said Pearl, speaking mostly to herself.

Signe stared at her. 'Why did you say that? What do you mean?'

'I'm sorry, I didn't mean any offence. I just meant – I don't know. It's something my mother used to say when someone died. She said that this world, for all its wonders, can be heavy. It can weigh us down, box us in. But afterwards, we're free. We're like birds, and we can fly to anywhere we like.'

Signe sat back on her heels, her hands still holding the shape of me.

'Signe, I really am sorry. I didn't mean – I can't begin to understand how –'

'I was thinking about my girls. About me and their father, how we were always pulling them back here.'

'Mara loves you. That's why she came back. You were here and you needed her – you didn't force her. You didn't even ask.'

'I've given my girls all I have,' said Signe, 'and I've taken too much in return. How can they make their choices when I'm still making them? How can they freely decide whether to leave or to stay? That's no choice at all. But I can set them free.'

Signe turned towards the cliff, then turned back. 'You're good,' she said. 'For Mara. I should have said that before.'

'Thank you,' said Pearl.

'Will you look after her for me?'

'She doesn't need me to. You were right before. She needs to be free.'

Signe and Pearl walked their separate ways. Birds must fly and selkies always leave.

Soutenu

Ballet dancers are unavoidably aware of the forces of the world. Gravity, friction, balance. Every movement they perform is a deal made with the world.

Signe reached the base of the hill and began the trek upwards. Above her, the moon shone as bright as polished silver. The air smelled of grass and clean earth. Everything, even the wind, was silent.

The benefit of the solo dancer is that she copes alone with a physical environment that is, if not always controllable, at least predictable. The floor of the stage or practice room will not suddenly change its position, and gravity will not suddenly release or strengthen its hold. This is not the case when she dances with a partner. With two people controlling the movement, the potential for conflict arises.

Signe emerged at the top of the hill. For so long she had been feeling heavier and heavier with each passing day; now she felt as weightless as moonlight. She passed the silvered statues without looking at them. There was only one that mattered.

Traditional ballet operates with strict gender roles. The woman is delicate and dependent; the man strong, supportive and in control. In a paired dance, or a *pas de deux*, much of the male dancer's job is to support his partner and display her to the audience in the most effective way. The female dancer must feel free and able to move, and to do this she must be able to rely unthinkingly on her partner's strength and stability. In any dance there is a complex interchange of trust, support, and acceptance. But the most important thing for both dancers is that their effort must never show.

Signe made her weightless way through the statues, closer to the edge of the cliff. There was Peter: his strong back; his grounded feet; his arms raised to the sky, ready.

The climax of a *pas de deux* is the male dancer supporting the female in a climactic lunge, fall or lift. To achieve this, the female dancer must accept the possibility – even the likelihood – of falling. The female dancer cannot control how she is lifted and held; only her own position in the air. She must surrender control and let her partner support her.

Signe approached her husband. She slid her arms up his back, curling them over his shoulders. She pressed her body against his.

A successful dancer follows rules. There are strict rules even for a standing dancer. When at the barre, the dancer must not roll her feet. She must straighten her knees, pull up her thighs, lift from her hips, stretch her ribs, lengthen her back, loosen her neck. Lastly, but most importantly, she must raise her eyes and look outward.

Signe was ready. She was as light as a bird. She wanted to stay forever, cast in stone, looking into her husband's eyes. She knew that they would hold their pose there together on the cliff, until the rain and wind and snow and sun wore them down finally, after years.

She took a few steps back, feet tickling on the grass, and bent her knees. Putting her weight onto her right leg, she raised her left foot, toe pointed. It did not matter that there was no one there to see; her form would still be perfect. She pushed off the ground with all her strength: with her leg, the ball of her foot, her toe, right up into the air. She was so light that the wind might snatch her away.

She twisted in the air so she was facing back to the island, and landed perfectly in Peter's upraised hands. Her body was raised up above his head, and he was looking right into her face. At the last moment, before her muscles ground to stone, before the whites of her eyes turned grey, Signe tilted her head down to look at Peter. He was smiling.

Drookit

The first great boom of thunder woke Mara and Islay at the same moment. By the time they'd blinked awake, lightning lit the room silver. Less than a second later, thunder shook the house again. Mara's first half-sleeping thought was to roll out onto the floor, dragging her blankets with her, and hide under the heavy wooden bed. Islay's first half-sleeping thought was to run through to her mother's room, which was empty.

'Mum? Mummy, are you here?'

In reply, the wail of the storm.

Islay ran instead to her sister's room. That bed was empty too, the sheet rumpled.

'Mara,' she said, 'bloody God damn you, Mara,' speaking only to herself, a tiny fierce whisper in an endless empty house.

'Under here,' came the muffled reply. Islay, heart pitching, dropped to her knees. Together the sisters huddled under the bed. Lightning lit up the other side of the house. Somewhere, cannons.

'Why are we hiding?' Islay's laugh shook. 'This is ridiculous. We're not children.'

'I know,' said Mara, not even pretending to laugh.

'It's only a storm.'

'Still.'

Thunder boomed again, and Islay let out a squeal, which she immediately covered with a cough. The windows rattled in their rotting frames, the wind and rain screaming into the room. There seemed as much weather inside the house as outside it. In the sudden flash of lightning, Mara put her arm around her sister and pulled her further under the bed.

The next crash of thunder was lost as the wind slammed open the front door of the house. Islay screamed and didn't try to hide it.

'It's okay,' said Mara, though she had no idea if it was.

'It's not,' said Islay. 'Mum's not in her bed.'

'Okay then, it's not okay.' Mara wriggled out of the covers and waited for Islay to follow. Already the edges of the window were emitting a steady drip. Outside the bedroom door they heard the wind hissing and screeching down the hallways.

'Dad.'

'I know,' said Mara, wishing that she didn't.

In the grip of the storm the island was unrecognisable, a land from a forgotten myth. Mara and Islay, wrapped in patterned oilcloth, staggering in pairs of Peter's too-big boots, leaned into the wind and fought their way up the cliff.

Through the sheet of sideways rain, in the quick flash of lightning, right at the edge of the cliff, they saw a man with his head tipped back and his palms raised to the sky – and a woman balanced on his hands, legs raised, toes pointed at the storming clouds. The stone figures were locked together in a perfectly balanced pose. They were looking into one another's eyes, unknowing of the storm around them.

'That's why,' murmured Mara to herself. 'That's why he stood like that. He was waiting for her.'

'I don't think it's safe in the house,' shouted Islay. 'We need to find somewhere to wait out the storm.' She hunched under the rain's assault, the wind stealing her breath. She laughed, and the rain on her face made it more like crying. 'There's nowhere we can go. If only we could go under the sea, or underground.'

Mara shouted back: 'We can.'

They fought the storm down the cliff and between the fields and walls and gorse and empty land and battened-down houses, all of it invisible to them, all of it clothed in rain and blown twistwise by wind, right to the centre of the island. Mara held tight to Islay's arm and pulled her to the door of Pearl's house. The wind had ripped open the door of the library bus and torn book pages flapped around them, sodden with rain.

They pushed and pulled and twisted the doorknob, but the door remained locked. Mara, despairing, smacked her fist against the door. She'd pushed Pearl away, off the island and back to her old life, and now this home was nothing but a shell.

There must be another way in. Maybe she could find a rock to bash the door open. Maybe she could walk around the hill and look for a vent that she could dig around. There must be some sort of chimney for the fire. Maybe if she –

The door opened. Pearl stood in the doorway.

'Mara,' she said.

'I'm sorry for coming here,' shouted Mara against the roaring wind, against the squall of blowing pages. 'And I'm sorry for letting you leave. And for being shitty to you, and for not listening to you, and for –'

'Shut up, Mara,' said Islay. She pushed her sister out of the way and stepped into Pearl's house. She shook her wet hair. 'It's ridiculous out there!' She pulled Mara inside, shutting the door behind her. 'You can do your bloody apologies when we've dried off and had some tea. I'm sure Pearl won't mind. Right, Pearl?'

Pearl shrugged. She reached into the cupboard and handed clean towels to Mara and Islay. 'Kitchen,' she said. 'I'll make tea.'

Inside the house, the storm was nothing but a distant knocking. The air was warm, the candlelight soft. Islay disappeared into the bathroom to dry off her hair. In the kitchen, Pearl filled the copper kettle with water and put it on the hob.

Mara patted her soaking hair with the towel, taking a moment to let the memories throb through her. The fire flickering in a wood-burning stove, the music swooning from a record player, the buttery-soft light from the candles. And Pearl, Pearl.

Her seal-sleek hair. Her shined-penny skin. Her sweetness, her bravery, her strength. How could she have forgotten this? How could she have endangered it? She was an utter fucking idiot.

'I'm sorry. Pearl, I'm so sorry.'

'I heard you before,' said Pearl. 'Don't lurk in the doorway like that. You don't have to ask to come in.'

Mara sat at the kitchen table. 'I thought you'd left.'

Pearl sat beside her. 'I meant to. I was going to. I was all ready to, and then ...'

'Then?'

'Then I didn't.'

Mara took her hand. 'At the end of the story. In that book you gave me.'

'You remember?'

'I always remembered. The end could be happy or sad, and I didn't like that. I wanted them to love one another still.'

'But they did, Mara. They do.'

'Is that enough?'

'I don't know,' said Pearl. She squeezed Mara's hand. 'But it's something.'

Cowp

Mara and Islay and Pearl were all safe from the storm – but what did that matter to the storm? They were not what it wanted. Just as Mara and Islay reached Pearl's door, rain slip-sliding their steps, airborne books flapping around them, the storm reached the door of the Ross house. It did not knock. It did not ask. It went inside.

The storm raged like fire through the house. It flung open doors and smashed every window. It raged up staircases and through rooms, surging along hallways, swinging light bulbs and shuddering furniture. The last thing it did as it left the house was rip the front door off its hinges (it did, though, leave the shark's jaw). Now the house looked exactly the same as the day the Ross family had first moved in, all those years ago. There was no front door and no back door. There were no windows in the downstairs rooms. Dead leaves blew along every corridor.

When it was finished with the house, the storm headed for the bridge. It toppled stonework and whipped out cables and bent railings, then forced whatever debris it could lift over the rest. It destroyed as much of the bridge work as it could. Islay, had she not been wrapped in a ball of blankets in her sister's lover's house, would have been reluctantly pleased, as would the rest of her Landlovers protest group.

Next the storm went for the cliff. It gathered its forces, creeping up to the highest point of the island, holding its breath. It let out a tiny puff of air. The heavy layer of grass and soil on the clifftop scattered across the sea like a blown dandelion. The storm exhaled with the full force of its lungs, with the rage of years, with the burning of a wish unfulfilled. The cliff crumbled into the sea. Dozens of stone figures took flight, flipped spinning across the water. They landed with a staccato of splashes. A statue of a burly man holding an elegant woman in the air was thrown the furthest, airborne the longest, getting closest to the sky. They were flung far from the island, their bodies still attached. Together, weightless, they flew.

Land fights with sea, just as stillness fights with change. But in this storm, in this fight, both won. The change was that everything went back to how it had been once, long ago.

The wind dropped, the sea calmed, the sky cleared. As quickly as it raised up, the storm was gone.

After

What happened to Mara and to Pearl and to Islay? I'm sorry to tell you that I don't know, because when the storm left, I did too.

When people are just stories, they're easy to predict. Their behaviour has to follow logically from what they've done before, has to follow a proper story arc, and so there's only one possible ending. But in real life, people can always surprise you. There's no telling what they'll do next.

Maybe Mara and Pearl got married in the library bus, with one celebrant and no guests, and Islay as their witness. They moved into the wreck of the big pink house, and slowly they built it up again – starting with repainting it so it wasn't pink. In the meantime the bridge was rebuilt, and by the time the tourists began flocking to the island, the guest house was perfect. It was a success, and Mara and Pearl lived there for the rest of their lives, and finally retired, leaving the guest house to their two sons, Peter the landscaper and Barra the cartographer.

Or maybe Pearl left the island and rejoined the mermaid show. Islay and Mara built the house up again. They kept it pink. The bridge was rebuilt and lots of tourists came and stayed at the house; or it wasn't rebuilt and only a few tourists came but paid lots money to stay there, because isolation can be valuable, and sometimes we're all willing to pay just to make everyone else go away for a while.

Or maybe Islay took Mara and Pearl's place in the mermaid show. She was just a girl, like the other girls, and she couldn't breathe underwater, but she grew out her long red hair, and it was so beautiful, burning there under the water, and everyone wanted to see her, and was happy to pay extra to do so, and every marquee shouted her name – her new stage name, of course, not the old name she abandoned – and she was wildly successful until the day she retired to somewhere warm and dry and many miles from the sea.

Or maybe Pearl and Islay left the island separately, and never came back. Mara stayed alone in the house. She intended to fix it up, to get rid of the ghosts to make room for guests. But the longer she stayed in the house, the heavier the air became. One day she went into a room to pull up some floor-boards, then paused. When she blinked, it was night. She sat in her father's armchair, and sometimes she stayed so still that she'd look down at her hands and see the silky powder left by moths' wings.

Or maybe Mara and Pearl left the island together, and never returned. They rejoined the mermaid show and performed every night, saving all their wages in a copper coffee tin that they hid under their bunk. They stuck so many pins in their map that the names of the countries weren't visible any more and the lines between them were completely obscured. They didn't live happily ever after, like a couple in a story. But they were happy for a while, and perhaps that's all we can ask.

Glossary of Chapter Titles

SCOTS WORDS

Bairn: child

Barra: a small child

Besom: broom; also a woman of loose morals, or cheeky child

Bidie-in: a romantic partner you live with but are not married to

Birling: spinning

Bonny: pretty

Brae: steep slope

Braw: fine, pleasant

Cannae: cannot

Canny: careful

Chapping: knocking

Clype: tell tales

Coorie: to cosy in

Couthie: sociable

Cowp: knock over

Dram: shot of whisky

Dreich: dreary, bleak (usually meaning weather)

Drookit: drenched

Drouthy: thirsty for a strong drink

Dunt: to hit something with force

Dwam: daydream

Fae: from

Fankle: tangle, mess

Fash: worry

Fouter: a fiddly, tiresome job

Gallus: self-confident, cheeky (usually derogatory, as in a rascal)

Glaikit: silly, senseless

Gloam: to become dark

Greet: cry

Haar: sea mist or fog

Hame: home

Haver: to talk incessantly

Ken: know, understand

Laldie: to undertake an action with vigour

Loupin: aching

Mauchit: dirty

Messages: groceries

Numpty: idiot

Pokey-hat: ice-cream cone

Scunnered: exasperated

Shoogle: wobble

Skelf: splinter

Skelp: slap

Skite: slip over

Sleekit: smooth and shiny; sneaky

Stooshie: uproar

Stour: dust

Stramash: a fight

Stravaig: to wander

Swither: to hesitate

Tae: to

Tatties: potatoes

Telt: told

Thrawn: twisted, obstinate, or sullen

Toty: very small

Tumshie: turnip, silly person; also term of endearment

Wheesht: hush or shush; telling someone to be quiet

Willnae: will not

BALLET TERMS

Balançoire: repeatedly swinging the leg from front to back; also tilting the upper body slightly forwards or backwards, opposite to the direction of the leg

Cabriole: caper

Détourné: turned aside; turning once completely around on both feet

Divertissement: enjoyable diversion

Ecarté: separated; thrown apart

Entrelacé: interlaced

Fouetté: describes the quick whipping action of a dancer's leg or body

Ramassé: picked up

Répéter: to repeat

Reverence: an elaborate curtsy

Sickling: used to describe a dancer's foot that is incorrectly placed

Soutenu: sustained
Volé: flying

BOXING TERMS
Bareknuckle: fighting without gloves
Palooka: a clumsy, second-rate boxer
Shadow-boxer: fights an imaginary opponent as a form of training
Sucker punch: an unexpected hit

Bibliography

The selkie and mermaid stories are adapted from versions in David
Thomson's *The People of the Sea* and Duncan Williamson's *Tales
of the Seal People*, as well as my own memories of stories I was
told and read as a child.

For the boxing details I am grateful to Edith Summerskill's *The
Ignoble Art* and J. W. Graham's *Eight Nine Out: Fifty Years as a
Boxer's Doctor.*

I am also indebted to Lennard J. Davis's *The Disability Studies
Reader*, Kenneth Laws's *Physics and the Art of Dance*, Kimberley
C. Patton's *The Sea Can Wash Away All Evils*, and Dominick
Tyler's *Uncommon Ground: A Word-Lover's Guide to the British
Landscape.*

Acknowledgements

Much of this novel was written and researched in libraries. Thank you to all the librarians I met, and the ones I've still to meet. I love your work.

Helen Flood, Elizabeth Foley, Bethan Jones, Cathryn Summerhayes: thank you for being the best publishing team I could have imagined.

Paul McQuade, Andrea Mullaney, Heather Parry, Angela Sutton, Ryan Vance: thank you for the writing dates.

Jen Campbell, Lynsey May, Susie McConnell, Katy McNair, Helen Sedgwick: thank you for first-draft feedback.

Alison Hennessey: thank you for advising me to cut that character from Part 3.

Catherine Gallacher: thank you for the ballet-dancer foot demonstration.

Mermaid Citrine and Hannah Mermaid: thank you for the mermaid information.

The Wellcome Collection Library: thank you for the dance and boxing information.

Eleanor Jackson, Ida Mantere, Reeta Pekkanen, Temu Räsänen, Helen Thurloe, Mary Elizabeth Yarbrough: thank you for the month at Arteles in Finland.

Angie Crawford, Xavier Jones-Barlow and Caron MacPherson from Waterstones; and Markie Deleavey, Effie Flood and all the librarians at Langside Library: thank you for loving your local authors.

All the Logans, Bennetts, Cairneys, Jinkses, Adairs and Sopers: thank you for being my wonderful family.

And Annie, always.